WAITING FOR CHILDHOOD

Novels by Sumner Locke Elliott

WAITING FOR CHILDHOOD

Sumner Locke Elliott

1817
HARPER & ROW, PUBLISHERS, New York
Cambridge, Philadelphia, San Francisco, Washington
London, Mexico City, São Paulo, Singapore, Sydney

FIRST EDITION

Copy editor: Marjorie Horvitz
Designer: C. Linda Dingler

Library of Congress Cataloging-in-Publication Data
Elliott, Sumner Locke.
  Waiting for childhood.
  I. Title.
PR9619.3.E44W35   1987   813'.54   86-46306
ISBN 0-06-015797-6

87 88 89 90 91 HC 10 9 8 7 6 5 4 3 2 1

For Pucky,
constant friend

PART ONE

There they were.

All of them together, looking mildly surprised, as though they had been intruded on, a door opening suddenly onto their family enclave in what seemed to be this Grecian temple overlooking a mauve sea, graceful marble pillars rising behind them, velvet curtains drawn back on brass rings, mountains revealed, somber, crystalline, glades and waterfalls inviting fauns, satyrs, unicorns and naked celebrants, drinking from conch shells.

But which was the canvas backdrop at Mr. Le Mer's photographic studio. Everyone quiet now, very still, Mr. Le Mer pleaded with them, removing the shutter and covering his head with a black cloth. One, two, three, four, five, counted Mr. Le Mer. "But shouldn't it be *La* Mer," Jess had asked. Jess was precise. It sounded ungrammatical. But then his real name was Fortescue, which did not look as well as *Le Mer Studios* curled in Victorian copperplate in the right-hand corner of the photograph.

There they were, for the first and last time, immaculate, combed, laced, beribboned, transfixed by the single eye, converted to sepia forever, arranged in two rows around Mother and Father, who sat in gilt chairs, the girls in stiff white muslin shirt fronts with black velvet bows and leg-of-mutton sleeves;

3

Fred, being the only boy, in the middle, his right arm bent and resting on his father's shoulder, dapper in his double-breasted jacket between Lily and Mary, Adnia on the flank, arms to her sides, Jess, nestled next to Mother, seated with her hands in her lap in order to show her white gloves, Sidney and Mignon, being the youngest, in little cream dresses threaded through with blue ribbon, at Father's feet.

They had come in from St. Kilda on the cable tram, rocked and shaken in the little red and yellow car, whisking the dust off their long skirts; they had hurtled to Melbourne, over the dirty Yarra River, over Prince's Bridge, past the knacker's yards and the hot smoke of factories raining cinders, past wrought-iron balconies and heavily ornamented stone buildings, banks and haberdasheries, dim arcades and little two-storied hotels with names like Bijou and The Five Feathers. Into Swanston Street.

How beautiful it was. How passionate. Inviting, stimulating. The city. Horses and carriages. Ladies half hidden under parasols in open landaus, the horses gleaming, currycombed and with polished silver and leather on the reins. Great Clydesdales heaving steaming flanks over cobblestones, hauling giant wagons with kegs of beer, the stinging sweet smell of manure in the sun mixed with other scents, flowers, oranges, eucalyptus trees and Mother's cologne.

But be careful, Lily said, cried out because Sidney had stood up, holding on to the strap in the tram, engulfed by the beauty and excitement of it all. "You shouldn't let her," Lily said to Mother, but they laughed at her, silly Lily, the worrywart.

Because what harm could come to any of them on this spotless morning, born miraculously cool in a burning February, gentle with breeze in this merciless midsummer? What could go wrong? Later on the day might turn brutal and storm with outrage at the heat, but not yet. Not yet. Nor would anything noxious come their way.

4

Serene, they turned mildly to see who interrupted their Grecian enclave.

But wait, Mr. Le Mer cried out, one more, no one move, steady now, don't anyone move, steeeeady!

Again Mr. Le Mer ducked behind a black velvet cloth, again the shutter moved, the eye winked. They were caught in a moment of truth. This time the eye had not been deceived by caution or serenity, they had been ambushed, and in that second of unpreparedness they were revealed naked, for what they were in their true selves, heartbreakingly innocent.

"Now are we safe?"

"Yes, my lamb."

"Are we hidden away?"

"Yes, yes."

"Where? Where?"

"Where would you want to be, dearest heart?"

Mignon and Father sometimes played asinine games in the dusk in the dusty back garden, she perched in the low hollowed-out bole of the horse chestnut tree, he leaning on the paling fence.

"Coral island?"

"Yes, my pet."

"But are you absolutely certain no one can see us?"

Father looked around the darkening uncut lawn.

"No one, precious."

She laughed then. It was always so if Father said it and she felt the safety, the warm blanket of night around them, their secrecy. Beyond in the lighted kitchen, figures moved, pans and dishes were being got out from cupboards, but here in the quickening dark was the secret tower.

Their trysting place; she and Papa; the sultan's mosque.

In practical terms, 420 Victoria Parade, within a stone's throw of St. Malvern's, where Father was minister, another stone's throw to the ocean sweeping in and out.

5

The manse stood, two-storied and a dirty peach color, ashamed of itself in its shabby garden (but funds were not provided for gardeners and the lawns and overgrown privet, the huge hydrangea and sticky pepper trees, remained unpruned, uncut except when Fred was home from the university), and turned its wooden shutters with half-closed eyes to the street like a once indomitable duchess come upon seedy times.

Only the numbers 420 on the front gate remained polished with Brasso and faith in some future, however rocky, or perhaps a pale belief in God's house being represented here to the congregation of St. Malvern's, who came to visit Father in early evenings with their troubles and vexations. But it was only a pale presumption, because frankly God was not mentioned midweek, much less invoked except at the table during grace. Father kept God for Sundays, which was only meet and proper, He being exclusive in the extreme, and it tended to render the Creator more significant. Other ministers could prattle of Him day and night, materializing Him and trivializing His omnipotence, but not Father. When Father said, "Let us pray," an infinity was felt to be present. It had been said that some of the more creed-bound members of the congregation had huffed and puffed that the Reverend Mr. Lord was too abstract and, halfway hinted, that he was too easygoing on sinners.

Mother would have liked to have her say. She was inherently Victorian and obeyed her marriage vows to the letter; but she kept her mouth shut about God in front of Father.

Because he ordained it.

Mother's lips were sealed about the presence of God in the house. Mother's lips had been so severely sealed for years that her mouth had virtually disappeared. Although this had been partly because in a rage of continual toothache and when they had been situated in outback Queensland, where a visit to the dentist involved a horse and buggy ride of forty-eight miles over a dirt road in any kind of weather, she had put an end to her torment by having all her teeth out and an upper and lower plate inserted.

It was a strange thing (and Mignon sensed it), this separation between Mother and Father. Because although they were seemingly together, slept in the same wide cedar bed, dressed in the same room, emerged from it in the mornings and disappeared into it at night, they were like alien creatures to each other, speaking a different language. Yet they had had nine children (two had, some people thought mercifully, died in infancy, Myfanwy having been dropped by the nurse onto the stone kitchen floor, the baby Alice succumbing to croup), six girls and a boy born out of their seeming indifference to each other, seven earthlings bearing the testimony of their genetic forebears in their startling red hair, which ran a gamut from sunset auburn to bright cerise.

Oh, there was respect between the reverend and his wife, deep respect and even mutual admiration, but somewhere beyond that, a dark sea lay between their two continents.

Mother was seen to bite her vanished lips, Father was seen to smile a sad smile.

Alienated. But nevertheless nine children.

"What'll happen," Mignon wanted to know, "when another one comes?"

"Another what?" asked her father.

"Baby."

For they were crowded now, even in this big old house; the girls slept two to a bedroom, Fred when he was home had to sleep in a little box room under the stairs. Mignon had to share with Sidney, which she occasionally regretted: Sidney was apt to be bossy.

"There won't be another," Father said and reached out his big hand to touch her hair. "You are the very last."

"How do you know?"

Because he was always telling them that God's ways were

past finding out. Or was that just one of those excuses? The Bible seemed to be full of them, something for every conceivable occurrence.

"Because there won't be any more, child. You are the last, my love."

Father rubbed the back of his ring hand against her cheek as though she were something precious. And perhaps she was. That was why her name was strangely different from the other girls', who could trace their names back to past generations, Lillian to Father's great-aunt, Adnia to Mother's older sister, and so on all the way down to Sidney, who had been named for a distant male cousin. But Mignon was Mignon de Beauvoir after a mystery, after some girl Father had met on a bicycle tour of France during a summer when he was still at Cambridge and long before he met Mother. So, Mignon de Beauvoir. Mother had wanted Edith, after someone in her family, but "I would like, if you don't object, for her to be named after Mignon de Beauvoir, whom I knew in France and who died young," Father said. And nothing more, not a word ever. And thus Mignon de Beauvoir was snuffed out like a candle and nothing further was ever known about her. Except that it had been long ago in France, in the Dordogne. Before Father had been discovered to have the incipient tuberculosis and had been warned that he must get out of the English climate forever and settle in some warm place like Arizona or Queensland and, choosing the latter, had wound up in Rockhampton, where on the pier he had first set eyes on Miss Annie Seddon stepping up out of a pleasure boat in a lilac dress and, looking up at him under her straw bonnet, she had given him a warm smile almost of recognition, as though she had been waiting for this young clergyman. Mother had given him her hand there and then to help her out of the boat, later given it in marriage.

So now after this long marriage there were to be no more children and Father had said so in the tone of voice reserved for things like the Holy Ghost, the tone of voice you didn't question, and now here in the dusk, with the lamplighter coming down Victoria Parade to light the gaslamps, there was an invisible thread between Mignon and her father, spun out of their mutual respect for each other and perhaps out of the very fact that she, being the youngest, had a priority over the others. Dearest heart, Father said to her, precious lamb. To the others, my dear. But to Mignon he said my love.

And the way they talked to each other about the stars, about the sea, about rainy weather, gathered shells on the beach, and walked hand in hand in the late afternoons, their shadows growing longer and longer in front of them until they were as tall as trees, sometimes saying nothing but as close as peas in a pod. Nobody else quite understood their relationship and her oldest sister, Lily, would often say, "Now, Mignon, you're not to worry Father right now." "But I am not worrying him," the child said truthfully, aware of the beautiful calm that always spread across them when they were alone together. Every night except when it rained, she went and sat in the hollowed-out bole of the horse chestnut and waited for him, waited to see his tall, slightly spent figure come out of the house and make his way across the lawn to her and then stand by the picket fence as the exciting darkness began folding its blankets around them, stars pricked holes in the black sky, and here they stayed together, sometimes talking about deep things which she didn't understand and which he attempted to clarify for her (like what did the Holy Ghost look like, because she didn't dare tell him that to her the Holy Ghost looked exactly like Mr. Drewe, the baker, who had a protuberance on his nose like a great gooseberry and was floury white; and puzzling things like why shouldn't you commit adultery? why not grow up?) until the kitchen window shot up, sending a yellow beam across the lawn, and Lily or Mary would call, Come in to supper, you lovers, a family joke that although attenuated still brought titters.

9

"What do people find when they die?"

"The peace that passeth perfect understanding."

She was thinking of her two baby sisters, one dropped on the floor, the other suffocating with croup.

"Even if they're tiny babies?"

"There is no age there, dearest."

"But if they were only babies, would they understand that?"

"Darling, you mustn't question the peace that passes all *understanding.*"

No one else would have dared. He was the rector, the emissary of God. But that was how close they were: Mignon could ask such a thing and did.

"Will God understand I only want to be with you?"

"Yes," he said.

But he sounded unsure, like somebody who is asked to clarify a notion, something seen in a dim light. It was one of the times when she knew that she had gone too far. She got out of the tree and put her arms tight around his waist, feeling the gold chain of his vest pocket watch against her cheek. He put his long arms around her then and they stood in silence together until he gave a sigh and said, "God," said it bitterly, like blasphemy. "God," Father said, shockingly, like a bad word written in chalk on a fence that she had been hurried past, and looking up in surprise to his face way above her in the glimmering dusk she thought she saw that his cheeks were wet.

The kitchen window shot up.

"Come in now, you lovers," Mary cried.

And three weeks to the day after they had had the family photograph taken, Father died.

At the breakfast table, piece of toast in hand, cup to his mouth, he spurted hot milky tea over the tablecloth and the cup dropped.

They thought he had choked on a crust; Jess thumped him on the back, Lily brought water. He had turned a strange blue color like the underside of a crab.

It wasn't until after the horse-drawn ambulance came that they could finally accept the staggering, unbelievable fact that there was no need for hurry because the body that was being carried out of the house was only lifeless matter (the ambulance men closed his staring eyes) and that, incredibly, when the ambulance drove off, it was to the funeral home. It was not yet even ten o'clock in the morning.

It was, of course, on Lily that the burden fell of making the arrangements and making them hurriedly. Because now that there was no need for hurry, everything had to conform to haste because of the hot weather. Quickly their black clothes had to be measured and sewn, hastily the bishop summoned to conduct the service, speedily Fred called home from college in Geelong ("Father desperately ill, come at once," Lily telegraphed, writing shakily with a blunt pencil in the post office, thinking to cushion the blow); then to prepare a dignified announcement for the papers, choose the hymns, hire the carriages, be polite to the endless-seeming parade of parishioners who came shocked to the door to offer condolences. Lily had no time for sorrow, only glad to sit down for five minutes and have a cup of tea between errands, her hair needed washing, no time, was that Mother calling? What, asked Mary, are we to have for dinner tonight? I don't know, Lily gasped, drowning in minuscule decisions.

Blessed are the dead who die in the Lord from henceforth. Yea, saith the Spirit, that they may rest from their labors and their works do follow them. So intoned the bishop. They rose. Rock of Ages, cleft for me, they sang. Father's favorite hymn. Let me hide myself in thee.

The Lord hath taken his servant William who bore our cross for us. And as they knelt to pray, poor Mary hiccuped, could not stop, it was always the way if she was nervous. Mary hiccuped in between the responses and prayers (now they all knelt in a row) like any old street drunk, and worse, it was plain to anyone knowing her that behind the handkerchief stuffed in her mouth, her brimming eyes and shaking shoulders, she was hysterical with laughter. Mary saw the comical in any situation.

After that they were all piled like baggage into the two carriages following the hearse, the horses with the black plumes, to the St. Kilda Cemetery, where they stood in the now broiling sun grouped around Mother at the open grave to hear about the Resurrection and the Life while wild magpies in their widow's weeds squawked and chattered in the gum trees; gravediggers, leaning on their spades, wiped sweat from their faces with burly arms. When it was over, Mother turned to go as if she had heard a bell ring somewhere, and they followed her obediently, not turning back to see the earth being shoveled, back to the waiting carriages and drove away.

Came home to that dark suffocating airless house where the comforters were waiting with cakes and pies. Virtually the entire female population from the surrounding neighborhood come to pay last respects to Mr. Lord with cakes and pies; they crowded out of the drawing room into the hall with their fruitcake, seed cake, sultana cake, lamingtons, sausage rolls, plum and cherry pies, custards. It was as though this avalanche of flour and shortening could stem grief and each pie had to be cut and tasted, praised. Through all the shining mockery of well-meant condolence, Mother sat silent and dry-eyed. And Fred stiff as a poker, and of course poor Adnia no help whatever, Mary in the kitchen and Jess looking after the two youngest girls, everything left to Lily, Lily beaming, bestowing praise and seeing to everyone, pouring tea (would they run out of cups, would the chipped ones be noticed, would people ever leave?), Lily submerging her suitable grief for Father under enthusiasm for rainbow cake, remembering names in desperation until at long last, the street gaslights being lit, the last of the overstayers got the hint and the family was left to loosen their pinching new shoes, open the windows to let out the miasma of the overheated condolences, and to finally realize that Father was in his grave.

Now, who was to go upstairs to Mother? Lily, of course, being the eldest. Mother, freed at last from the solemnity of being the newly widowed, was sitting in a wicker chair by her bedroom window in the now dark. She was leaning on her elbow, looking out over the tenebrous garden, when Lily came quietly into the room.

"Don't you want a lamp, Mother?"

"No," Mother said, "I like the dark."

Lily sat down on an ottoman and thought suddenly: I don't know what to say to her. I haven't ever prepared myself for this moment, but something is required.

She fidgeted with her skirt and said, "Is there anything I can bring you?"

"No," Mother said.

"People were kind."

"Yes."

"Did that cousin of the bishop's speak to you?"

"I suppose so."

But something was *required*.

"Try to think of what a good life he had—" Lily began, but there was a stiffening of the back in Mother as if Lily had made some giant faux pas.

Mother stiffened and Lily was left stranded in midsentence with her commiseration left unfurled between them like a wet flag.

"—and that you have no reason whatever to regret anything —a perfect marriage—" Lily blundered on hopelessly, whatever sincerity she wished to express lost in the soup of platitude. It was often the way with her; she remained untranslated.

"Made—" In heaven, Lily was about to say, but the words

13

died on her lips of malnutrition, were so pitiful that they were an affront to Mother. Because when you thought about it, no words were sufficient for a marriage that had been either heaven or hell and nobody knew which except Mother. Surely nobody except Lily, the light sleeper, getting herself warm milk in the dead of night, had heard the voices dimly under the crack of the bedroom door, Mother pleading. For what? Or against what? Please, please. So much the antithesis of herself in daylight, solid, constrained. Then Father's voice and then Mother actually crying, "Oh Will, Will," shockingly because she never referred to him so familiarly in public. It was like seeing them undressed and Lily had crept back into her room, infused with shame. You simply could not, did not, ask your mother had everything been as it was supposed to be, conjugally harmonious; you might as well utter some blasphemy in church. Your mother was tight-mouthed, all mothers were, it seemed. Some older girl might take pity on you and calm your fears about the horrendous mutations of your body; your mother was mute as a statue.

But surely now, surely death could be, should be, the alchemy to bring about understanding between them.

Yet Mother was deadly silent. Lily went toward the door, feeling that the silence, at this time, was unwarranted and the unfairness of it shook her to her depths.

"What are you thinking about?" she asked.

Mother stirred, turned toward Lily in the dark. Perhaps she was smiling; it wasn't possible to see anything beyond her stoutish figure framed in the faint luminescence of the open window.

"Calves' brains on toast," Mother said.

Like logs, they would have said. Slept like logs. Worn out from piety and stuffed with Mary's delicious tripe and onions as only she could cook it in cream sauce and parsley, the family slept, funeral tired, exhausted by the new possibilities, the changes that were being rung on them. Temporarily avoiding tomorrow, they slept like logs except that during the night Mignon woke up from a dream that she had been walking down a dark street with Father and that the pavements had turned to water and he had said to her, Let us walk on the water, darling. They had walked on the water quite easily and then she awoke to her terrible reality and wept, stuffing the pillow into her mouth so as not to awaken Sidney.

Jess was ironing a blouse to wear on the journey to Sydney when Lily burst into the kitchen and said, "Oh, don't bother with that now when there's so much to do." Why not? One still liked to be neat no matter what the catastrophic changes. They were moving. There were lighter patches on the wallpaper where the pictures had been taken down. They had to be gone from the manse after all these years to make room for the new minister, the young Reverend Mr. Jollocks and his family, who were putting up temporarily at a local boardinghouse; and "putting up" was what described Mr. Jollocks's ill-disguised impatience and forced amiability, conversing flatly with them while his wife looked into closets as if they were already hers. It had been a period of drifting uncertainty as to what they would do, where they would go, left homeless with a small pension and stacks of hymnbooks until bold Lily took pen in hand and wrote to Mother's well-to-do cousin Jacquetta Moss (Lily disdained the word "rich," preferred not to be a cousin of the rich; she was already an inherent Socialist) and reported their plight.

"I would have preferred Jackie not to know," Mother said.

"We had to do *some*thing." Lily was on the point of screaming. "We have to be out of here by the tenth of the month."

"My dear Lillian," had replied Cousin Jackie quaintly from Sydney on mauve notepaper edged in black (for the young husband, killed in a riding accident, twenty years ago), "you are a good dear to write and tell me all your news, sad as it is." Cousin Jackie wrote in her Germanic handwriting made heavy perhaps because of diamond rings. Her heart went out to them all over the passing of dear William, that saintly man. Your sweet mother will remember I was with her when she met him on a beach in Rockhampton all those years ago, flowers of yesterday, rambled on Cousin Jackie for eleven pages until at last she came to a point. One of her several properties, a largish house in Turramurra, was becoming vacant and she would be glad to let her dearest Cousin Annie have it for a "minimum rent." What the rent would be she failed to say. They knew nothing of Sydney environs; they asked about this place called Turramurra. A long distance out, they were told, secluded. Oh well. They waited for Lily to say it. "Beggars can't be choosers," Lily obliged. They packed.

Father's precious sets of Macaulay and Walter Scott went toward paying for Fred's continuing at Geelong University, where he was in his first year of Philosophy and Latin. He saw them all piled into the Sydney night express. He kissed his sisters damply and embraced his mother emotionally, then stepping off the train he waved to the wrong window. It was like him.

They rattled through the night, being awakened at the New South Wales border by the conductor and shepherded onto a long, dimly lit platform at Albury, where they were directed onto another train. They could not get the window to shut and suffered a black snowstorm of cinders all night.

They looked hopefully around the cavernous smoky interior of Sydney Central Station but there was no sign of Cousin Jackie, no helpful chauffeur, only hundreds of stern-faced people rushing this way and that in the green-glass twilight. A porter snatched up their luggage and piled it onto a cart. "This way for a cab. You want a cab, don't ya?" He helped them into two hansom cabs outside in the fierce racketing street. Sydney was terrifying, all right. "A good cheap hotel," Lily said to the drivers. Quite respectable and safe, ladies, the first driver told them outside the Royal Oak next to a tawdry theater which luridly advertised that it was presenting Mr. Bland Holt in *A Race with Life*.

"Well now, it can't be helped," Lily said about the two awful rooms, wallpapered in liver-colored roses. "It's only for a night or two." The spectacle of highly rouged, ornately hatted women drinking in the ladies' saloon was not reassuring.

Just the same, Jess laid out her imitation-tortoiseshell brush and comb on the dressing table in the way she thought a lady would. She and Mary went across the street to buy sandwiches and they were followed back by two beery rowdies from the pub downstairs. "Show us a smile, dear," they roared. "Show us your lace panties." Roughneck jackaroos down from some outback station to spend their pay, they pounded on the door and bawled out suggestive invitations until young Sidney opened it a crack and said with great aplomb, "Would you please stop that; we have somebody here very ill with smallpox." The rowdies fled. Sidney had already developed a strong creative bent.

The water in the communal bathroom down the hall gushed out brown and thick as mulligatawny. The horses and carts, the tramcars, began under their windows at five in the morning.

"But we didn't expect you until *Thurs*day," Cousin Jackie simpered in mock tragedy as they came into the great scented drawing room in Point Piper. "Oh, you poor lost things with no one to meet you at that horrible Central." In reply to Lily's feverish telegram, Cousin Jacquetta had sent her new motorcar and chauffeur.

"Luncheon," said Cousin Jackie, "after which Yeldham will drive you back to this awful hotel and pick up your luggage and then take you directly to Turramurra."

How blissful it was, charming little lace doilies on their laps, plates of exquisite china ornamented in roses, all of them at the long mahogany table in the big windowed dining room outside which the garden burst with rhododendron. A uniformed maid discreetly brought cutlets dressed in paper frills. Jess thought that if only she could be seen now by her friends, having her crystal water glass filled for her, she would die happy, and she frowned at Sidney when she thanked the maid. One didn't, Jess knew, thank servants.

After lunch they were shown around the garden, where a respectful gardener touched his sweat-marked hat to them. The Lords admired everything: the towering pergolas of wild roses, the beds of canna and scarlet salvia, a hedge cut into the shape of a swan. "I must have plants, living things," Jackie said and then, leaning down and as if it were an everyday occurrence, plucked a clover from the grass and said gaily, "Look, a four-leaf clover." Just so, Lily thought; when most people never find one in their lifetime, one is at her feet, like everything else.

And Jess in the little guest washroom, finding the perfect cake of delicate pink soap (French, was it?), wondered for a second if anyone would notice if she dared take it, keep it to smell as a reminder of this rich day, but thought better of it.

As they were all putting on their black straw hats in the front hall, Cousin Jackie, who seemed to be ruminating on something, maneuvered Mother aside from the girls for a moment and Lily thought, hoping, is she going to tuck a hundred-pound note into Mother's hand, she would never miss it, and Jess heard Jackie say, "Annie, my dear, let me help you. Let me take one of the girls off your hands. Think it over, sweet lamb."

Which one? They all went down the steps to where the shiny red motor waited, gleaming with its brass lamps and spotless mudguards. One of them to be a companion to Cousin Jackie?

They pretended innocence going down the steps, but Jess said to Mignon, who dawdled, "Don't linger, it's rude," as though she had advance priority.

But no wonder they had been given the Turramurra house for a red sou. The neediest family might well have looked at it askance. Prevented by curmudgeon oak and beech from any sun, it stood in perpetual gloom, a fake two-storied Tudor with flinty mean little windows and a roof shedding tiles. The sign on the gate read "Piedmont" but it could as easily have acknowledged itself as Atreus or Usher, under the heavy odor of lilac and jacaranda, the perfume of sorrow. A rusted gas lamp with a broken glass bowl hung lopsidedly over the entrance. The chauffeur unloaded their luggage on the weedy footpath and, saluting them, drove off down the rutted muddy dirt road. "Well," Mother said without naming their benefactor, "she was a Stark and the Starks never spent their money on any place where they didn't live themselves." Inside it was as cold as Jacquetta Stark's charity. The house had a dampish smell of old mattresses, the bare floors creaked under their feet. In the big kitchen there were sinister dark stains on the stone floor which suggested brutality and in the quickly gathering twilight it would not have surprised them to find something dead, a possum on the cold iron stove or an iguana in the dirty wire meat safe hanging in the larder. So sepulchral was the thick gloom (they pulled open kitchen drawers to find candles) that when a clock in the front hall chirred and beat six clacking strokes they jumped. And when Adnia lifted the plug of the kitchen sink she disturbed a large brown spider that ran across her hand. In a crock on the Dutch dresser was something gone into gray decomposition.

Not to look the gift horse in the mouth, Lily said, settling Mother in what seemed to be a less tomblike room upstairs, where the flaking wallpaper had once been a splendid yellow. They were unrehearsed in change, they needed time and orientation. All they needed was to put up their own dear pictures, get out their own nice spoons and forks. The reality of beautiful cups. All they needed was a good night's sleep and now here came Mary, all smiles, with a lamp lit and Adnia had got a fire going in the iron stove, Jess had found sheets and blankets. "Be it ever so humble," Lily said.

They all knew it would be Jess. Long before the letter came from Cousin Jackie, everyone knew that Jess would be chosen to be the companion to rich Jacquetta and go live in style; it was the way some people are born to their lives, in the way some people are born handsome and some not. It could have been in the way her miniature hand pushed away, with a certain look of gastric derision, the baby bottle, later snatched off the offending woolen bonnet, the way that her child's body grew graceful as a water lily, or that Jess's hair was burnished into a kind of flaming splendor, never grew lank with the humidity or dry with the wind, remained thick and glistening. No matter how uncomplimentary the fabrics of her cheap dresses, Jess always looked as though she were in brocades or velvet. It was just that thing about her. Nobody could put a finger on it. Not luck, a quiet power sustained her, gave her an inborn elegance that no academy of linguistics or domestic science could imbue her with.

Moreover, she knew it.

She had a way of coming into a room as though she were obliging it. Yet she was not emotionally frigid. Books and music could send her into transports of joy or into tears. She was more deeply affected by the death of Little Nell than by any calamity in her own family. She wept for Heathcliff. But only fictional characters could disarray her exceptional calm.

It had to do with her secret. Jess's secret (not told to anyone) was that she was really English. She may have been born in Sandgate, Queensland, in the middle of a tropical downpour on a tin roof, but some mistake had occurred, some metaphysical mix-up had transported her infant soul to Australia. That was why she secretly detested her wide primitive homeland. Let others carry on emotionally about the great pavilions of blue sky, the mighty spreading gum trees, the blaze of golden wattle, the smell of the earth, the billabong and loneliness of the outback. Jess turned up her nose. In her mind she saw the sun set over the Wiltshire downs, she saw Somerset and Cornwall. She found in a secondhand bookshop a tatterdemalion map of London streets and she studied it intensely, district by district. She could locate Cockspur Street for you in a second, Cork Street, St. Pancras; could differentiate between Eaton Place and Eaton Mews. In her long solitary map walks she took in the East End and Holland Park, she dreamed she was going up the steps into the Victoria and Albert Museum. Sat upstairs on a red Kensington bus.

But all the time she was getting ready, quietly preparing for the day when her fate would become activated and she would be delivered from her absenteeism in this violent country where people were apt to behave with vulgar exhibitionism, without the English caution about their emotions, with public displays of affection or dislike.

She was ready for England anytime that God decided to rectify the mistake that had been made about her place of birth. The girls at Miss Garner's School teased her about her highfalutin "Pommy" accent. "My father is English," she told them haughtily.

She had her suitcase secretly packed and ready under the bed, with little cakes of camphor around two frilly blouses she had made, a pair of black silk stockings, white cotton gloves, her map of London, and a piece of rose-and-glycerin soap said to be French. She was ready. She knew accurately all the sailing dates of the P&O and Orient liners with thrilling names like the *Narkunda* and the *Orontes,* departing from Wooloomooloo in Sydney to Liverpool via Colombo and Port Said. She was ready.

When it happened it wasn't exactly as she had planned it, some shining angel, a handsome millionaire stepping down from a hansom cab to take her hand in his, trumpets blowing;

it was Lily rustling into her bedroom, where she was sitting reading *Little Dorrit* for the fifth time; Lily had a mauve and black-edged letter in her hand. Lily sat down on Jess's bed (never a may I come in, just barged, sat on the carefully made bed) and said, wrinkling her nose, said in an intimate coy way, "Well, you've made a hit, dear. Guess what? Cousin Jackie's asking you up to Mount Wentworth for a week. Mum just got the letter this morning." Lily often referred to Mother in this colloquial fashion behind her back. Jess wished she wouldn't, it was so awfully like just common tradespeople talking about "Mum and Dad."

" '. . . how overjoyed I was to see you all' "—Lily was flipping pages—"and so on and so on. 'Now I want to ask you something, I wonder if young Jess would like to spend a week with me up at Mount Wentworth, the first week of April? I keep seeing her fresh young face in my mind. She would need to bring one warm coat as the evenings in the mountains can be chilly.' "

Jess said nothing, sat very still.

"So, would you want to go, dear?" Lily asked halfheartedly. This family was unused to frivolous journeys. Jess could hardly speak.

"Oh yes."

"Would you really? You don't sound very keen somehow."

"Don't I?"

As if Lily would know about how hard it was not to sing aloud with joy. *She* had been chosen for a trip with Cousin Jacquetta. It could lead to *any*thing.

"You don't *have* to go, dear, there's no one forcing you."

"I'll need an evening dress," Jess said. That settled it.

"Are you sure?" Lily had begun to fret her fingernails against each other.

"She stays at the Majestic in the mountains. It's the big old grand hotel."

"Who told you?"

"She told Mother that day at lunch, she said, 'I always put up at the Majestic in Mount Wentworth.' They *dress.*"

The insuperable, Lily's face said, not admiring the thought of poshness. The incipient Socialist looked askance at the thought of Jess being obligated to the slothful rich.

"I wonder," Lily said, regretfully, "if we could do over the white dress Mary wore when she sang in the *Messiah* with the choir that time at Melbourne Town Hall. Perhaps we could take it in at the waist for you."

So Jess had settled it. She was to go.

Mary was deputized to see her safely onto the train, not that she wasn't capable of getting on a train by herself. She was almost seventeen.

She wore her best dark green wool skirt and a white blouse with a little black bow for Father and in her suitcase with her pink flannel nightgown was the evening dress they had run up for her out of Mary's *Messiah* robe.

"Send us a postcard, love," Mary shrilled. Mary had no sense of moderation in public and her hair was adrift under her hat, crumbling under a loose pin. She looked like the White Queen. She waved goodbye as the train chugged out.

Jess was alone in her second-class compartment and able to give complete attention to the novelty of her expectations unfolding before her eyes just as the air was changing from ordinary to exotic, perfumed with the dark ferny smell of bush and mountains, and as they passed waterfalls and through smoky tunnels turned from mist into rain and she had to lower the window.

At Mount Wentworth station, she sat among hanging maidenhair ferns under the tin roof in the torrential downpour until a man in a white coat on which was stitched *Majestic* gruffly asked her, "Are you for us?" and led her under an umbrella to where a disconsolate gray horse covered in canvas stood with a hackney in which a lady and gentleman already sat, wearing expensive looks of annoyance at being kept wait-

23

ing. Jess knew by their tight patronizing smiles that they guessed she had come in second class, like somebody's maid.

But the Majestic was like Buckingham Palace (she imagined). Turrets, balconies, grillwork. A striped canopy sheltered the entrance from the heavy rain. There was Cousin Jacquetta in the cardroom.

"Jess." She was kissed fervently. "You got here. My dear, the terrible weather; we've had a week of this. They keep promising—" Gongs sounded.

"Dressing bell," Cousin Jackie said. "Go and unpack, dear, and we'll meet here for dinner."

A housemaid, stiff and starched, led Jess down endless corridors to her room, 77. The giant key was like something out of *Ivanhoe*. "Your first time here? You'll like it if the rain ever stops; everyone's been marooned for a week now," said the maid.

Her room was exquisite, all shining white and pretty cretonne, spotless. The gleaming white jug and basin for washing your hands, the soap dish in the shape of a nesting bird, great white huggy towels, the pink eiderdown quilt folded on the bed. All hers for seven Arabian nights.

A tap at the door. "Come in," she said with her aplomb.

The night maid. "Turn the bed down, miss?" Oh, this was the life, like Emma Bovary at the chateau, servants, courtesy. "Thank you, miss," the maid said, going out and closing the door softly. Then she put on the evening dress.

Horrors. She looked like Deirdre of the Sorrows in this passionless white crepe de chine with eyelet work and a watery pink sash. She would be discovered to be the inexperienced daughter of the poor minister being treated to a dose of the good life by her mother's philanthropic elderly cousin, she would be instantly tolerated for her temporary status. Something desperate must be done. She sat down at the dressing table mirror and heaped her red hair up in combs for the first time, exposing her long white neck.

Now if only she could maintain the look it gave her, quasi scorn, she might not be looked on as an interloper. She went downstairs and into the dining room with Cousin Jackie like a young queen.

Nobody laughed or stared at her, they were too courteous, these people in their nice clothes, the ladies dressed in sparkling stuff, mysterious and beautiful under the little gaslight chandeliers shaped like rosebuds. In fact, Jackie paid her a compliment, "How nice you look, dear," and when they sat down and Jess unfolded her napkin shaped like a lily, half the unfortunate dress was hidden under the table. Now, what on earth was jambon? What was entrecôte? The menu was typed in French. Well, she would learn, by God (excuse me, Father). They had a beautiful clear soup which to her great surprise Jackie slurped up like a wharfy. Jackie asked her questions about herself, had Jess many friends and so on, while stuffing bread into her little mouth. They seemed to be reaching toward each other without effort and Jess felt a surge of well-being, felt solid and confident in the rose-colored light, with the crystal and silver, while all around them was the subdued chatter of affluent people who had never had problems with mice or worries about roofs leaking, and then in the middle of their roast lamb, suddenly, a tall thin girl all in tweed appeared at the table and had scrounged the chair between them.

"—terribly late, sorry, the motor broke down, haven't even had time to change," she said in a high-pitched rather too la-di-da voice.

"Oh, here's our Bettina," Jackie said, smiling, and made introductions. "Bettina Boxer, another cousin, different side of the family. And this is our dear little Jess."

Bettina had been visiting friends in nearby Blackheath, Jackie explained, and Bettina fanned herself with the menu and said to their waitress, "No, nothing, Nellie, just a cup of tea and maybe later an ice. I've been eating all day. Hello,

hello," Bettina said, nodding to people at nearby tables, on intimate terms with everyone, it seemed. Their ices came with the most delightful little paper Japanese umbrellas on them. Jess carefully took hers and folded it to keep, but Bettina just crumpled hers up and left it on the table.

After dinner they wandered into the cardroom, where Jackie and Bettina played a sharp game of whist and there was nothing for Jess to do but turn the pages of a magazine. Somehow the glow of her arrival had dimmed. Bettina beat Jackie at whist and laughed a well-bred whinny. "Got you," she neighed. Jackie didn't seem to mind. Later she said to Jess, "I'm sorry there aren't more young people at the hotel." Bettina saw Jackie off to bed. "Good night, good night," Bettina sang out to Jess, taking Jackie off by the arm. It took Jess quite a time and down several wrong hallways before she located room 77.

In the morning she was up and washed and dressed and in the dining room for breakfast, where she found herself almost alone in the forest of tables and army of starched waitresses. It seemed that Jackie took breakfast in her room. Half an hour later Bettina arrived, cool and crisp in pale yellow, and with her came everyone else. She had, it seemed, a gift for timing. She was always a trifle late and yet always on time. She was convivial ("How are *you* this morning, early bird?") and yet detached ("Ugh, no, I don't want *eggs*"), fashionably bored and yet inquisitive.

"How many are there of you?"

"Seven."

"Seven. Good Lord, all girls?"

"I have one brother."

"My gracious. *Sev*en."

Reallly? Bettina drawled in her well-bred voice, disdainful of anything she would rather not be bothered with. But she could be learned from, Jess knew, watching her being eloquently aloof when, in the ballroom, dancing with the boys, she held herself away from their embraces with a languid indifference. Bettina knew when she was at her own best and followed her perceptions of herself to a T. That Cousin Jackie approved of her was evident in everything they said and did together, and Bettina seemed able to predict accurately what Jackie would like to do at any given moment. Dear, Bettina would say, frowning, do we *really* want to get caught up with the dubious Jacksons? or What about a before-lunch sherry?

Bettina was the rift in the lute, the unforeseen snag in Jess's confirmation of this life with a room of her own and with polite maids to turn on her bathwater, her becoming accustomed to the luxury of beautifully mannered people who took it for granted, like flowers on the table. It was an opalescence, not to be put into mere words. It was a form of life.

But suddenly Jackie would say when she and Jess were alone together, "Go and see what Bettina wants to do, dear."

The dreadful thing afterwards was that Jess had had moments of wishing Bettina dead.

But all Jess could think of were the diminishing days. She only had three more, then two more left.

Meanwhile it rained. Morning, noon and night. They awoke in the morning to it and went to their beds with the not unpleasing sounds of rain on the roof.

There were little teasing pauses for a brief sunshine but not long enough for people to stir out of their apathy and to put out the deck chairs before down again came the torrents. The guests at the Majestic were clearly sick to death of their enforced life indoors, of each other, of the billiard room, the stale novels and magazines in the library.

"What a wretched time you've had, poor child. Nothing but rain and now you have to go home on Saturday, do you?" crooned Jackie and before Jess had time to say she didn't absolutely have to, Bettina broke in with savage amiability.

"Saturday," Bettina said, biting off the word like a cotton thread. Then miraculously on the Friday at the last trump,

God repealed the weather and they awoke to a morning of shining sky and sun.

Even Bettina seemed to respond to the utter astonishment of fine weather. She leaned across the breakfast table and smiled at Jess. "Let's get outside for a bit. Have you seen the Chinaman's Hat?"

"What's that?"

"Oh, it's a great rock, quite a nice walk. Have you got a pair of good walking shoes?"

Opening Jackie's bedroom door an inch, Bettina poked her head in to say, "Darling, Jess and I are going to Chinaman's Hat. It's a superb day. We'll see you at lunch."

Outside it was verdant, the mountains emerging from mist, the faint haze of blue, the sharp smell of wet eucalyptus. Off they went, Bettina walking briskly in her strong-heeled golfing shoes, Jess slightly hampered by her town pumps. The hotel with its gingerbread turrets was left behind tall firs as they took a circular path that led gradually away to a sudden feeling of violent cliffs of light and shadow which dropped to uncertain depths in deep valleys. The air was intoxicating and almost mauve. When you drank it in, it was like dark sherry.

They followed the pathway around towering rock interspersed with fern until they came eventually to a fenced-in lookout where Bettina leaned backward over the valley and pointed up. "There," she said.

"Where?" Jess asked, craning.

"Chinaman's Hat, silly."

What sounded like a shot in the unearthly stillness was a rock falling under their feet, the crack of a rifle shot over the valley, but it was the crack of fate, of tired earth capitulating after a thousand years, ready to give way to the temptation of a great fall. It was the earth around them having a heart attack.

"I say," said Bettina, clutching at the fence, which hung for a minute or two with her clinging to it, hung over nothing while to their unbelieving eyes the pathway disappeared and trees were wrenched out by the roots as the feeble lookout gave way and everything was echoing, echoing, and the rocks tilting and falling, and Bettina had halfway disappeared, only her head and shoulders were visible above the chasm where the fence had been and with one arm free and the other around a sapling she was waving to Jess.

"Help me. *Help* me," she repeated as if she were screaming to a deaf fool, and Jess had lunged forward with her arm out and stopped frozen at the sight of the broken earth. It was as though a giant with a cake knife had cut a slice out of the cliff and Bettina was a birthday candle on the slice.

Then as Jess leaned over toward the screaming girl (her felt hat had tipped over Bettina's eyes as though to shield her from the last terrible moments), she froze, not so much in horror at the sight of the chasm but at her own impotence. She could not catch hold of the tweed shoulder or the outstretched arm. Her fingers were inches from the lapel of Bettina's buttoned jacket but she could not thrust her hand further, she was immobilized. Here was this girl, her hat tilted over her eyes, now hanging between life and death with only a thin sapling to hold on to, and Jess could not move, *would* not move, became still as death itself, the sweat pouring down her face, the seconds ticking by. Then the sapling broke, Bettina fell away. There was an airy silence and then, miles below, it seemed, crashing sounds and then only the splashing of a waterfall which had been dropping for thousands of years. Thy will be done, Jess said silently.

Men came with ropes later in the afternoon and one, climbing down onto the niche of rock where Jess was crouched, tied himself to her in an embrace and they were hoisted up, holding each other, swinging out over the valley and back, bumping, bruised by rocks and branches, onto a plateau above the landslide. "You all right?" the men asked. She was given water to drink; she was still too shocked to speak. Shocked beyond credulity. At her gross culpability.

She was to be punished by concern. Reaching the hotel in a buggy, bundled for some reason in blankets, she was greeted like a heroine rather than a murderess. "Here she is," the head porter called into the hallway as the buggy drew up and she was carried up the steps and set down in a chair while people came with brandy, with eau de cologne, with smelling salts. A doctor had been summoned. Cousin Jacquetta was being helped downstairs. Cousin Jacquetta, yellow without her rouge, held out arms.

"Jess."

Thy will be done, Jess had said as the girl slid away, but this is what she had meant, Cousin Jackie's arms around her, holding tight, Cousin Jackie's tears dampening her neck. This is where Jess knew she was wicked.

"Oh, my dear God," Jackie said, "thank God you're safe. Oh, is it true? I can't yet believe it. I can't believe that only this morning the poor darling angel was alive. It's those wretched unsafe lookouts. But are you all right? You dear good thing, risking your own life trying to hold on to her. You did hold on to her, didn't you?"

Jess said nothing.

"You good thing. But the doctor comforted me quite a bit, the doctor told me she wouldn't have felt anything. He says at that height—she would have suffocated before hitting the ground."

Cousin Jackie reeked of brandy.

"I want to go up to my room," Jackie said. "I have to compose a letter to Bettina's mother. Will you help me?"

As they went upstairs, people drew aside to let them pass, smiling sheepishly as though they were in some way peculiar. People drew aside as if Jess and Jackie had some communicable illness, bad luck.

"Good evening," the people said.

In Cousin Jackie's large bedroom, where Jess had never been before, attention had to be paid to Jackie, pillows found, notepaper found, spectacles, drinking glasses. The brandy bottle was on the dressing table. "Have a small tot, it will steady your nerves," Jackie said, "and I'll have one too."

The brandy stung the throat horribly. Jess had a coughing fit.

"On second thoughts, I think I'll put off writing to Lenore, that's Bettina's mother, my cousin by marriage, until tomorrow. I'll have a better grasp of things tomorrow, don't you agree?"

"Yes," Jess said. It was the first word she had uttered since the earth gave way.

There was something just the other side of Jackie's bed. It was a girl with her hat pushed over her eyes, a girl in a tweed suit; she was slipping behind the bed. There she was again behind the washstand, hat over her eyes.

But you got over such fantasies, you rose above them. She took a long swallow of brandy.

There was a gentle tap on the door and she heard herself say in a carrying voice, "Who is it?"

The door opened a slit and the maid looked in. "Could I put the fresh towels in the bathroom, miss?"

"Not now," Jess heard herself say sharply. "Come back later. Mrs. Moss is upset."

"Yes, miss."

The maid withdrew.

"Oh, you are a comfort, Jess," Jackie said, pouring another brandy. "You might have read my mind."

"Now, dear," Jackie said later, a tray having arrived for them with cold chicken, "you mustn't think of going home tomorrow in the state you're in. You can stay a little longer, can't you? And you're such a comfort to me. Can you stay a week or so until . . ."

Newspapers reported that a girl had fallen two thousand feet to her death in the Blue Mountains landslide. A splotchy picture of Bettina was captioned "Vivacious debutante, daughter of Sir Hugh and Lady . . ." Geologists suggested that heavy rain might have contributed to the loosening of the basalt.

Typically, Lily telegraphed on a pink urgent telegram: "Family frantic at your silence. Are you all right?" and Jess telegraphed back by ordinary telegram: "Yes." She continued to see Bettina slipping from time to time, Bettina's mouth open, gaping, in the bathroom, on the dais behind the musicians after dinner. Curiously enough, when the body was finally recovered ten days later, in dense undergrowth in the as yet untrodden valley, Bettina stopped haunting her. She was able to come into her bedroom without finding Bettina sitting on the bed with arms outstretched and she awoke in the morning feeling cleansed and young, hungry for a good breakfast. But it wasn't as though she was without conscience, cold-blooded. She was perfectly aware of what she was. It was engraved in her and the awareness was that she was wicked.

"Now," Jackie said, humming, "would you like to learn to play whist?"

"Oh *yes.*"

Three weeks later, wearing expensive new shoes, when she arrived back home in Turramurra it was only to pack her few remaining things.

Adnia was the quiet one.

If you were looking at the family photograph she was the one on the extreme left standing to the right of Father and wearing a long dark skirt of some heavy material laced through with dark ribbon. She was the second eldest and named for Mother's sister, but the meaning of the name had been forgotten. It meant faith or goodness. One or the other.

For goodness knows she had need of faith.

Adnia was as naturally lovely as an earthenware jar or a white stone in the sun. Without adornment, the mere fact of her quiet gray eyes and perfect skin, the rich auburn hair against her whiteness. Seated with her sisters, she was another flower until you noticed that protruding from her long skirt was this parody of a foot strapped into this ugly special shoe designed to assist her walking but in reality a hardship because it drew attention to her mortification.

Because of some mishap at birth, she was told, either in or out of the womb, the baby leg was twisted behind her. She was never told how or why, only that she had this handicap, she limped, she lunged, rocked like a ship in heavy seas. Steps and stairs were her anathema, hills a curse, poor Adnia, her small-proportioned body tapered gracefully down to a twisted leg and a foot knobbed like a cauliflower.

She had begun life kicking and laughing in her cot and grown from that as in a spell of good weather to believing she was like her older sister Lily and her younger sister Mary, perfect as all children are perfect. Until she had risked comparison and begun to notice that she was in some way extraordinary, that the grown-up people treated her differently, excusing her from this and that, saying, Oh, let the nice lady pick the pretty flower for you, or No, no, you can't run after the doggie. Then when the minister's children began being asked to parties, she was subjected to special attention, people said, "Oh, come and sit with us, Adnia, while they have the egg and spoon race," or "Let's look at the stereoscope pictures of Egypt while they play musical chairs."

It hadn't dawned on her, she was so confident that she was sweet and perfect by the way people delighted in her and chose her to be special.

"Addie, you look like a little daisy in that hat," they said, or "Gracious me, what lovely curls." They beamed at her.

Not even coming into church, marching behind Mother up the long aisle to the front pew, little Adnia with her heavy shoe going ker-plonk, ker-plonk all the way while heads turned, not even then did it occur to her that her specialness was that she had a disability. She wasn't conscious of any sham

33

enthusiasm when Miss Prute, their nurse, came gurgling in saying, "Oh, you're going to have a treat today, ducky," and then dressed her to go into Melbourne in a hansom cab with Mother and the treat turned out to be just another doctor who looked at her foot under a strong light and talked double Dutch to Mother over her head.

Much later, after things had happened to shake her security, when she was no longer safeguarded by her childhood, she realized that it hadn't been so much a matter of being dense (she was quick as a whip) as of dodging the issue in the way most people put off thinking about death. Whenever she heard her condition being discussed, she remained impervious, instantly disassociating herself so as not to disarrange her intense happiness. Like the time she had heard Lily saying to Miss Prute, "You know, that nurse we had who dropped my baby sister on the stone floor—well, I've often wondered if she mightn't have been responsible in some way for Addie's condition too, because Mrs. Ames, the midwife, swore that as far as she could remember the baby had been born normal."

Me?

Adnia shook it off, the way she shook her ringlets. No nurse had dropped her. When the time came she would be alerted to her "condition" and she would accept it, not before.

In the meantime she clung to the raft of her childhood, thriving on the attention she got from people who groped under chairs for the things she dropped or up on mantelpieces too far above her, saying, "Let me get it for you," or "Don't bend down, I can reach it." They held doors for her, waited while she floundered up or down stairs, smiling encouragement. A few overdid it, like the oxheaded Miss Prute, whose humor was heavily roguish, saying things like "That's a good girl, eat up your peas and we'll have you playing on the cricket team in no time." Those Addie ignored. Some she questioned. Like Mother, who never said anything beyond "Good morning, Adnia." "Good night, Adnia." "Your sash is coming untied, Adnia." Mother never gave her the benefit of any doubt and the only time she felt that Father had singled her out for any special attention was when one Sunday in the sermon he paused and looked down directly at her during his reading about the lame man waiting by the pool of Siloam for the angel to trouble the waters.

In the long summer afternoons she read to her little brother Fred under the peach tree heavy with acidy fruit. She was an actress, assuming various voices for the characters, threatening, cajoling, innocent, vile. They were reading *Treasure Island*. "Do Long John," Fred would exclaim and Adnia would get up and clump around on her own uneven walk, assuming the wooden leg. "Do it again," Fred would cry and Adnia would stomp until she had no more breath and the two of them dissolved into laughter, she so pleased by his approval, he so childishly fulfilled that they never once paused to consider what they were laughing at. Nor that they were conspirators in a guileful innocence.

Ker-plunk, ker-plunk, went Adnia around the tree. "Hearken to me, Jim Hawkins," she would bellow, better than a play. She would be anything he wanted: Oliver Twist, Mother Hubbard, Noah, Ned Kelly the bushranger. She was best as evil or deranged people; Fred screamed in delicious terror. Although there was the difference in their ages and in many ways he was still a baby, they had a common understanding and a world of their own that no one else entered into. "No, no, I want Addie," the little boy would insist when one of the other girls tried to give him his cod-liver oil or bandage a cut knee, and he would wait furiously while Adnia clumped up the stairs. Nobody but Adnia could get him out of a bad sulk. Miss Prute was often beside herself. Strapped into his high chair and commanded to eat his supper of mushy bread and milk, he resisted all threats; even when in defeat Miss Prute took away the lamp and left him to think it over in the dark, would not touch a mouthful until Adnia came in with a candle and said kindly, "I'll eat it if you don't want it."

Both of them being obstinate in different ways, they found an accommodation together against an uncompromising world. Both were impervious to certain facts, he that he was a boy amongst these girls, she that she was critically damaged, and together they translated their innocence to their games. She let him be Pocahontas, he made her dance.

"There's too much pretend," her older sister, Lily, said. Lily tended to be grown up and didactic even then. "You'll have him getting nightmares. Too much imagining's not good for the child."

"So's not enough," Adnia said firmly.

What harm was there, for goodness' sake, in ants being pixies and in seeing the faces in the Bad Banksia Man tree? If she and Fred wanted to believe the dreadful Scissor Man came to cut off their thumbs and they hid from him, thrilled with fright, under the sheets, what then? As if some clairvoyance hinted to her that she might not be intended to have what was generally known as a normal life, might never have a child, he became her baby and she performed the natural functions of a mother, feeding him, dressing him, comforting, cherishing. Like any normal mother, she was to lose him. Before anyone had time to notice, like a summer passing, he was out of his high chair, his little shoes no longer fit, his first milk tooth was gone. In the natural course of events he began to look further than the back garden for his world and over the fence came Jay and Alan Biden from next door. Slightly older than Fred, the Biden boys played cricket pugnaciously, climbed trees after birds' nests, swam noisily in the St. Kilda bay and had between them the imagination of a gnat, all of which proved to be irresistible to Fred, who, once helped over the paling fence, found the Bidens' backyard a playground of mysterious boyish pleasures. Adnia, coming home in the afternoon from Miss Garner's School for young ladies, would find no little boy in the swing, waiting, no sign of him until among the shrieks of the attacking bushrangers next door she would recognize the excited tones of her missing child. Patiently she waited at the fence, most tactfully she would pose the question.

"Would you like some bread and guava jelly?"

"No, thanks. Mrs. Biden gave us some banana custard."

"Look, I've got some new picture books for us."

"Mmmm. We're playing."

Then desperation.

"When will you be home?"

"Don't know."

The Biden boys naturally thought girls were extraneous and boys who played with girls were sissies. It had at last been pointed out to Fred that he was a boy. What did he think his little wee-wee was for? Hadn't he noticed that girls didn't have one? They all presented their little pink and mauve faucets for inspection behind the lantana bushes and Alan grandiosely let go with an arch of golden water, standing straddle-legged, and Fred was masculinely indoctrinated. Thrilled at his little difference from girls ("They sit down to wee," Jay said contemptuously), he pecked out of the egg in which he had been imprisoned under so many female feathers since he was an adored baby. No wonder he had been treated with such deference; he was a boy, he was a prince, he deserved it.

"When are you coming home?"

"Don't know."

Fred Lord? Oh yes, he knocks around with the Bidens and some of the boys from Highgate Prep. Little Fred Lord, he's one of the larrikins who play cricket Saturday out the back on the vacant lot behind the gasworks.

He came in hot and grubby, his hair plastered on his pink brow, socks falling down, sometimes cupping a green and gold beetle in his hand which he would not let go. Adnia would be waiting with the glass of milk.

"Ta."

"Don't say 'ta,' dearest."

Didn't like being called dearest. Assumed the Biden-like Australian accent: "Moi naime's Fred."

One day she dared to attempt to infiltrate this hostile country of cricket bats, fishing lines, scarred knees and perspiry little bodies.

She had seen, to her discomfort, spying through the fence, that the Bidens' sister Jill occasionally bowled for the cricketers. Well, Addie could bowl for them, it didn't seem to require that much effort. She practiced throwing a ball on the side lane until she felt she had achieved a good aim. Cautiously broached the matter. Fred seemed more interested in a squirming locust he had caught.

"No," he said.

"Why not? I can bowl underarm."

"Not on our team."

"Why ever not?"

"You're lame."

Oh.

She turned and went across the lawn to pick up the watering can and resumed watering the juicy big red cannas. She felt nothing, felt extraordinarily airy and light.

Then, as if God had struck her in the face, she was suddenly as scarlet as the red cannas right down to her neck. All the garden was silent around her, not a bee hummed. Lame.

Not that she didn't know. Just that it was suddenly as clear as lightning striking that she was a hindrance. She was distorted. The real reason for the solicitude given her was pity. Lame girl. That dreadful shoe she wore, no matter how pretty the dress. Now it had been said aloud. She could weep with shame and exasperation for all the special attention she had been given, the doors held open, the reaching under chairs for things she'd dropped, the patience. All for pity. Well, the wheel of pity was not going to break *her* spirit. Let other cripples hang on to every ounce of solicitude they could get, let them be saturated with attention and forbearing; not she. No amount of compassion was ever going to demean her. The more she floundered like a seal, the taller she would grow; the uglier her boot, the more dignified she would become. Just watch.

"I can pull out my own chair," she said that evening, snatching it away from the helping Mary. "I can reach it," she said, snubbing Lily passing her the glass cruet. They stared at her, disconsolate that their superiority was being taken from them.

They stared at her as though she had grown antlers.

"Are you feverish, Addie?" Father asked from the head of the table. Even Mother condescended to look at her curiously.

"No," she said. "Why? Do I look strange? I'm perfectly *normal.*"

But it was obvious that there was some psychical change in her; to touch her might have set off an electrical shock, she was so scornfully alive. She smiled at them pityingly because in the changing of her perspective, they were the ones to be pitied, not she. They had this vulgar need of superiority and goodness. They needed goodness to support themselves, like a crutch. So they were the handicapped ones, not she. Goodness. All this need of goodness. Maybe that was the reason there were murders. People couldn't stand the ever-present need for so much goodness.

That was what hell was, everlasting goodness.

Now she knew for certain, looking around the table at all these good kind people.

They were eating their soup, they were bent over their plates as if in prayer. They would do anything for her in their gracious superiority. They could also be murderers.

She was only nine when this occurred to her, but it was profoundly affecting, like a miracle. As if she had found herself skating.

39

No, Mother said. No to everything. Well, almost everything. She didn't need this, want that.

He was gone.

She was vastly alone. Vastly. On the cold moon.

Come, dear, they had said. Shall we get dressed now? What about your pretty pink bed jacket?

Always this condescending child-talk, as if they were all good chums, and always this disagreeable amiability. *Well* now, they said, bursting in on her contemplation of the moon around her. *Well* now, they gurgled with humiliating cheer.

She had been violently uprooted. Without a by-your-leave she had been bundled out of her house. Bag and baggage out of the house she had lived in all these years. She had been helped to dress in her black bombazine with her cameo brooch and her little black pillbox hat with the veil. Then she had been put into a carriage and then onto a train without a word of explanation or a second's consideration for her preference. Later at night she was hustled off this train and down a long gaslit platform onto another train, very small and wooden with hard seats where they had sat up, drowsing, all night until the morning stars showed through the cindery windows and a grim gray morning unfolded over ramshackle suburbs and they came into a huge smoke-filled terminal, roaring with noise and people, carts of oranges and pies, where she was dislodged into a cab and driven through the streets of an inhospitable city.

"Where are we?" she demanded once.

"Why, Sydney, Mother," Lily chirruped. "You're going to love it once we get settled in."

Ensconced in a vulgar hotel somewhere, three to a room, she asked no more questions. She ate what was put before her. She got into her flannel nightdress and into bed without argument. What was the use? The blind on the window next to her bed would not pull down and one of those new electric signs went on and off outside like fireworks. She slept only in little snatches, filled with troubling dreams. But what did it matter? For what activity did she have to be rested? For what appointment did she have to look refreshed? Time had become meaningless, four in the afternoon was the same as midnight. He was gone.

He was gone.

It was the only fact that helped her to die. The only fact that meant anything to her and continued to mean something so that she repeated it silently to herself, first thing in the morning, over lunch, pretending to read, watching sunsets, last thing at night. He is gone.

Not long after he had died, she began by not caring what day it was and then by not knowing. Things began to lose shape rapidly; she accumulated vacuums and, like a person who is losing consciousness, she became successful at compressing time: awakening from a morning nap, she would be told that it was nearly time for supper. Then where had she been? What had she been doing all those hours? Very quickly, alarmingly, she began confusing spoons and forks and, shortly, people. "What is the name of the smaller girl?" she asked Mary, honestly at a loss. "Which smaller girl, love?" "The girl who brought me in the newspaper just now." "Why, darling, that was *Sidney.*" But Sydney was the name of the city they now lived in. Was there a person too? She encouraged her own willful amnesia, she opened the blank windows of her mind to the mists around her. She was discovered just in time about to step into a tub full of hot water fully clothed.

They had called in Dr. Sayers, who was inordinately cheerful, therefore pessimistic about her condition. Shock, said Dr. Sayers, falling back on the flimsiest diagnosis. Or it could be, he said, stroking his little vestigial beard, premature senility. We had better be prepared for it if that is so.

Shortly after they had arrived at this ricky-ticky lavender-walled hotel, she had been fussed and fumed over, bathed, brushed and combed, and put in a surprising automobile and driven some miles out of the city to a splendid house where obviously nobody had ever misplaced anything and where she instantly recognized her cousin Jacquetta, though they had not seen each other for years.

"Annie, you lamb," Cousin Jackie had said and kissed her. Consciousness stirred, a reminder of something sweet, of youth and prettiness. Of stepping out of a boat onto a pier. Of a man. She was temporarily roused out of her apathy-in-extremis. She turned to her cousin when for a moment or two they were left enisled on a sofa together and said with the purity of her sincerity, "Help me."

But Jackie either hadn't heard her or completely misunderstood, for she merely smiled that polite iridescent smile she had for people and objects that should be admired ceremoniously and remain in their place. But later, as they were apparently leaving, in the hall, Jackie leaned toward her and said, "Annie, my dear, let me take one of the girls off your hands. Think about it, sweet lamb."

Can I help you?

One of the girls!

Take all of them, she had wanted to say. Just let me die. I want to die more than anything, don't you see?

Then they had been driven away in the car without anything being settled to some new house which was just another prison. She was again fussed over and as usual brought supper in bed lovingly. She felt by this time that her unpopularity with her children must have reached some peak, but the more they tended to her, the more they made her their priority, the wider the gulf between them. But how could they know about passion when all they had experienced was pleasantries and niceties, discretion and some worry thrown in for good measure? How could they possibly envisage what heights and depths she had traversed? Such conjugations of the human heart could not be explained to them, they only had a somewhat circumscribed viewpoint, severely limited not only by the fact that they were virgins but by a suffocating logic. On the very evening of the funeral, while she had been communing with the void in the darkness of what was going to have to be her new life, her eldest daughter, Lily, had intruded into her room, bringing a lamp and platitudes. Some drivel about her not having anything with which to reproach herself and encouraging her, actually having the audacity to encourage her to think what a good life *he* had had. *He* had had.

It was appalling, like being comforted by a total stranger in the street, by a bus conductor. She would have liked to grab her bath sponge out of the washbasin and push it down Lillian's throat.

Can I help you?

Once, in church, the organ notes vanishing into the air around her, she had looked down along the pew at their empty faces, Lillian, Adnia, Mary, Fred, Jessie, Sidney and Mignon. In total eclipse. They could have been anyone's children, there was this unfamiliarity, except in their various likenesses to her face, the evidences of her deep red hair and here and there to William's smooth glacial forehead. She was caught by the strong sense she had of a terrible vacancy. It was as though she were looking at somebody else's children. His. As they stood up all in a row to sing the hymn, she faltered, with a hand to her feathered hat as if it might blow off in the cold wind she felt suddenly right through her body and the implications it brought of destitution, of not loving one's own children and at the same time the need to get her breath in such a wind and to admit it. I don't care about them. She swayed.

"Are you all right, Mother?" Mary asked.

She had stepped out of a boat, she was wearing a lavender dress with French pleats and she had a parasol, she was typical of the day. She could have been in an illustration of a romantic Victorian novel and the young man who caught hold of her eager hand said, "Can I help you?"

43

Later they sat at a long wooden board table draped in Union Jacks, having tea out of a scalding metal pot. It was Empire Day. Later on there would be fireworks. Children ran with flags and hoops along the beachfront.

The young man with the long serious face and handsome side levers was William Lord, "newly arrived from England to be the curate at St. Cuthbert's." (It was significant and perhaps traumatic that Annie forever afterwards recalled it in the phrasing of a Victorian novel; she even visualized the frontispiece illustration of the two of them seated demurely at a flag-draped table, the young man bending toward the girl, the caption reading: "He sensed her bashfulness in her downcast eyes. 'Have I said anything to disconcert you?' he asked.")

Better for her, for all concerned, if they had remained in a book illustration. If she could have ended her life fictionally at the bottom of a page by simply remarking, "Reader, I married him." In reality, the refreshment tent was warm as a greenhouse, the tea was bitter, the sandwiches damp, the noise deafening. They had to almost shout to be heard above the din of clashing china cups, laughter and a brass band playing outside. In abbreviated sentences they heard from Mr. Lord that he had been at Cambridge, where he had done exceedingly well, rowed against Oxford, decided on the ministry, been ordained, fallen ill. In a brief respite from the brass band, he said in almost apologetic tones, "They found that I had a spot on one lung and advised that I get out of the English climate." The dryness of Arizona had been recommended, but in a moment of more logical consideration for the Empire (as if to emphasize his loyalty, the band struck up "Rule Britannia") he had chosen Australia. All this he addressed to Jackie, barely glancing at Annie. He seemed subtly to be proposing to her. But there was nothing new in that. Annie was quite accustomed to being left abandoned while young men paid court to Jackie. Jackie was proposed to on the average of once a month and once a month she sweetly dissented. She had bigger fish to fry, certainly with more than this consumptive young clergyman had to offer. She snuffed him out with extravagant gaiety and laughter. On their way out of the tent, he paused a moment at the table where sweets were being sold and said unexpectedly to Annie, "Miss Seddon, do you care for barley sugar?"

Next morning he appeared bright and early at the boarding-house where they were staying (they were in Rockhampton to take the warm sea air and escape the Melbourne winter) and proposed a walk in the public gardens, which they politely refused. But in the afternoon, while they were taking tea at The Cup & Saucer, he appeared suddenly from behind a potted palm, teacup in one hand, and asked might he sit with them.

He made observations about his work, his voyage out, his bishop, his living quarters. He hoped (when Jackie suppressed a yawn) that he wasn't boring them. He quivered with a suppressed sensitivity and eagerness, Annie noted, his fine nostrils showed white with tenseness, his eyelashes flickered.

"Miss Stark, Miss Seddon, won't you allow me to take you both out to dinner?" he asked, nervous as a lost cat.

He was lonely; it would have been evident to a blind person. Once they spotted him walking along the beach alone in a blustery wind, holding on to his hat while sand blew in his face, his liturgical clothes making him an unlikely beach-comber. His elastic-sided black boots squished in and out of the sand.

"Call out to him," Annie pleaded.

"Oh no," Jackie said. "We'll only hear more verse. He has a verse for every occasion."

"He recites most beautifully," Annie said.

She was to be shaken to the depths.

Young Mr. Lord seemed impervious to Jackie's cold-shouldering, or else her methods were misinterpreted as encouraging. He turned up almost wherever they went, at beach concerts, in the park. The more Jackie gently snubbed him, the more attentive and eager he became. He dashed ahead of them to get carriages or benches, he was left behind as they drove away. When they came out of the boardinghouse, there he was, leaning against the jacaranda tree. It was his very harmlessness that disarmed them, his frank eyes, his sincere smile; his profession made it impossible to take more drastic steps to get rid of him. And whoever heard of having to discourage a lustful curate?

Then Annie got word she must come at once to the bedside of an ailing mother who suffered on and off from an excitable heart. Not that Annie hadn't also acquired excitement of the heart. On the afternoon that she was to leave, she bade good-bye to Jackie, who was unable to come to the railway station because she was in the midst of having what she called her "unmentionables," which brought on painful headaches.

There on the platform was standing the Reverend Mr. Lord as if he had been deputized to see Annie off by the mayor of Rockhampton.

"Miss Seddon."

"Mr. Lord."

She had almost said My Lord.

"But how did you know I was leaving?"

"Your landlady told me when I just happened to call this morning, Miss Seddon."

"It's extremely considerate of you to come and see me off."

"Not so at all."

"Very flatter—"

"I needed to see you."

"How agreeable."

"When I heard that you were leaving today, there was nothing to do but to come to the station and to hope that perhaps Miss Stark would not accompany you. Do you understand, Miss Seddon?"

"I don't think so, Mr. Lord."

"Haven't you the faintest notion of what I am trying to say?"

"No, I'm afraid not."

"Haven't you any conception of my feelings toward you?"

"No."

"Then may I ask, had you thought I was perhaps more concerned with your cousin?"

"It had occurred to me."

That this conversation had taken place in these stilted and moth-eaten phrases was unlikely, paralyzed by her dim recall, and could have been due to the influence on her at the time of the novel she was reading by Mrs. Henry Wood. But nothing could distort the memory of his young urgency when he took hold of her hand there on the crowded platform and said:

"Oh my dear, I love you. I have loved you and longed for you from the moment you stepped out of that boat and I was standing on the pier. I have been tongue-tied with love for you, and so I had to address myself to your cousin and hope that you would understand it was because I was too shy. Oh my dear, my dear, you are the beat of my heart, so will you give me some hope? Oh Miss Seddon, Annie, here comes the train and I only have a minute or two to dare to ask you is there a possibility? Do you understand?"

"I—I think so," she had said. She had picked up her basketware suitcase and the wooden platform had begun to shake under her, but whether because of the train or her own beating heart she couldn't tell.

"I mean—may I ask you—in all seriousness—is there the slightest hope?"

They were standing together, looking at each other as if, amazingly, they had been lovers. People bustled by them, doors banged along the train, a whistle blew.

"I must get in," she said.

He assisted her into a first-class compartment and as she let down the window and leaned out, he took hold of her hand again.

"May I hope you will think about me?"

"I very likely *will,* Mr. Lord."

"Miss Seddon, I am due a fortnight's leave next month. May I come down and visit you in Melbourne? May I ask Miss Stark for your address?"

"Oh yes, ask Jackie. I mean—whatever you like, Mr. Lord."

The train had begun to move. He walked beside it, let go of her hand and then began to run.

"Would you begin by calling me William, Annie?"

"Goodbye, Mr. Lord—goodbye, William."

"I love you, Annie. I love you."

He was running, dropping behind, his panama hat blew off. He became a dot waving, wrapped in smoke, gone.

She thought that she had sat down and laughed and taken off her hat in a state of rapture but probably none of it was true, probably he had not said those things precisely in the manner that she remembered, probably he had been far more reserved, more liturgical. He may have even bought her a box of glazed fruit from a vendor. It was all lost in memory and now disguised as happiness.

One thing was certain, the Reverend Mr. William Lord had taken leave of his pastor in Queensland for two weeks and appeared in Melbourne on her veranda the following month and whatever took place between them, now omitted from her memory (she did not keep a diary), it resulted in their engagement and their wedding the following winter. Whatever took place between them on the platform at the railway station in Rockhampton, whatever transpired between them later, what actual words he used to propose to her in the stuffy dark green parlor of her parents' home in stultifying East Brunswick, she had subsequently translated into passion.

Just as someone might contract smallpox, she had contracted love. At first she could not have been more surprised to find her contentment in him ravished by an insatiable hunger. Long before their brief honeymoon was ended, while they were still enjoying the subtle but wanton spring flowers of their early intercourse, she became transformed by love. Before they left to go back to Queensland, she was abiding in a cocoon of bliss. It was incredible to her that she had so underestimated her own sensual prodigality. She was entranced to learn that she was pregnant.

There was ecstasy and mysticism and sometimes dazzling joy (she was overcome with the sense of it, she reached for his hand under the table) and she cleaned and scrubbed their plain little house with abandonment. She shook out the doormat. How beautiful upon the mountains were the feet of him who wiped them on it.

As an expectant mother she thrived, she grew, waxed fat and fruitful as a Biblical pomegranate tree. The climate of Queensland seemed perfectly to agree with her mood of expectation, the warm early spring brought gentle rain and in their small garden, shoots of young greens appeared. When he took over the duties of minister for the Reverend Mr. Salmon, away on vacation, she sat proudly in the front-row pew and gazed up at him in the pulpit. This portion of her early memory was mostly intact and essentially true to what happened. She could remember, twenty-five years later, exactly what sermons he had preached, what sort of dinners she had served, the names of parishioners who visited them, and she could visualize the little house set up on pilings above the ground so as to give some air and relief from the northern heat in summer. The outdoors lavatory, as though to hide its embarrassment, was rampant with honeysuckle.

What she could or would not remember was when the loving stopped. Sometime, there was no date in memory, no day seared into her consciousness, it was not as though a door had banged shut, William left her as surely as though he had packed a rucksack and driven away in a horse and buggy. The reason that it was not more savagely remembered was that she had not been stunned, she had not been cruelly bludgeoned, no bitter words had passed between them, no threats of divorce or accusations of infidelity were flung; the realization dawned slowly on her with terrible conviction that William no longer loved her.

She had her baby. They named her Lillian Sophia after Annie's mother (who had died two months previously of excitement of the heart), and he seemed gently grateful and pleased. Almost immediately their sexual unity resumed and at first she felt comforted by its renewal and his seeming gluttony of her. Except that (but this was in looking back, when all symptoms of some digression appear magnified) he was not precisely as romantic as she had remembered, or so it seemed. If it was possible to be physically aroused and yet preoccupied, so he seemed. But it was as intent and continuous as it had been before she had the baby, and for a while everything in their private life seemed as firm as the solid rock on which their marriage had been constructed.

When the second child was born with a twisted foot that the doctors pronounced incurable, Annie wept and William comforted her. Even though to be told that the child's deformity was God's will seemed to her to be evangelically unfair. But he was the clergyman, he sat professionally, at any rate, on the right hand of God. At times she had become (God forgive her) a trifle impatient that every excuse to be made was usually the will of God, which to say the least was a holy nuisance.

When he immediately resumed their bedroom life with what seemed to be ardor, she responded with overwhelming elation. She desperately wanted another child soon, a child perfect in every way to make up for the disabled little Adnia. Thus to assure her there was nothing wrong between them in their procreative life, that there was proof their ecstasy was God-given, which was what he desired. Incredible to her later that she could have taken such avoidance of the truth that it occurred to her only subliminally that he always turned away from her bodily the moment she was pregnant.

She had thought it was occasioned by his sweet forbearance, out of consideration for her, but gradually a pattern emerged that was too deliberate to be dismissed. She was becoming pregnant about every fourteen months; she could almost have marked it on the calendar in advance. It was as though he was activated by some ritualistic phase of the moon. She was ravished, possessed in a wildness that had the elements of rape, as if she had been waylaid in the forest at night and taken by a something horned, with cloven feet, and she responded to this fantasy with a wild joy, only to be thrown away and subjected to courtesy. Being conservative, she had an overweening sense of the romantic and she was assured of William's love by the way that he took her in bed, but unable to reconcile the ferocity of his lovemaking with the dull-edged figure who sat opposite her at the breakfast table and cut off the top of his boiled egg with such precision (it seemed to give him gratification) and introduced her as "Mrs. Lord." "I believe you have met Mrs. Lord," William said, presenting her, never referring to her as "my wife." Earlier, the sweet words had been said in bed, in the dark, sweetest words, dearest and my love, my true love he had said, reaching for her mouth in his, their sweet coming together, the magic of their impeccable timing, their bodies responding to each other, my dearest they had said. But now he came to her like a footpad, saying nothing but just as ferociously performing the ritual on an April or October night or whenever she was supposedly ready for quickening, and almost stumbling over him once, naked but bent in prayer in a slit of moonlight, she was tempted to ask him if he was importuning divine approval.

But all she said in the silence that followed the uproar of their union was "I'm cold. Let me have a bit more of the eiderdown."

"Yes, my dear."

Always Yes, my dear.

"Is the haddock cooked to your liking?"

"Yes, my dear."

"Was the bishop encouraging?"

"Yes, my dear."

"Would you read us the Twenty-third Psalm? Will you be away long in Toowoomba? Will you look at me?"

"Yes, my dear."

Look at me, she wanted to scream. Or to wear a low-cut scarlet dress like a harlot. Which she occasionally felt like. She let down her wonderful hair and stood naked in front of the full-length mirror and saw again that her chiseled body was thickening with childbirth. She had barely time to cherish a child, to get to know and love it, before it was snatched away from her by a nurse and she was becoming heavy with another. Gradually she receded from her children, they became noises upstairs in the nursery, she became faintly intimidated by them. When she came face-to-face with them, they seemed at a loss as to what to say to each other.

"Oh hello, Mother."

*"Hel*lo."

No matter how she tried to infuse some warmth into the greeting, it sounded hollow and perfunctory.

It usually ended with her saying that they had better go back now to Miss Humphreys, Garside, Prute, whoever was the current nurse. Not so with William. They fought to get to him, they tumbled down the stairs to greet him when he came in the front door. Oh, Father look, Father see, Father listen to this, they begged, and he responded with profound interest to their childish prattle and passing rivalries. He was no longer the parson. They laughed and played pranks on each other, but when she came into the room the revelry ceased. They all stared at her, patiently but with the quietly repressed annoyance of being intruded on. "Good evening, my dear," William would say, and she would take her seat among them like Banquo at the feast.

Then two children died in infancy. Bereaved, she was told again that it was God's will. She hoped vainly that he would turn to her in their mutual grief, if only for his own comfort, and she whispered this hope in her prayers. But when the second little girl died at only two months, suffocated by croup, she prayed for William's compassion and tenderness, this time through clenched teeth, prayed avidly for him to come close to her for reasons other than childbearing. Then she saw him through the dining room window, standing in the shadow of wisteria with his arms around both Mary and Lillian, who were sobbing. He was saying something to them, or perhaps quoting from the Bible, while the three of them swayed together in a comfortable rhythm, as if all three were suspended by invisible threads to an invisible Deity. Annie felt the full force of her jealousy pass through her like an electric current. If she had come upon him in bed with another woman she could not have been more affected.

There was no one she could turn to, no understanding preacher or woman friend to whom she could make her confession. If she'd only been Catholic, she would have been able to seek the sanctity of the confessional to say, "Father, I have sinned. I hate my own children," and ask for forgiveness. As it was, she had to swallow it and in swallowing it she became more poisoned and corrupted. The wall between her and William grew higher and more unscalable because of the children. She began not to be able to be with them for long because of a rising feeling of physical discomfort, an actual visceral shortness of breath which began in her chest like a tight ball of wool and expanded until she felt that her heart and lungs would burst. Outwardly she gazed at her children with cool detached eyes like somebody faintly bored, but inwardly she watched them through fires of resentment for what they represented. They were the living embodiments of his love. But not his love for her. For every caress and kiss on her mouth there stood a child that was his passionate reassertion of himself. This was the fact of life with which she was forced to live and yet continue to love him. For she lived to love him and that was the sentencing to life imprisonment by the Supreme Judge of heaven and hell, that she would love him forever.

So they grew on together like a crooked tree, so they bore fruit and reached out branches and grew more gnarled, went on into middle age, into another century. Seven children survived.

"Yes, my dear."

She felt that she could have accepted his death more accommodatingly if she had had some last word from him, the eleventh-hour word of love, or if he had at least said her name. If he had said "Annie."

What he had said to her was "Please tell Katie once again that she doesn't cook the bacon crisp enough." A minute or so later he spewed tea all over the table, dropped the cup and had died before they could get up from their chairs.

So she was punished by being left with her children and to their tender mercies and in her loneliness and ingratitude she longed to die. But that luxury not being granted her, she prayed for amnesia and got it. Gradually a white cloud encircled her and she withdrew into exclusion, she forgot her name and the words for simple utensils. Day and night merged into each other without clocks. People came and went in the haze. She was provided with plates of food and with pillows, she was coaxed into taking her medicine. Who was sitting by her? Was it Lily? Mary? What did it matter? They all had the same features, they were all big white rabbits as far as she was concerned. One rabbit gave her a bath, another rabbit helped her to dress. Rabbits sat her down in a chair in the garden under the whatsit tree until it was time to be taken inside again. In this cloud world, the only reality was William. She saw him vividly, far more clearly than the newspaper or knitting put into her hands. She was waiting for him and he was coming to get her.

"What are you looking at, Mother?"

"The harbor, the boats."

"Can't see the harbor from here, Mother."

Yes, she could. She was in one of the little boats, he was holding out his arm to help her out, he was quite young, they both were.

Or they were at the railway station. "Oh my dear, my dear, you are the beat of my heart."

Now that he was no longer here to contradict her assumptions, they flew into each other's arms. As long as there was no further need for logic, he became her true lover and she came to believe it, she saw him coming toward her across the lawn, they ran toward each other, they were enveloped in stars and she no longer knew that this was fiction.

Only he didn't come. Sometimes she thought she saw him arriving on horseback or driving a carriage up to the gate, but the horse, the carriage, disintegrated into thin air as somebody placed a plate of sausages before her and she was informed that it was time to wake up for lunch.

It was a quarter past ten in the morning when he came. She was sitting outside being read to, and the sun was in her eyes so that she did not see the yellow pony cart approaching until it was nearly at the gate, and the driver's face was obscured by the dazzle until the pony cart passed under a tree and in the second's shade she saw that it was William. He had on a white panama hat, one he used to wear on the beach at Rockhampton when they had first met. He was driving fairly fast. She got up and ran, she pulled open the gate and ran toward him through the noise of wheels on the gravel and the shouting, perhaps the rejoicing of angels. As the cart came on, she looked up toward his young smiling face, he was calling out something to her and holding up the reins. She held out her arms for him to lift her up. It was no dream, she could smell the horse, the cart was real. Glory, glory, hallelujah. . . .

At the inquest, the baker's driver testified there had been no time to stop the cart, Mrs. Lord had come running out of the gate directly in his path. Her lame daughter had been with her at the time and had not been able to catch hold of her quickly enough to stop her getting out into the road. The baker's boy was absolved of any blame.

The silence at home was really terrible, there was no one to criticize and dance attendance on, to be put on the potty, to be a nuisance, to be whispered about behind her back. Her quilt was neatly folded on her immaculate bed and there was a blank where she had been. The girls sat around the kitchen table and had tea and fruitcake and everyone felt that something ought to be said and finally, to break the awful silence, Mary said it:

"Poor old Mum."

Lily was dreadfully seasick on the S.S. *Waratah* on her way to Tasmania. The little coastal vessel, top-heavy with a tall blue funnel, yawed and floundered in the troughs of sea in the Bass Strait on its voyage from Melbourne. Lily lay, fully dressed, on her bunk in the tiny cabin while the stewardess brought her ginger ale which she then immediately vomited.

"*Us*ually it stays down. I've found it's the only thing that stays down, usually," said the stewardess, whose name was Brigid. "Mind you, the sea's a little heavy tonight," Brigid said, "but I've known it worse. I've seen them all laying in their bunks from one end of the boat to the other." Thank God there was only one night at sea. Sometime tomorrow, if she ever lived through this purgatory, they would be safely in the calm waters of the Derwent.

"Is it your first trip to Hobart now, Miss Lord?"

"Yes."

"Oh, you'll find it a lovely town. People I know tell me it reminds them of Scotland, the country around, the mountains and sheep and so forth. You ought to see a bit of the country while you're there. You ought to see the lovely Derwent valley where they grow the hops."

Hops! The very thought of them made her iller.

"Have you got friends there?" Brigid pursued.

"No. I'm here to speak for the Women's Socialist Movement."

"Oh, reely?"

"Have you heard about our crusade?"

"Can't say I have."

"I'll give you one of our pamphlets. I'm going to be speaking at the Trades Union Assembly tomorrow night, that is if I'm recovered enough to stand up on the platform."

"Oh, you'll be right as rain, Miss Lord. Will it be in the paper and all?"

"I should think so, Brigid. Mrs. Daphne Oxhard is the chairman of the committee arranging everything."

"Oh, I've heard of *her,*" Brigid said in a tone of thorough disapproval.

It was funny how these young workers, frequently underpaid, resisted the Movement. Some of them were more right-wing-minded than the plutocratic bosses.

Lily was about to ask Brigid some questions about her employment and time off, but a surge of nausea swept over her again and she had to ask for the basin. She felt too weak to talk and closed her eyes. Most of the night she retched and heaved with the plunging ship while Brigid brought basins and towels, bismuth and dry biscuits. Toward dawn the heavy seas seemed to abate and the ship stayed miraculously on even keel. Lily slept, and awakened to the sight of Hobart through the porthole and Brigid bringing her a cup of tea which to her amazement she was able to swallow, asking for a second cup while she sat up and combed her hair.

"Brigid, you are a pearl. You've hardly had any sleep."

"Oh, I'm used to that."

"How much do they pay you, may I ask?"

"Two pound ten."

"A trip?"

"Oh no, a month."

"But that's disgraceful. You have to be on call all night. How many trips do you make a month?"

"Oh, about ten, I s'pose. But I get a week off every three months."

"I'll write a very severe note to the shipping company."

"Oh, please don't, Miss Lord." Brigid was wringing her big red hands. "I love my job. It might cost me my job if they'd think I was complaining. And I get my meals and I'm allowed to sleep in my cabin in port. Oh, don't go complaining to the company, please, Miss Lord. I'd much rather you didn't, if you don't mind."

Lily put five shillings in a saucer on the dressing table.

"Are there many of you girls?"

"There's about eighteen of us all told."

"I don't suppose you have a union?"

"Oh no, we don't have anything like *that.*"

Brigid looked scandalized. Well, sometimes there was no reasoning with these girls. They almost asked to be exploited. The Irish seemed especially prone. There were more Callahans and O'Rourkes doing abominable jobs for rock-bottom wages and being cheerful about it. Think of all the Irish washerwomen toiling over copper tubs for a few shillings for the idle rich of Sydney. Well, that was part of the reason Lily was here in Hobart. To spread the word about the new awakening. Just look what had recently happened in Russia. If that wasn't going to stir up the working classes everywhere, then the moon was green cheese as far as Lily was concerned. She had never been surer of anything in her life. You only had to have seen the way they clapped her in Wollongong and Kiama, the wives of the coal miners. She had the press cuttings with her to prove it. "Ovation for Miss Lord."

She put on her new hat with the brown bird on it and fixed it with a hatpin. It was too tight for her and made her scalp burn, and her button-down shoes were apt to pinch. These new clothes had been bought for the trip in too much of a hurry. But there was never enough time for personal things. They had to go by the board for the New Advancement. With a deep sense of the significance of her arrival, she followed the cabin boy carrying her straw suitcase up on deck. Miss Lillian Lord of the Women's Socialist Movement to address the Hobart chapter. She pulled on her gloves and gazed over the water at the stone buildings built the century before by the convicts. Well, here she was. But there was no one to meet her. There was no sign of Mrs. Daphne Oxhard or any of her henchmen. In her letter, Mrs. Oxhard had written, "You will be met by either I or one of my henchmen."

Lily went down the swaying gangplank, feeling the aftermath of her grueling night and a sense of a new uncertainty. Up until now, wherever she had ventured to speak there had always been a little bother taken to meet her, one or two women at the railway station or waiting at the hotel. She stood in the bustle on the quay and looked around, half hoping to see Mrs. Oxhard, late and apologetic, bustling toward her. She picked up her suitcase and made her way through the crates and bales in the cavernous shed to where she hoped there would be a taxi. The other passengers from the ship were being greeted, embraced and put into hansoms and cars. As she looked around uncertainly, feeling the tightness of her new hat and the pinching of her shoes, feeling unwelcome in this strange town, a man crossed in front of her to get into a cab, turned and said:

"Look here, can I give you a lift?"

When she hesitated a moment, he lifted his hat politely and said, "Where are you headed for?"

"The Mount Wellington Hotel."

"Going right past it. Hop in."

He gestured to the driver to pick up her suitcase and then gallantly held open the door of the cab for her to get in.

"This is most kind of you."

"Not at all." He tapped the driver on the shoulder. "The Mount Wellington first, driver." He sat back; she noticed he was wearing the most elegant boots. "Excuse me," he said, "Miss Lord, isn't it?"

"Yes. How did you know?"

"I've seen a photo of you in the newspaper. Do you mean there wasn't anyone to meet you?"

"I think they may have been detained."

Again he raised his hat. "Roderick Loftus."

"How do you do."

"I think I read you're here to speak on behalf of some movement or other?"

"Women's Socialist."

"Ah yes."

"Mrs. Oxhard is the president here."

"Jessica is?"

"No, Daphne."

"Oh. There are several Oxhards here in Hobart. We once had an Oxhard as governor."

"Oh, really?"

She hardly thought that Governor Oxhard would have been sympathetic to the Movement. But then neither perhaps would Mr. Loftus be, with his fine boots. They were now driving past rows of whitewashed stone cottages with little gardens laced with daffodils and spring flowers. Well, if these were the homes of working-class people, they certainly had it better than their comrades in the sooty environs of Sydney and

Melbourne. She looked out of the cab windows until Mr. Loftus coughed and said:

"Quite an undertaking, your movement."

"Yes, we feel very strongly about it."

"I'm sure you do."

"We do indeed."

"I do hope, Miss Lord, that you won't take this discourtesy of not being met as an indication of the lack of Tasmanian hospitality."

"Of course not."

"Curiously enough, I happen to be in the exact reverse of your situation. I happen to be president of our Geographical Society, and I was at the dock to meet a Mr. Quinlan, who was scheduled to speak to our group this evening, but who was not on board the night boat from Melbourne and could have, I think, at least sent a telegram to save me having to get up so early to meet him."

"Yes, how thoughtless."

"Ah well, for every thoughtful person there is a boor."

"How true, and again how kind of you to go out of your way to drop me at my hotel."

"Actually, Miss Lord, it is not out of my way because as a matter of fact Mr. Quinlan had also been going to stay at the Mount Wellington. And here we are, right on cue, as they say."

Mr. Loftus, president of the Hobart Geographical Society, was well known here, obviously. The doorman touched his cap. A bellboy rushed to take Lily's suitcase. Mr. Loftus gave his arm for her to alight. At that moment, a photographer wearing a leather cap came running up.

"No, no," Mr. Loftus said, waving away the man with the camera. "There's no need for pictures, Jack. Sorry, but Mr. Quinlan was not on the ship. Unless—" Mr. Loftus turned with a dazzling smile to her. "Miss Lord, would you do me the honor to have a picture taken with me to show our club members?"

The least she could do. They smiled at each other while the photographer snapped them once, twice. Mr. Loftus held out his hand.

"Goodbye, Miss Lord. Good fortune attend you, as Shakespeare says."

"Goodbye, Mr. Loftus, and my deep thanks to you."

She was laying out her toiletry articles in the hotel bedroom when there was a knock at the door.

Two women, dressed in cheap brown and green cotton dresses, stood outside. Each wore the tin badge of the WSM and they were holding on to their handbags as if they had been warned about bag snatchers. Their hats were tragic. The older woman gave an unsmiling nod.

"Mrs. Oxhard?" Lily asked. She could hardly believe it. Mrs. Oxhard was so nondescript.

"Yes."

"Oh, come in, won't you?"

They sidled in.

"This is Miss Love," Mrs. Oxhard said. "Miss Love is our secretary."

Miss Love was staring at Lily's hat. Perhaps she was a bird lover. Lily unpinned her hat and laid it on the dressing table.

"Won't you sit down?"

They took the two chairs, leaving Lily the bed.

"You musta been pretty sharp getting off that boat," Mrs. Oxhard remarked with a tiny but unpleasant laugh. "You was gone by the time we got there."

"Well, I waited for about five minutes and there was no one around and so—"

"The trams take a while getting down to the wharves and, you see, I had to pick up Miss Love first and she lives quite a way out. Got here by yourself then, did you?"

"A gentleman gave me a lift in his cab."

"That was lucky."

Mrs. Oxhard had the whining voice and suspicious watery eyes of the undertrodden. You'd have thought they might have chosen someone with more dash for president. Miss Love looked dubiously at the hotel curtains.

"Well," Lily said, "here we are then, the three rabble-rousers, ready to do battle."

They stared at her silently.

"Well, I'm all yours for the day. What do we do first?"

Mrs. Oxhard coughed and murmured, "We thought you'd probably want a bit of a breather after your trip, as you've got your speech tonight."

"Oh, I had a little touch of the mal de mer but I'm all right now, right as rain and ready to begin."

Mrs. Oxhard gripped her bag tighter. "Oh, I see," she said. "Well, we didn't have anything much planned, really. We thought we'd wait until you got here."

Really! Everywhere else they'd had her running from the moment she got off the train, meeting people, visiting the slum areas, helping to raise money, championing the cause. Wasn't there even going to be a lunch for her? She'd sketched out a speech. Wasn't she going to meet the famous Mrs. Tyrrel, the wealthy patroness who had given so much time and money to the cause?

"Whatever you think you'd want to do," Mrs. Oxhard said in the same defeated tone, as if the cause were already lost.

"Well, I'd like to meet some of the women."

"Oh yes."

"I'd like to see the substandard housing here, how they live, that sort of thing." Naturally.

"I s'pose we could." Mrs. Oxhard seemed mildly surprised.

And what about the famous Mrs. Tyrrel? "And Mrs. Tyrrel?"

"Mrs. Tyrrel?" Mrs. Oxhard looked blank.

"Aren't I going to meet her?"

63

"She'll be at the meeting tonight."

"I daresay, but I thought so much could be gained if we could have ten minutes to chat. I'd be so grateful to get her viewpoint on women's conditions generally."

Mrs. Oxhard fidgeted with the strap on her handbag. "I s'pose we could, but the thing is she's got Mr. Barnes on her hands."

"Who's Mr. Barnes?"

"He's the main speaker for tonight."

She had come all this way across torturous Bass Strait, suffering incalculable physical distress, not to be the main speaker?

"Oh?" Lily could not help her own cool tone.

"He's the Labor member of Parliament for the Illawarra district in New South Wales."

"That isn't in Hobart."

"No, but he's Tasmanian born. And he worked in the coal mines as a lad. He's come a long way, you see."

"I see."

"There's going to be quite a crowd for him tonight," Miss Love put in, speaking for the first time and to the wall.

"In fact"—Mrs. Oxhard leaned forward—"we were going to ask you, if you wouldn't mind, to keep your speech to about ten minutes so as to give Mr. Barnes more time."

So as not to advertise her growing dislike of Mrs. Oxhard and of the whole situation, Lily smiled prettily.

"My speech is locked into my head," she said, "in such a way that if I tried to delete any of it, I would lose my way and forget the continuity and possibly the whole sense of it."

"Oh yes?" Mrs. Oxhard again gave her pitying laugh. "Oh, well, if it can't be *helped* . . ."

So then, as it now looked as though they were going to sit here all day like rag dolls, Lily grasped hold of nettles, rose and said, "Time's ticking away, ladies. Shall we go? What's first on the agenda for me?"

Mrs. Oxhard and Miss Love exchanged a glance, then Miss

Love said in an undertone that perhaps Miss Lord would be interested in the soup kitchen.

Mrs. Tyrrel had started it for the survivors of an explosion and it had grown so that now they had more than a dozen volunteer workers and fed more than a hundred poor people a day.

"But that's what I'm here for," Lily said and put on her hat with the bird, pinning it on determinedly. "That's exactly the kind of work the Movement should be doing, that's enterprise. Lead the way, ladies."

Discount the fact that they had no transport for her, that no arrangements had been activated, nothing planned. Forget the fact that nobody at the soup kitchen had been forewarned that she might appear, let alone knew that she was one of the founding members, and that all she was asked at the kitchen was please not to stand in the way of the swing door. Forgive them for taking her to meet Mrs. Tyrrel through the gate marked "Servants' Entrance" and standing her at the kitchen door, where they were met by a fearfully uppity maid who glanced at them as if they were lepers and then informed them that her mistress was at lunch with Mr. Barnes, her houseguest from Sydney, and that she couldn't see anyone now. Dismiss the humiliating manner in which Mrs. Oxhard laughed this off and retreated like a mendicant out of the gate as though she were accustomed to being thrown out of fine houses. Overlook the way Mrs. Oxhard and Miss Love brushed aside Lily's sincere wish to visit some of the very poorest of the poor in order to see how they survived. Lily was already so accustomed by now to the lack of cooperation and just plain politeness that she was not in the least surprised when Mrs. Oxhard suddenly squawked that oh, look at the time and we've got to be at the Trades Union Hall to help with the chairs and moving the piano and can you get back to the hotel on your own, Miss Lord, we'll see you tonight then.

Now you mustn't, Lily said to herself, *expect* gratitude, you mustn't look for respect. That isn't what you are in the Movement for.

But just the same—when it came to absolute duds like Daphne Oxhard, it made you think of all the hours of work you put in for no salary whatever and then got not an ounce of recognition. She dressed most carefully for the meeting as she always did. She combed her dark red hair upward into a black ribbon and wore her long brown velvet trimmed in black. Usually a cab or a car was arranged by the local committee to take her to the hall but when seven o'clock struck on the Town Hall clock outside and nothing, nobody appeared, she went downstairs and asked at the hotel desk how far it was to the Trades Union Hall. At least the desk clerk was civil enough to go with her to the street and point out the direction. A very light rain was falling and she had no coat or umbrella so that she arrived at the brightly lighted hall looking rather disheveled. She stood neglected in the lobby of the old wooden building, wondering what to do or whom to ask what she was to do, and looking through the doors she saw that the hall was indeed crowded and she was about to catch hold of one of the women going through into the auditorium when Mrs. Oxhard, all in peach voile and with a dying chrysanthemum pinned to her shoulder, came toward her waving a newspaper.

"Well," Mrs. Oxhard said, hardly able to conceal her triumph. *"You're* in trouble."

"Am I? In what way?"

"Just look at *this* in tonight's paper. Quite a few of the crowd have seen it, I'm afraid. Oh, you're in a bit of trouble, all right."

Lily took the newspaper being prodded at her. The unsettling events of the day had partly obscured what had taken place so long ago this morning, but gauzily she recognized the splotchy photograph of herself wearing her bird hat and smiling at Mr. Loftus. The caption read, "Captain R. Loftus wel-

66

comes Miss Lillian Lord, a Sydney Visitor to our Shores."

Sydney visitor indeed! As if she were some trumpery socia-
lite.

"Well? That's the gentleman who so kindly gave me a lift
from the pier."

"Roderick Loftus; don't you know who *he* is?"

"How could I possibly?"

"Don't you ever read the fliers we send over to you people?"

"We get so many from all the—"

"Roderick Loftus. 'Skullbreaker,' we call him. He's the boss
of all the bosses. He's out to get the unions. He owns two zinc
mines and he's the worst strikebreaker there is. His men musta
broken a couple of dozen heads down near Port Arthur recently and he's got scabs and spies working everywhere. He
was probably lying in wait for you and you walked right into
his little trap."

Because, Lily wanted to say, there was no one to meet me.
But Mrs. Oxhard had now been joined by several women who
were staring at Lily with apparent skepticism.

"I didn't *know.* It was just an innocent mistake. How would
he have known *me?*"

"Oh, he's sharp, all right."

"He reads our stuff," one of the women said. "He knows
everything that's going on at our center, you can be sure."

But in an instant the women were turning their heads away
and their interest was being deflected from Lily to the arrival
of a large horsey lady and a gentleman who were being bowed
into the hall.

"Just a minute," Mrs. Oxhard called out to Miss Love, who
was escorting the new couple. "They've got to meet Miss
Lord."

The horsey lady turned a painted face around and Lily was
hustled toward her. "Mrs. Tyrrel," gasped Mrs. Oxhard and
pushed Lily almost directly into Mrs. Tyrrel's ample bosom.

Mrs. Tyrrel, benefactor deluxe of the Tasmanian chapter of Women's Socialism, drew herself up like a ship docking and stared.

"Miss Lillian Lord," Mrs. Oxhard said, "our speaker from Sydney." Not a word about her being one of the founders.

"How do you do." Lily extended her hand politely, but Mrs. Tyrrel ignored it and said, "Oh yes," in the tone of one who had read the evening *Herald* and who knew a fool when she saw one. "Miss Lord, Mr. Barnes," Mrs. Tyrrel introduced. She was overdressed for this democratic occasion, in blue lace. Mr. Barnes looked young to be a member of Parliament. He smiled briefly at Lily.

They were being directed now into the hall and up steps onto the platform, meagerly decorated with the Tasmanian flag and some pots of fern, where several chairs were arranged behind a lectern. Mr. Barnes and the ladies were seated and then, with the crash of a chord on the piano below the stage, everyone rose while a thin woman wearing pince-nez bullied "God Save the King" out of the old keys.

Really it was disgraceful. Not that Lily had anything personal against the king; it was just that now the Great War, as everyone called it, was over, there was no need to keep up this symbol of colonialism and the vestigial link to the royal family. When you thought how much it cost to keep the royal coffers going and you looked around at this threadbare group of women standing obediently, while the national anthem was played, in their patched shoes and pathetic hats, it gave you pause. If she had her way, she would rouse them with the *Internationale.* Now *there* was a tune full of blood and hope, and none of your "long to reign over us" nonsense. Lily sat down a second before it was over just to show her repudiation of this German royal family who had had to change their name to Windsor.

But then, not only the king but the rambling. The first part of the meeting was taken up with a long discussion of why and how the Women's Socialist Movement offices would have to move from the space kindly donated to it by the Fish and Game Preservation Society to another location in a less desirable part of Hobart.

"Miss Lillian Lord."

She had almost been drowsing when she heard her name announced by Mrs. Oxhard. She stood up and went to the lectern in a splatter of applause.

"Let us be*gin.*" Lily began, as she always did, dramatically, taking them all in from one side of the hall to the other, and from one side of the hall to the other there was silence. But not the silence that she was used to, respectful, hushed, an amicable bridge between her and the audience over which she would carry her message to them and to the world. Almost at once she recognized something sinister in this silence, there was hostility in it. Somewhere in this silence rats scurried in the dark of an old unfriendly house and although the women pinned their faces on her, there was the sense of sidelong looks and disbelief.

She wished now that she had not been so obstinate in refusing to cut down her speech. It extended before her like an endless promenade of windy rhetoric. Her few little jokes fell flat on the floor. Her story of Marx in Paris with his poor broken shoes and the difficulty he had in getting up the stairs to meet Engels (no matter that it wasn't verifiable, it usually got a reaction, they leaned forward, they were held) was received in sullen silence. She was not going over! The first time that she had not held an audience in her palm. Meeting their accumulating dislike of her was much the same as smelling smoke just before finding that the house was on fire, and a slow resentment infected her so that she knew she was speaking badly, her points were not well made, and her enthusiasm for the cause, instead of being convincing, sounded high-pitched and petulant. At one point (she might just as well have been making a speech from an iceberg in the Arctic), she dried up completely and in the quick frozen silence while she fumbled for the line a woman toward the back of the audience called out something. Ignoring it, Lily went on gamely. But they had her now, they had seen her falter and the fact that she had been affected by their doubts of her sincerity spread through them mischievously and, like a mob becoming inflamed, they picked up stones. Another woman called out and then another. Lily had stopped speaking and was blinking at them. Now they started to stand up. "Who are *you* to preach?" someone called. "Friend of the bosses," a woman cried, and now several of them were waving the fatal newspaper and the ugliness grew much plainer. "Bit of a fake, aren't you, Lily?" crowed an old woman in the front row and the nastiness of it was taken up by them. "Fake, fake," they chanted while Mrs. Oxhard stood and made feeble efforts to quieten them by waving her arms. Fake, fake, *fake,* they intoned. A dreadful joy was infecting them now; they were grinning at her.

Catcalls had begun to sound and Mrs. Oxhard had resorted to banging her gavel, but the louder she banged the rowdier they became until the meeting was totally out of hand and Lily could only stand there with her arms pinned to her sides. At this point Mr. Barnes, the young parliamentarian, stepped forward boldly and holding out his arms to the crowd called in stentorian tones, "Quiet, *quiet,* please now, ladies, give her a chance. I'm sure there's been some mistake, but either way Miss Lord's a true friend to your cause and it's only fair to let her speak." A hush came over the hall, but it was rebellious now and as cutting as bayonets and Lily resumed her speech haltingly into it. Whatever power and authority she had started with had gone and she sounded almost apologetic as she invoked Louis Blanc as the father of Socialism and sounded his cry, "From each according to his abilities, to each according to his needs." But it was the mew of a kitten and she sat down to perfunctory applause. The rest of the meeting went by with an ache in her neck from holding her head up bravely.

Mr. Barnes seemed to go over like the aforementioned house on fire. There wouldn't have been a war if the women of the world had united against it, Mr. Barnes assured them, and part of their duty was to make sure it never happened again. A minute's silence was called for the war dead, followed by the announcement that refreshments would be served in the basement.

Somehow shortly afterwards she found herself outside in the street, walking home. She had escaped by a side door; nobody having spoken a word to her, no one having uttered a syllable of regret for what had happened, being left alone in the confusion of urns of tea and nude-looking saveloys, she had simply walked out the door.

Back at the hotel, she let herself into her room and without even taking off her dress, she lay down on the bed and stared at the ceiling. There was more to think about than the unfortunate photo in the newspaper or that Mr. Loftus had turned out to be a conniving scoundrel and that he had lured her into the trap designed to sabotage her appearance at the meeting. Something else was becoming painfully clear to her in the aftermath of the evening's fiasco. She had never in her life (she was now twenty-eight years old and it seemed like a hundred) been truly appreciated. Never given the assurance she so much needed and deserved. The word of thanks. Not even by her own family. Oh, lip service. Ta, Lily; thanks, dear. But she couldn't honestly remember one occasion on which she had been recognized for what she was, a tower of strength.

Not that she had been one by choice. It had been foisted on her because of being the eldest. Therefore she had the key to the medicine cabinet, she had the iodine and the bandages; naturally they came to her with their wounds. If anyone was to be taught how to stuff the goose, it would be she. If someone was to be called out of her warm bed at two in the

71

morning to see who was crying, having nightmares, had been sick on the floor, it was Lily. Get Lily, everyone said. Ask *her* where it is, how it is, why it is. The housekeepers, the nurses quickly learned they had a willing horse and left her their unwashed cups in the sink, their uniforms to be ironed. No one else was going to bother. And who else knew how to wheedle Mother into taking a bath once she had lost hold on reality? Who else was ready to give up seeing the new Mary Pickford film because one of the younger girls had a temperature? Much of it was Lily's own fault, she knew quite well. She was a born doer-unto-others. Even as a small child she had begun by picking up people's dropped umbrellas for them. Soon she was opening the front door to callers and ushering them into her father's study. Please won't you come this way, she said and expected their serious compliance. Oh, the little angel, people said, what a little treasure you have, Reverend. And her father seemed to agree. Lily had unconsciously taken on the role that her mother had vacated. Mother, who was constantly in what was referred to as a delicate condition, lay on sofas behind closed doors and was excused from bothering with visitors and parishioners. So the serious-faced little girl hung up coats and hats and asked would people kindly come into the parlor.

As, year by year, sister after sister was added, she expanded her role of motherhood and in the course of her truncated childhood (for really she had no time for dolls, she played no games with other children) she grew up long before she had to. Infected with the need for caring, she thought at first of becoming a nurse but the mere smell of hospital disinfectant turned her faint. Besides, it had become natural for her to be at home in case Adnia or Fred or Jess needed something, in case Sidney was coming down with a cold. No eligible young men hovered in her background. But she was contemplating a horizon without knowing yet what it was, and in the mysterious way God operated, her life was changed in the least expected manner. Once a week, Emmy Greenop came in to do the filthy work, which was to clean the big iron oven, hang out and beat the carpets and wash the kitchen floor. Naturally this involved more work for Lily, who could be found scrubbing the grease marks off the linoleum so as not to make such hard work for Emmy.

Lily fed Emmy on scraps of leftover veal-and-kidney pie and Emmy fed Lily scraps of information about the tide turning when the working classes would claim their rights over their oppressors. Emmy attended meetings organized by a Miss Partridge, a Socialist. She handed on little pamphlets to Lily, who, although skeptical, was nevertheless intrigued by the vision of a society based on an extraordinary simplicity of equality. "Oh, it's going to come about, Miss Lord, we're going to get our rights," Emmy said, chewing on her lunch with the few teeth she had. She had persuaded Lily to come with her into Sydney on the little steam train to hear Miss Partridge hold forth, and Lily accepted only so as not to offend Emmy. So it was a revelation to her that she was immediately drawn to the cause. She was riveted to her hard wooden chair by the dazzling pyrotechnics of Miss Partridge and the feverish reaction of the women who crowded into the little room. It was Lily's transformation overnight to feel that she was one of them, that her way of life had been made clear to her. When Miss Partridge asked for volunteers to do office work in their spare time, Lily held up her hand. From typing envelopes, she went on to submitting little pieces for *The Worker,* the penny paper issued by the Socialist Democratic Party, and then one evening Miss Partridge was indisposed, and Lily took charge of the meeting and shook fire and brimstone into the ladies. She was electric with words, she burned with sincerity, and they cheered her and stamped their feet on the bare floor and had been doing so ever since.

Until now. But then tonight had been an accident. Or had it been? Could it have been designed to punish her for secretly wanting the recognition she had always craved, first from her family and now from the people whom she had committed her life to helping? Wasn't it that she really loved the deafening applause and the nice write-ups in the local newspapers, the comments on her appearance, the way people introduced her as *the* Miss Lord? And how much did she really like going into the dirty smelly little houses and greeting the unwashed people in their sour clothes, the mangy children who were often stricken with unpleasant diseases, rickets and ringworm? Sometimes she was afflicted by a revulsion which had more to do with disgust than with pity. Once or twice lately she had come home nauseated by the smell of the poverty which she could not get out of her nostrils. So had this evening in Hobart been the method with which God or the devil meant to face her with the fact that she was a fraud?

She twisted and turned in uneasy sleep, dreaming that she was trying to pet a filthy oily seagull. Its gummy feathers tore off in her hands and she cried out in her sleep.

While she was dressing in the morning there was a knock on her door. For a second or two she could not place the man in the gray check suit and polished boots, and then, "Oh yes, of course," she said to Mr. Barnes, the parliamentarian from the evening before. She had so successfully erased the terrible meeting from her mind that he had vanished with it.

"Won't you come in a minute? Do excuse the room; the maid hasn't been in to do it yet."

Oh, should she have mentioned a maid coming in to make her bed? She and her speech about equality? Mr. Barnes sat down. Twisting his homburg hat in his big hands, he seemed at a loss, so she said as warmly as she could, "How nice of you to call on me. I thought perhaps I was a pariah."

"You were caught in a trap anyone could have been."

"I daresay I should have been a bit more wary."

"Oh, if you're on our side of the fence, there's always someone out to get you."

"I suppose you've had your scrapes too."

"Oh, you bet. I'm the bloke who's proposed the Minimum Basic Wage Act in the House. Well, naturally the Nationalist Party and big money's against it. I'm for an insurance plan and old age pension for workers. Oh, the big boys'd like to skin me, all right."

"I'm sure."

"Look, Miss Lord, I'm on a tour of inspection this morning to see Boyle Street and Waterloo Road."

"What exactly are they?"

"Bad section. Like to come along? I've got a car waiting."

"Oh, it's just what I've been asking to see."

"We're in this together, and I thought after last night—"

"How kind of you, Mr. Barnes."

Feeling suddenly light and coquettish, she pinned on her hat with the bird on it. She went downstairs with Mr. Barnes, convinced that the fight was still on and that she had an ally. She liked his candor and really, for a man who had started out in the coal mines, he sounded so well educated. Though one mustn't mention it, of course. Seated in the dark blue sedan was Mrs. Oxhard, and judging by her greeting, something had been said to her about Lily's treatment.

"*Good* morning, Miss Lord. Hope you slept well."

Mr. Barnes, Lily thought, had been busy on her behalf.

Waterloo Road was a stretch of hobbledehoy wooden houses holding each other up by huddling together like cattle.

Thin raggedy children were playing in the open drain that ran muddily down the unpaved street. They stopped to stare at the big car turning unexpectedly into their cul-de-sac. Slatternly women leaning on fences looked with glazed uninterested eyes at the three people alighting at number 10. Had they been told that the gentleman was a member of Parliament from Sydney, they would not have cared much, they were long past caring; it was evident on their yellowish pasty faces and in the way they slouched at their gates. They were the defeated.

"Name's Radcliffe," said Mrs. Oxhard, referring to a slip of paper. "Widow with five children, one of them a Mongolian boy. No pension. Eldest girl supports them by working in the local paper mill. Husband got caught in some machinery and died of injuries so they gave Roma a job sweeping up in lieu of compensation."

Mr. Barnes gave Lily his arm to step over the piles of refuse in the gutter. Even before you got into the house you could smell it. The smell. It was always the same; indefinable, sweetish-sickening, it stank of drains and bad food and unwashed bodies. Of a glum boredom with despair. It anesthetized.

Lily prepared herself for what was coming. She put on her best egalitarian smile when the thin broomstick of a girl appeared in the doorway and Mrs. Oxhard said brightly, "Well, hello, Roma, not working today?"

"I got a sore arm," Roma said in the dull voice of someone accustomed to plagues.

She led them into a cramped room where an older woman was sitting by a wood stove with a child on her lap. Two other little girls looked curiously at the visitors. "Here's the ladies and gentlemum," said Roma and the older woman nodded. "Now, Mrs. Radcliffe, did you get any help from the Workers' Aid we sent you? Has anything been done about your roof?" asked Mrs. Oxhard briskly, and the mother gave her a look of intense distrust and clasped the child to her as though Mrs. Oxhard might be going to snatch it away. "Don't reckon," she said in a low voice and Roma said, "They come and talked to the landlord to give us more time to pay the rent, that's all they done."

The child on Mrs. Radcliffe's lap began a wail and at the same time there was a snuffling noise from a corner of the room, half snort, half snigger, as though someone had a bone caught in the throat, and Lily turned to see the Mongolian

76

idiot boy sitting on a wood box, his melon head nodding on the thick barrel chest from which his short arms protruded like lizard's legs. A long green tear of saliva hung suspended from his open mouth and his piggy eyes seemed to be excited at the entrance of visitors. He made tiny jabbing movements in the air with his little turned-backward hands. Squinting upward toward them, he let out a stream of gibberish until Roma said, "Shhh now, Frankie, it's all right, here's your toy," and handed him a wooden spoon. She produced a rickety-looking chair and at the same time indicated the wide double bed, on which there were remnants of blanket. "Won't you sit down?" she said, and there was a vestige of ceremony in the gesture, enough to touch Lily's heart, and she smiled at Roma and sat down in the chair, swallowing and trying not to reach in her bag for her handkerchief to repel the odor—it was like a gas leak.

Strangely enough, Mrs. Radcliffe had begun to sing. She rocked the child on her lap and in a low sweet tone she had begun to croon what sounded like a Scottish folk ballad or a sea chanty. She crooned and rocked the child and her thin hard mouth took on a gentler, younger look so that Lily was struck with the thought that this gnarled woman was possibly still in her thirties. Something about the sea and a lost ship Mrs. Radcliffe sang in a pure crystal water voice and underneath the singing Mrs. Oxhard was saying in a matter-of-fact voice, "Turnips. All they've had to eat for a week is boiled turnips and a little stale bread. They haven't seen a pat of butter or an egg for months. And the two younger girls got sent home from school because they were wearing no underpants. Tell Mr. Barnes about your job at the mill, Roma. Mr. Barnes is a member of Parliament. Speak up now, Roma, don't be shy."

Roma said apologetically that it wasn't too bad, they gave her a place to sit and have a mug of tea at lunch, the boss's wife gave the girls some of her left-off old clothes. They had

Christmas and Boxing Day off. Roma looked frightened that Mr. Barnes might be going to report her for telling him anything bad about the mill. Her big hungry eyes looked at him reproachfully for being a member of Parliament. As if they didn't have enough trouble without him coming here and asking her all kinds of questions. She replied to them in monosyllables and tried to brighten the corners by adding that although her pay wasn't enough for them to make ends meet, they often got a free fish off the trawlers down by the wharf when the nets came in. It's not bad, Roma said to everything, not bad.

Suddenly the singing stopped and Mrs. Radcliffe said in a scalding voice, "Who are you?" She was staring at the three visitors now with unconcealed dislike. "Who are you people? You come into our home with all your talk and everything and what do you do for us? Who said youse people could just come walking in like this? We don't want you poking your noses in here. This is our *home.*"

"Now, Mrs. Radcliffe . . ." Mrs. Oxhard began, but her remonstrance petered out in the silence created by Mrs. Radcliffe's denunciation. In the silence of her pride, *they* were the beggars, Lily thought. The two little girls in their thin shifts had moved toward their mother and were standing one on each side of her chair, completing the picture of want like an engraving, but the atmosphere was laden with Mrs. Radcliffe's private affluence. And in the grievance they were causing, Lily looked around desperately for some sign of forgiveness for their clumsiness and at that moment she caught Roma staring at her hat, the hat with the brown bird on it. The look on Roma's starveling face was a marvel of sweet wonderment. If an angel had appeared in the room, Roma could not have been more transported. Without a second's thought Lily took off the hat and put it into Roma's hands and then ran out of the house.

"The shame of it," she said to Mr. Barnes outside, meaning

them and the Radcliffe family and everything. "Not to be able to do anything," she said and without warning she was weeping into Mr. Barnes's waistcoat, not only for the hopelessness of their cause, the whole unfed wilderness of the world, but for her own lost self.

Ferdie, he called himself.

He was a girl, like all the others.

Or so he thought, little Fred, Ferdie, Piggle Wiggle.

It was an eternity of childhood before it had been broken to him that he was a boy.

In his first baby picture he is wearing a frilly baby dress left over from his sister Mary because Miss Prute, the nurse, just hadn't the time to get into Melbourne on the tram to buy him little-boy duds and besides, he was so adorable with his russet curls which they had left long that she liked to dress him in the little smocks and patent-leather button shoes discarded by the older girls. So he was photographed all in frothy lace with a pink ribbon around the waist, gurgling with delight. In this beribboned world nobody questioned or enlightened him. When he came prettily into the room in this gaggle of girls, he was accepted as one of them. "Oh, here come the children," someone said and visitors clucked and told him what a darling he was, what a little sweet. Nobody ever said what a fine boy, and if they had it wouldn't have disillusioned him. In the bathtub nobody ever pointed out his little pink proclivity to him. That was never referred to and the absence of it on the others never occurred to him. In his joyful innocence he and his sisters were as alike as peas and as sexless as cherubs on a weather vane. He was Piggle Wiggle in a world of all-encompassing affection and laughter, of innocent children who never referred to his difference of gender and a nurse who deflected sex by alluding to him as "it." Oh, here *it* comes, Miss Prute would sing when he appeared. *It* wants its face washed, doesn't it? And when they all went to the beach he ran down into the sea with a little rubber cap on to keep his hair dry just like all the girls. They all held hands and ran with him into the sea, where they became neuter bubbles floating in rubber caps.

Then, coming out of the water, someone would cry, "Come on, Piggle, race you," and they would all pretend to run faster than he up the beach while he skittered after them, gurgling with delight. He imagined they would play this game forever because everything went on forever, they would come splashing out of the water and run, on and on and on. Until one extraordinary summer when they actually ran away from him and disappeared. Just suddenly. It seemed to him that overnight he no longer seemed to please them quite as much, suddenly he became Ferdie rather than Piggle because there was a new baby for them to coo and cluck over, little Jess who was being put into the lace dresses and baby bonnets that had been his, and although he was still hugged and kissed, it was with less exultation and as if they were impatient to get back to the baby, to see what the baby wanted, darling little Jess. Then to his surprise he heard them singing "Sweet and Low" into the cradle, which had surely been his song, made for him. And what they saw in this red-faced thing covered in its own disgusting spit he could not imagine. When he threatened the baby with her own rattle he was actually slapped and told he was naughty, told to be very careful with her because she was "only a little girl." Well, so was he, wasn't he? What was so special about *her?* That was also the summer that Miss Prute left to get married. So everybody had run up the beach and left him except his crooked sister Adnia, who couldn't run. But she was marvelous at reading stories and acting out the parts, and the two of them stayed alone together, perhaps because Addie couldn't walk any faster than he.

As he grew older, but not conscious of growing, he began to notice that the older girls, Lily and Mary especially, turned away from him to the wall when they undressed at the beach to put on their bathing suits in the big old wooden Ladies' dressing shed and once while Mary was getting the sand off him under the shower, a fat older lady who was drying her big bottom said, "That child's staring at me and he ought to be in the Men's," and Mary said, "There's no man to take him in." Probably because Father never went in swimming.

As far as Ferdie knew, Father never got undressed because he was a minister and if he didn't have his collar on then people might not know him. Mother and Father were like the gods that Addie read to him about, like Wotan and Fricka. You hardly ever saw them except at mealtimes. Every so often, Miss Prute dressed him up in his best smock and combed his hair and they went upstairs and she knocked on Mother's door and a thin voice would say Come in and they would go into the big room with the enormous bed and find Mother lying down on the velvet couch, reading. Usually the blinds were pulled down so the room had a greenish light that made Mother look ghostlike. He hated it when Miss Prute left the room because then he and Mother were alone together and didn't have an earthly thing to say to each other and Mother would put down her book with a sigh and ask him how he was and what he had been doing. Nothing much, he would say, covered in shyness, and stare at the fancy wallpaper wishing it were over. Sometimes Mother would say, "Come here and give me a kiss," and he dutifully went over and reached up to her face with his mouth and one time while they were kissing, she pulled him toward her fiercely and said, "Be a good boy now and be grateful you're not a girl in this horrible world." But surely she knew. "Yes, I am," he said, correcting her, but she smiled dimly, misunderstanding him. She closed her eyes, which meant Go away now, I'm tired.

But was he a girl? He began noticing that the kids ("kids" meant the rougher element, rude boys and girls who picked their noses and spoke in twangy Australian accents) snickered and nudged each other when he came into Sunday school in his neat little smocks and bow-tied shoes, and one older boy asked, "What's your name? Beryl?" and he said sweetly, "Ferdie," and they guffawed and hooted with laughter. "No, it's Beryl," they chorused, pulling at his smock and rumpling his curls but not daring to go any further because he was one of the Lord children, the minister's family. But word must have got around because next thing he knew he was being taken into Melbourne on the tram by the governess and fitted out in little gray flannel pants and black boots and then (just as Addie had warned about the dreadful Scissor Man) he was taken into a shop and sat on a high box and snip snip his long red curls were gone.

So what a boy he was, his sisters loved him again, showing him off to the neighbors and the deliverymen in his new trousers. But he didn't feel any different, merely cut off, slightly hurt. The thought of being a boy was lonely when the only world you knew was girls, and the fact that he would soon have to go to school at the boys' primary, where the shrieks and hoots in the playground were enough to wake the dead, filled him with terror. He wanted to stay being a girl, being a girl was safe and delightful because you were like everybody else. In his dilemma he turned to the only person who seemed to understand, his sister Adnia. They had something in common: he was a boy and she walked funnily.

And they clung to each other with fairy stories and love and a bit of fright.

Then as naturally as daylight coming, he saw the facts and they were not so terrible, they were the Biden boys next door, and instead of being repelled by their raucous behavior, their whoops and dirty knees, he was interested. Something was stirred in his small being by the smack of the ball on the cricket bat and by their voices in the pepper tree catching locusts. "Want to see?" they asked him and opened their grubby paws to show him the fat green things waving their legs. Their smudged faces and heated smell came through the paling fence and reached into him as they began having little conversations and interchanges. He told them his name and that his mother was lying down and they told him their dad was a fireman and that they didn't believe that rot about Father Christmas. They helped him climb over the fence into the new world and then he was Fred and Ferdie was left behind in that dull world with Addie and her fusty stories and he was let bat and best of all they held a secret conclave behind the toolshed and showed their wee-wees and Alan actually wee-weed right there on the lawn as if to show his superiority over all girls and grownups, and in that thrilling moment Fred accepted his own dewy scepter as his mark of manhood.

"Say cock," Alan commanded.

"Cock," said Fred, thrilled.

"Say piss."

"Peece."

"Say bugger."

"Bugger."

Gosh, gee whiz, crikey, it was fun being a boy. He got to be later and later for supper, refused to go to bed while it was still light, made the basin dirty and gave poor Mary the fright of her life when she found a live locust in the soap dish.

Fred, the sisters called into the twilight, over the fence, down the road. Fred, come in now. Fred, dinner's on the table. Bedtime, prayers. And the face that greeted them was often hot and indifferent. But they were still lovey-dovey, cuddling, chiding. Oh, how did you get so dirty? They couldn't accept him as growing up. Wherever have you been to get a caterpillar in your hair? The difference was that he now saw them for what they were, girls, and the difference between them was vast.

Even the growing up was different. He learned something happened to the girls when they were twelve or thirteen which they couldn't mention it was so shocking. But it kept them from swimming and that was how you knew it was going on and not to ask. And both Mary and Lily had developed little chest balloons under their camisoles.

The world was full of secrets; boys had them too, as he discovered in high school and was indoctrinated into the largest secret of all. Can you come? asked Archy Liggins. Where? Fred asked and after the giggling died down he was taken into the deserted school auditorium where five boys lined up along the edge of the platform and disported themselves rudely in a competition to see who could climax first. One of them was Fred's father's altar boy, Lionel Evans, and another was, to Fred's amazement, ethereal little Gentry Prudhomme, who had often come to the house for tea and was always being pointed out as the paragon of good behavior. Fred was goggle-eyed at the possibilities and shortly afterwards began to turn the key in the bathroom door and thus began his estrangement from his sisters and from women in general. Often then after school he indulged in feverish clandestine carryings-on with boys in cobwebby cellars and wash houses. There was nothing epicene in these sexual extravagances, no hint of effeminacy was ever permitted, and the act itself was performed in a bald travesty of masculinity, the ballsier the better, the more hulkingly male the less shame. So they swaggered in and out of their lavatory relationships, swearing and posturing with their arched phalluses, rivaling and succumbing and occasionally choosing an accommodating partner for a companion so that small marriages were consummated and later dissolved and the most flagrantly bullish was Fred Lord. Once his voice changed he solicited partners in a husky baritone and scoffed at his own indulgences in a hearty backslapping manner, using as coarse a language as he could. "Bullshit," Fred said to his lovers, to pals, to anyone showing affection for him. "Bullshit" was the password to Fred's isolation. And nobody could be tougher on the football field than this rugby-legged boy who once used to try on his sister's hat before the mirror.

True to form, he was among the first in line to join up with the Australian Expeditionary Forces when the war broke out. He actually perspired with eagerness to serve king and country, and snapped to attention every time a band passed down the street. ("Oh we don't want to lose you," pretty girls in red, white and blue sang at the enlistment rallies, "but we think you ought to go.") He took off his glasses and somehow managed not to bump into anything at the enlistment depot, but ironically this otherwise exceptionally well developed male who had conspired to safeguard himself from any emotional involvement was found to have a strained heart, a slight weakness but enough to find him unfit and to rescue him from possible death at the hands of the Turks the following year in the Dardanelles, where the Aussies were mown down like hay. Where both Lionel Evans and little Gentry Prudhomme were killed.

Fred, forbidden heroism and the football field, retreated into the brick cloisters of the University of Geelong. "My dear child," his sister Lily wrote to him, "this dreadful war is only a worldwide conspiracy by the Krupps and the international munitions makers, be grateful you didn't have to go."

But he wasn't comforted or appeased. No longer allowed boisterous exercise, he began to grow flabby, at least he felt flabby, and looking at himself in the shaving mirror he thought he looked it and that his fluffy pinkish hair was growing thin in front. He was feeling the pinch of middle age at nineteen and it occurred to him strongly that he needed a new direction. As he stood in the morning sunlight in the poplar grove outside the biology building, it occurred to him that he needed to fall in love.

What never would have occurred to him was that he would fall in love with his sister Sidney.

The house was deathly quiet when he opened the door. He had forgotten his key but remembered that they left a key under the loose tile of the low roof over the portico.

"Anyone home?" Fred called.

Nothing but the dripping of a kitchen tap. Usually there was a chorus of voices: Oh, it's you, Look who's here, Fred's here. Sisters would envelop him, coming from the stairs, from the pantry with floury hands, putting combs in their hair. But today there was only florid silence and a dripping tap.

The smell of the house was the same, a dull smell. His dislike of the house made him even more resentful that no one was here to greet him. Where would they all have gone? He had written to say he was coming for the Easter holidays and they all knew the Melbourne train got into Sydney at nine in the morning on the dot; why couldn't someone have been here to at least say hello, say welcome? It was part of the family's bone laziness that kept them still living in this ramshackle pretentious house full of airs and graces and drafts, full of gloomy corners and not enough sunlight, damp even in summer. Nothing but cold linoleum on the floor. Did they stay on in this mausoleum just because Cousin Jackie charged them little or no rent?

By Christ, Fred swore, didn't it make them squirm even to look at the front gate and think of Mother? Mother trampled to death and run over by the baker's cart right at the front gate and yet the girls lived on here quietly drinking their everlasting tea. By Christ, it was enough to give you the bloody shits.

Enough to give him the usual shivers of his secret shame whenever he became righteous and indignant over his poor Mum, considering that he had been devoid of grief over her death, had had to rely on a sharp wind at the cemetery to be able to wipe away a tear or two. Bloody fraud and he knew it.

Just the same, the woman for all her faults and coldness had been their mother and there they still were, looking calmly at the gate. Christ.

He carried his heavy suitcase down the hall and opened the door to the room he usually used when he was home and was surprised to find it orderly, with a new quilt on the bed and a pair of woman's shoes by the bureau. Who had moved in here? Where were his golf clubs and his ties he used to leave hanging on the mirror?

He was contemplating getting into a real bust-up with them over moving his things when he heard creaking sounds on the stairs, and going back into the front hall he looked up and saw a young boy peeping over the banister.

"Yes? Who do you want?" Fred asked.

"Oh, it's *you*," the boy said. "You're early, aren't you?" He poised a leg over the banister and slid down the bottom half, arriving in front of Fred. It was Sidney.

"Sidney, I didn't know you. You've cut your hair."

"Yes, as a matter of fact. How are you, Fred?"

She leaned forward and they kissed in an awkward bump. Sidney's hair was cut short like a boy's and she was wearing a sweater several sizes too large and a pair of old plus fours and dirty sand shoes.

"Oh, well, welcome home, Fred."

"Thanks. Those are my plus fours you've got on."

"Oh, are they? They're wonderful and comfy."

"Where *is* everybody?"

"They're at a peace rally. Lily's a speaker. She's wildly pacifist, so's Mary."

"Bloody stupid. Who's taken over my room?"

"Miss Rintoul."

"Who the hell is she?"

"Didn't they write to you? She's the boarder; she's rather ghastly but it helps out with the gas bill and whatnot. You're early, Fred."

"I took a taxi."

"All the way from town? How original. Oh, you're in Jess's old room."

She had grabbed his bag and went swaying with it up the stairs while he followed. Into what had been Jess's little box of a room before she left to become the great lady. Bullshit.

They were all arseholes, nobody to welcome him, nobody to give a bugger about him, he needn't have bothered to sit up all night on the express. But where else was there to bloody well go? He sat down on the bed and looked at strange Sidney.

"Why'd you cut your hair like that?"

"Well, you see, I'm *not* a pacifist and I thought I'd like to get a war job in a factory and I'd be better off with short hair, but it turns out I'm too young."

"Aren't you still at school?"

"I got expelled, sort of."

Some rigmarole of a story about how she had been discourteous when the headmistress had caught her smoking. She had called the headmistress an ugly word no nice girl should know.

He was punching the mattress.

"Bloody awful bed."

"How was your train trip?"

"Bloody awful. Soldiers on leave bloody sang all night."

"How bloody?"

She was like one of the boys, swore easily, you could be yourself with her, no bullshit.

"Did you hear I got turned down for the army?"

"Yes, Fred. I'm sorry."

"Bloody strained heart. Trust them to find out when I didn't even know myself."

Impish face she had, turned-up nose, comical except that when she was looking serious you saw she had really beautiful eyes, a darkish hazel. She was no beauty but yet you couldn't take your eyes off her because there was something she had to offer, a buoyancy. Fancy little Sidney turning out to be a whiz-bang like this.

"How's it going at the uni?" she asked.

"Oh, it could be worse, I s'pose, but sometimes it seems like a lot of bullshit to me."

Sidney looked at a toe peeping through her sand shoe and said seriously she supposed it would. "But I suppose if philosophy sometimes seems like bullshit the only thing is to be philosophical about it."

"Bloody right."

Shit, she was so easy to be with; they'd only been magging about ten minutes but already he felt they'd known each other this way for years. She brought out a very masculine protective strain in a bloke. Looking at her, he could actually feel a dominating maleness creeping through him. It even affected the way he was sitting there on the bed like a big wrestler, arching his shoulders. He grinned at her.

"Listen," he said, "how'd you like to pop into a frock and I'll take you into town for lunch?"

And it would serve the others right to come home and find nobody.

"At a hotel, you mean?"

"If you like."

"Bet your bottom," Sidney said and was gone down the hall in a flash.

Why not? Not one of your veal croquette lunches at one of those genteel ladies' tearoom places; they were enough to give you the jimjams with their Iceland poppies on the table and waitresses dressed as gypsies. Why not a good blowout at a posh place like the Carlton, white tablecloths and silver and being handed the menu by the maître d' and Sidney could have a sip or two of his beer while no one was looking.

"Here's to your very good health, Sid," Fred said, lifting the frosted glass of pilsener.

"And ditto," Sidney said. She looked more like his younger brother who had got into a dress for a lark. They had been given a window table and felt rather grand. Probably the best thing about lunch in the Blue Room at the Carlton was the way the iced consommé came in little glass dishes set in silver. The couple of beers made him feel important and expansive or maybe it was Sidney.

"How about we go for a matinee?" he asked.

If they hurried they might just get in to *Chu Chin Chow* at Her Majesty's. He'd heard it was a knockout.

Oh, gorgeous, Sidney said. She was good fun to take out, she appreciated everything so avidly. He took her bony little elbow in his hand going up all the stairs to the "gods." From the moment the crash of the cymbals started at the overture, she was gone, she was in make-believe China.

Waiting for the train home at Central in the dusk, she told him she was going to be a writer. It was all settled. Their boarder, Miss Rintoul, had sold her a little secondhand Corona typewriter for two quid and some ironing. She'd already written a story. It was called "The Passing Passion" and she'd sent it in to the *Bulletin.* Mum's the word, Sidney said. Nobody knows I write yet. On the train they sang "I'm Chu Chin Chow from *China.*"

"Sick," Lily said, meeting them at the door, "with fright and worry. You could have left a note. In ten minutes we were going to ring the Turramurra police station."

Only in town, went to a matinee.

"Found your suitcase, couldn't think where you'd gone."

Oh, I was all right, he said.

"Not *you.* It was Sidney we were worried about, she's only a child."

"Oh, silly," Sidney said, "you know nothing bad ever happens to the wicked." She winked at Fred.

Go and help Mary with the bread sauce, Lily said, all despair at the world and at people who casually went off to matinees. "Welcome home, Ferdie," Lily said glumly. Something was wrong with the stove, it wouldn't stay lit and you couldn't get anyone to come to repair it during Easter. Oh well. It was a typical homecoming. Young Mignon had to have a tooth out. Watch out for that spider, Mary shrieked.

That night he had tumbled dreams about rescuing Sidney from a collapsing bridge over a deep chasm, she clung to him and he held her tenaciously but then she slipped out of his reach and there was nothing in his arms except a lumpy pillow and he was awake in the first daylight. So it was consoling to find her in the kitchen in the morning before anyone else was up and that she had made them both a pot of tea. The tea was coal black; it had been steeping too long. She had been up hours, waiting for him. She'd doped out a story in longhand. She was a good sort.

"It's bonza," Fred said, tasting the bitter tea.

"I wish you could come home more often, Fred," she said.

What was nice was that she was brand-new, he'd never known her before when she was a kid. He began to make excuses to be with her alone. Couldn't Sid and him go and pick up the groceries? Sid and him would hop over to the post office for Lily. They sat up late after everyone had gone to bed and he told her things he'd never admitted to anyone.

"But why be frightened?" Sidney asked. They were on one of their long walks.

"Don't know; I just am, sometimes."

"You went to join up and I think that's as brave as *any* thing. What would you be afraid of?"

"Everything. Aren't you, sometimes?"

"No. I don't think I ever am."

She was getting that quizzical look.

"I'm all sorts of things, some of them not too nice, but I'm not afraid. Oh, I suppose I would be if something terrifying happened to me like being in a burning house. But you see, being frightened about something takes too much out of you."

And he could see her, in her knickerbocker pants and sweater and her boy's haircut, stubbornly not being afraid. Looking dragons in the eye.

"Now, poor Lily," Sidney said, "she *invented* worry. Don't invent worry, Fred, it's too damn tiring."

Bloody right. What he'd like would be to have her along when he got the mopes and worried about exams, about whether he was on the right track of things, about what would happen to him. She was like a little soldier. That was it. Sid was his little soldier-woman-mate. He took hold of her hand.

"You'll do me, mate," he said hoarsely and she turned her face up to him, he thought to be kissed so he kissed her and she kissed him back, lightly on the lips, and they walked on a bit until he said suddenly, "Oh, you don't know how lonely I've been."

He pulled her to him and this time they kissed like lovers. Then she broke away and began walking quickly down the road and when he caught up with her she said, looking at the ground, "I love you, Fred."

"And I love you."

"And that's all it is," she said with such purity and gracefulness that he felt his eyes prick with tears.

No, she could not see him off on the Melbourne express because Lily worried about her going into the city at night, a girl her age alone.

But she would write to him. Bet your bottom.

Dear Bro, she wrote to him, and sometimes My Worry Dear. I miss you somewhat dreadfully, old darling. Dear dear Elf, he replied, I ditto. They exchanged private tribulations, she told him that her short story had been turned down by the *Bulletin* with the flimsy excuse that her style betrayed an innocence too youthful to allow her to write of such emotions with conviction. How do they *know*, she asked. He confessed to a night of shameful drinking on the town with some "cobbers" and of how he had then overslept the next morning and missed a vital lecture. Safely apart and shielded by their pervasive innocence, they indulged in passionate affirmations of their affection. Yours till the end of time, she wrote and added kisses. Thou hast the pavilion of my heart, Fred reminded her.

Solid in their convictions, it never occurred to them that

their letters could be read by anyone else, let alone that they might fall into the hands of someone with a pitiless lack of irony. Their sister Mary was born without a trace of humor or irony in her veins, notwithstanding that she laughed the live-long day. Dear Mary, she could and would see you through any painful experience on earth, but she was incapable of seeing the joke. Dear Mary's hearty laugh would reverberate through the house but if you troubled to come two flights downstairs to investigate the merriment, it would have been to trip over wild geese.

Sweet Mary, her gaiety reached up to them in the attic, where they often stole time together in the duskiness of old tennis nets. It was Fred's first visit home since Easter.

Thought they heard their names in Mary's laughter coming up the stairwell.

Mary was leaning on the kitchen dresser and had her back turned to them as they came in. She was reading aloud from something in her hand while Lily and Mignon shelled peas and Adnia ironed a dress. The scene had a gentle family look of warmth and lambency until Lily saw Fred and Sidney in the doorway, when immediately it took on the overtones of con-spiracy. Lily seemed to signal silently to Mary, Mignon's hand stayed poised over the saucepan, only Adnia, ironing, seemed unaffected. And Mary. Mary read on from whatever was in her hand.

" '. . . even when you sometimes fret over my worrying when you are doing the worrying, sweet one. I lie on my hard dormitory bed and thank God for you, my darling one, and think how lucky I am to have my little elf—' "

What had been at first incomprehensible rubbish became horrifyingly, comically familiar.

"Mary, stop," Lily said, grasping at a dish towel as if to hide her shame behind it, and some scintilla of caution must have been transmitted to Mary for she turned her head and saw Fred and Sidney in the doorway.

"Well, and here they *are.*" Mary, undaunted, waved Fred's letter. "Here come the young lovers. Well, what are we to call you two? Daphnis and Chloe? Danty and Beatrice?"

"Excuse me, that's *my* letter," Sidney said and took it from Mary's hand. "Where did you get it?"

"I just was tidying your room and I recognized Fred's writing. I didn't think you'd mind." Mary's abject innocence.

"You're a sneak, Mary, and I think it's contemptible of you." Sidney was white-lipped, and she folded her letter.

"Oh gracious," Mary said, poor Mary in her typical way. "I didn't think you'd be embarrassed, love. I truly didn't. Look, I didn't know it was *serious.*"

A look went around the kitchen and in the silence Adnia went on ironing, ironing. Lily shelled peas, Mary flustered with her hair. Serious. The word landed like a grenade or so it seemed to Fred, and suddenly everybody was behaving with exceptional gentility.

"I'm very sorry, Sid," Mary said.

"How about a cup of tea?" Lily asked.

Nobody looked directly at them, at Sidney and Fred and at their scorching faces. As if they *were* lovers. Just as if they had been caught *in flagrante* in the attic. Adnia went on ironing, ironing. Then after a minute Sidney went briskly out the side door into the backyard and Fred said huskily, "I wouldn't mind a cup of tea," and so, grateful to move away from the situation, both Lily and Mary made at once for the sink to fill the kettle, bumping into each other and apologizing. Sorry, dear, sorry. Mignon turned away to a basket of laundry. Only Adnia, as if she were stone-deaf, went on ironing as though nothing had happened.

Nothing had happened. Not that their letters hadn't been foolish and syrupy for two reasonably grown-up people, but nothing had happened. Not really. Everyone knew nothing had gone on between them but—

Smiles were different. Their smiles to each other were too

bright. I'm sorry, he said to Sidney, I wasn't listening. What? she said to him, I was far away. Would you like to do so-and-so? he asked. Oh, I don't think I can today, she said.

They were too conspicuously unaware of each other in company, their glances turned away to other people. She got up from the table before supper was finished and was heard to slam her door upstairs, he ostentatiously put on a coat and went off for walks alone. It seemed to them that everything they did had significance; even avoiding being alone together seemed to transmit guilt.

But he knew the knock on the door before he said come in.

"Look," Sidney said, "we're a pair of fools, aren't we?"

"Are we?"

"Oh, Fred, please don't give me that bloody polite pretend-I-don't-know-you stuff, please."

"I'm sorry."

"Look, I mean, what are we hiding from? We haven't done anything, it was all stupid bloody Mary's fault. Fred, I miss you, I miss our bonza talks. I love you, Fred."

"Yes, yes, I too," was all he could say. His eyes were filling with tears at the sight of her, she looked small and defenseless in her too big sweater.

"Well then—can't we just say to hell with everyone else? I mean, suppose . . ." Only she could be this daring, he would never have dared. "Suppose it had been true, suppose we *had;* would it be anyone's business except that it's wrong in the Bible?"

The thought was beyond him, *she* was beyond him in some ways. She could accomplish this easy renunciation and they could go on as before, but he knew that he couldn't. The mere implication had been enough to make him feel as though someone had unbuttoned his trousers in public. Maybe it was because he was guilty. He *had* had thoughts about his dear little boy sister, he had thought about them perhaps swimming, away in a forest somewhere, bare as magpies under the sun, running hand in hand. It had never occurred to him that such thoughts were indecent but now this damned inference had been made, it spoiled everything. It made him feel dirty being alone with her and he couldn't help wishing she hadn't shut the door, couldn't help imagining sly looks and leers outside. He got up off the bed where he had been sitting, because just in case someone else came in, well, it might look . . .

"You're right," he said bleakly, not sure that she was.

"I say we're just stupid to let them do this to us. I don't think Mary intended it in the worst sense, it's just her bloody naïveté and innocence. But *we're* the innocent ones, Fred, why should we let them spoil it for us?"

"You're right," he said again but wished she wouldn't pursue it.

"So—everything's back to normal, isn't it? Oh, what a relief, I feel a million times better, don't you?"

"Yes," he said. He wished that she'd go.

"Want to go out tomorrow and have a picnic on the crag? I'll hard-boil some eggs for us."

"Yes," he said, "that'd be good-oh, all right."

She came over and put her thin arms around him and pressed her small body up against him. Oh Christ, what if someone came in?

"Good night, old darl," she said. "I'm off to bed early, hooroo."

"Hooroo," he said.

It was over, finished, kaput. Bloody people interfering. He thought suddenly of two lines of Samuel Butler and wished that he hadn't. "We were two lovers standing sadly by / While our two loves lay dead upon the ground."

He got up early and dressed and went next door to Mrs. Wardrop's to ask if he could use the phone and made a booking that night on the Melbourne train.

"I'm off," he said to Lily. "Too much work ahead, a paper to do, got to get back."

"Oh, I worry about you not getting the proper food and being overworked. You look thin."

Goodbye, he said to his sisters, kissed them automatically, had his bag in the front hall. Sidney had not come downstairs and he hoped he might get away before she did. *Damn* Mary, stupid Mary, didn't she have *any* sense of what she'd done? "Come on down, Sid," Mary was calling. "He's going in a minute, don't you want to say ta-ta?" She came down in her old bathrobe.

"I overslept," she said. "Oh, do you have to leave? I thought we were going for a picnic today."

"Got too much work to do before exams and I think I better grease the old elbow."

"Oh well," she said, hands on hips. She looked as if she hadn't taken it in, his going. "Well, I see. All right, mate. Hooroo."

"Hooroo," he said and went down the front steps.

"Be good," she called out.

Such relationships between people are so fragile and infinitely alluring that when they bloom they sometimes ferment jealousy in others.

After he had picked up his train ticket and checked his bag, he wandered about aimlessly, looking in shopwindows and considering the price of seeing a flick at the Crystal Palace, until he found himself outside the Carlton Hotel and thought about blowing himself to their pricey lunch. Thought better of it. As he turned away, a voice said "Fred," and he felt himself touched lightly on the arm. He couldn't think for a second who this young woman was, a rather stylish sort, well dressed, white gloves.

"Well, goodness, don't you know me?"

Could have knocked him over with the proverbial feather, it was his sister Jess, grown up and smart as paint.

"Well, crikey, Jess. What a surprise. I would have walked right past you."

"You almost did. What are you doing in Sydney?"

"Oh, I've had a week here, midwinter holiday, going back this evening."

"How's it going? The uni and all that?"

"Not bad, not bad. Hope to get my degree in December, fingers crossed, touch wood, spit eight times."

He was laughing sheepishly; she was so cool and collected it made him nervous. She wasn't like one of the family, but then Jess never had been.

"How are things with you, Jess?"

"Oh, all rightish." She turned to a young woman with her and said in the same detached manner, "Grace, this is my brother, Fred. Fred, this is Grace Coin."

"Pleased to meet you," he said.

"How do you do," said Grace Coin. They shook hands and Miss Coin looked away as if she were impatient for this meeting to be over. She had an arrogant manner, all right.

"Have you been staying with the family?" Jess asked.

"Yes. As a matter of fact, I was in your old room."

"How are they all?"

"Oh, fine, everybody's fine."

He was ready to let them go on their way and not delay such grand young ladies any longer, when Jess said abruptly, "What are you doing now? I mean, are you going anywhere? Grace and I are lunching here at the Carlton, why don't you join us?"

"Well," he said, "I'm just really filling in time. Well yes, Jess, I'd like that very much."

Surely she meant it was her "shout," only she wouldn't have used the word, and even if she didn't mean him to be her guest, he had a bit of cash left over. He felt suddenly eager to know Jess and her new varnished self. She walked with an assurance.

"You haven't been out to Turramurra much lately, I gather."

"No," she said. "As a matter of fact, I'm a bit offish with the family at the moment."

"Oh, I'm sorry to hear that. They didn't say a word."

"I don't think they know," Jess said and smiled.

"And how's Cousin Jackie?" he asked.

"Oh, Jacquetta's Jac*quetta*."

They had arrived at the door of the Raffles Room, copied it was said from the Raffles Hotel in Singapore.

"We're going to be three," Jess said to the maître d', and Fred said "After you" to Grace Coin, but she had already swept ahead. She and Jess had the same leisurely walk, gracefully acknowledging their umbrellas, as if they had attended a class on walking.

"For you, Miss Lord," the maître d' said, pulling out chairs.

"Thank you, Ra-*ool*," Jess said.

By Christ, you had to hand it to her.

She had always been putting on the dog, as they called it. Even as a little nipper she was quite the lady. She was the most prepossessing of all the girls with her neatness and her grave manners and had a way of speaking (he could hear it now as she asked him if he'd care for a cocktail: "Would you kerr for a cocktail, Fred?") that was faintly Pommy or as if she had had elocution lessons.

Lord, he could remember her coming down to lunch wearing her hat (she was about fifteen and cool as an archduchess; she had the family in fits) because she said "ladies" always wore hats to lunch. And then there was that thing in the Blue Mountains (she would never speak about it) while she was up staying with their cousin Jackie; a landslide had happened after a lot of rain and part of the cliff fell away and some girl taking a walk with her had been killed and young Jess had had to hang on until they rescued her with ropes and then after all the fuss in the newspaper about her courage, all she had had to say when she got home was "There doesn't seem to be a clean towel in my room." That was her, all right. You had to hand it to her. Went off to live with Mother's rich cousin Jacquetta in a big house in posh Point Piper and they hardly ever laid eyes on her, as rare as a lyre bird.

Here's to you, Jess, he said. Why not? Good old Jess, she'd shouted him to a sherry and they didn't stint you here in the Raffles Room. He smiled at her and Grace Coin. He was a bit surprised to see them both light up gold-tipped cigarettes. But after all, Jess was grown up now and with her fine clothes (you couldn't help but be struck by her hat; her hat was a bloody masterpiece, come to think of it) she was about as far removed from her sisters at Turramurra, from boiled beef and cabbage and putting the tea leaves down the lavatory, as she was from China. She was saying that she and Grace worked in the Red Cross canteen on Thursdays.

"Our bit, we call it," Jess said.

"Our bitter bit," said Grace.

"Oh, it's not too awful. The lads are jolly well mannered, considering. The only thing's the uniforms they make us wear."

"Grimmers," Grace Coin allowed, witheringly.

If anything, she was more upper-crust-sounding than Jess. She was aristocratic right down to her thin ankles and pointed shoes, long-legged as a stork in her black stockings and her long glen plaid skirt and the white silk blouse she wore with a droopy black taffeta bow. And whereas Jess was constantly aware of what was going on around her and seemed to be highly gratified by it (she took the menu from Raoul as if it were the Magna Carta), Grace chose to ignore it, but to ignore it by being accustomed to it, as though if the dishes were solid gold it would be no more than what was expected. She was a real toff, all right. But one little thing he noticed was that when the girls took off their gloves and laid them on the table, Grace Coin's gloves were frayed.

". . . and rather dread when they're on final leave because they tend to get drunk and be sick on the lavatory floor," Jess was saying.

"Which we have to clean up."

"Which is grimmers."

The picture of Grace Coin cleaning up a lavatory floor was hard to conjure up. Fred was looking at her thin lovely hands and as though she had caught him at it, she folded them on her lap.

She looked at him rather fiercely and said, "I suppose you'll be off to France once you've finished your university courses if the dashed war's still going."

"Fred was turned down," Jess interposed. "For what was it?"

"Something wrong with the ticker," he said and it sounded coy so he coughed to hide its insignificance. This Grace Coin could really make you nervous.

"I know a boy who was rejected for diabetes," Grace Coin said, "and they never gave him a badge or anything so he used to get white feathers handed to him on the bus all the time, poor devil. He finally caught some girl red-handed putting a white feather in his pocket and he couldn't stand it anymore so he yelled at her, 'Look here, I've done my level best, I've volunteered but I've got diabetes,' and the girl said, 'I'm awfully sorry but it doesn't show and we have to get after the slackers.' "

A sad little trio of middle-aged ladies, one of whom carried a cello, had taken to the dais in the middle of the room and after some chirruping and thurumping had broken into "Smiles."

Grace Coin said, "What with one thing and another, I'm sick and tired of the war."

"Oh, I'm ashamed of you, Grace," Jess said, smiling.

"I am," Grace said. "I'm sick of that song, I'm sick of

'Tipperary' and keeping a stiff upper. I'm sick of cheering them up. It just goes on and on."

"You're in a mood," Jess said. "Decide what you're going to have for lunch."

Grace said, "Don't start telling me how much better off we are than the nurses at the front. I know that. I sleep in a safe, clean, warm bed and I've never seen anyone with a leg blown off, but you can be miserable at home too."

She was rather awesome, rather touching. She looked at the menu scathingly and it was plain that something was bubbling up from deep inside her; it tightened her fine nostrils into thin white lines. Fred felt so suddenly strengthened by her ambiguity that he leaned toward her and said, "I know what you mean," but she jerked her head up and merely stared at him as though she had never seen him before in her life and said, "Oh, do you? Good *heav*ens." Then she turned to the waiter who was poised with his pad and said, throwing down the menu as if it disgusted her, "I'll have the curried lamb," which Fred had already noted was the cheapest dish on the à la carte. So perhaps there was a conjunction between it and the frayed gloves, this fine contempt, this disingenuousness which gave her such quality. Royalty was what she was and you knew it the minute you laid eyes on her. Here was the genuine pearl whereas poor Jess for all her airs was only the cultured.

> . . . smiles that make you hap-py
> There are smiles that make you sad

Once you had seen Everest you could never be content with just any mountain, and Grace Coin was, in a word, Everest. He was stifling with the heat of the room and a sense of fatalism as if some deity had spoken and said, Well, Fred, you have met the girl of your dreams, old fart. Whether you like it or not, this lovely, austere, troubled girl is the one for you, old cock, because it's written in the sands, it's what they call kismet.

Jess said, fingering the menu delicately and smiling at the waiter, "I feel oysterish."

Things could have turned out differently. But then there might not have been a world war, an earthquake might have missed San Francisco, various calamities might have been avoided by people not meeting or by letters not sent. Happiness is so often accidental, and if forthcoming events were to have been visualized by Sidney Lord, they would have reflected her boundless optimism. They might have formed the kernels of short stories for such periodicals as *Wildcat Weekly* and *Maiden,* for which she wrote palpitating fiction with one eye on commerce and the other closed in a wink (although her more serious eye was on the literary and conservative quarterly *Ovid*), but always committed to a satisfying conclusion. In Sidney's stories love was never unrequited, fidelity paid off, rascals copped their deserved fate, lovers were united. In Sidney's version, George Barnes, the bright young parliamentarian, got the Widows' Pension Bill passed by overwhelming vote and when he and Lily were married, the cheering crowds broke through the police barriers to acclaim them. Likewise, when pretty Jess tripped over the bulkhead on board the P&O liner carrying her to England, who should come rushing to her aid but the handsome son of the governor-general. Or by diverting a foreigner from getting on a wrong train, lame Adnia would come in contact with the brilliant Swedish surgeon who would effect her cure. Mary would be married in a traditional ceremony at St. Andrew's Cathedral with a choir and the bishop of Sydney officiating and nothing comical happening to set her off laughing. In a story (perfect for *Maiden* and probably entitled "His Comeuppance"), the foolish young Fred would have been shown the door by the high-and-mighty Grace Coin (whom the family had met during an uncomfortable prawn lunch), or better still by her butler, and shown out the back door and in a severe rainstorm, and serve

Fred right. But waiting behind the ledge with his mackintosh and a thermos of hot cocoa was . . .

So Sidney would have them all bathed in sophomoric bliss although it was contrary to her basically realistic nature, which was tinged with a cautious pessimism. Of course people didn't really win the Irish Sweepstakes and weren't often swept off their feet by perfect lovers; they blundered, they missed the boat. Look at *them,* her own darling pups, talk about missing things. They woke one night to the sounds of whistles and cheering and thought the Bronsons down the road were having a late party until the next day, when the butcher boy, delivering two pounds of pork sausages, said, "Didn't you hear, the war's over."

So things happened as naturally as rain. Grace Coin accepted Fred without the sky falling. Lily and George Barnes were married simply by a justice of the peace in George's district of Illawarra in a room in the Trades Hall in Kogarah, with only Sidney and Mary and George's elder brother present, and no crowds blocked traffic. When Jess and Cousin Jackie sailed for England, their P&O liner was delayed by a wildcat dock strike and prevented from leaving until three in the morning. Dear lame Addie, instead of meeting Sidney's proposed brilliant surgeon, ran into a fat acquaintance from her childhood on the local bus and saw light, the fat acquaintance being an employee of the Pacific Light and Gas Company in Chatswood, and Addie going to work for them in the accounts department, and Mary married her shy farmboy husband back from France with a couple of ribbons, in the little town of Bacchus Marsh outside Melbourne with none of her family present, and when the wheezy organ in the small church let out a series of preliminary farts, she had burst into a fit of giggles behind the propriety of her mosquito net veiling.

Yet in spite of their very ordinariness, these events had a certain mystic element: they had resisted unlikelihood.

What had seemed unlikely to Sidney were the empty rooms and things left behind in drawers, bits of elastic and ribbon, a cast-off hat or two, addresses scrawled on envelopes and left on the kitchen table with admonitions about forgetting to keep in touch when one by one the family dispersed and their pretense of keeping together was colder than the unused fireplaces in the almost empty house in Turramurra, the fate of which was now left up to the two youngest, Sidney and Mignon.

Left to the ants and the mice in the silent kitchen, the two girls scraped together apparitions of meals concocted out of tins and leftovers, bread and dripping and eggs. Left alone, Sidney typed and Mignon mooned. Until significantly the possums took over, nesting in the attic room where Sidney used to read her stories to Fred. For some time now, doors had begun to open mysteriously by themselves.

"Do you suppose it's Mother come back to apologize?" Sidney asked and they laughed.

As things worsened, windows jammed to let in the rain, pipes stopped up, the bathtub tap fell off; it was Sidney's opinion that the house resented them. Houses had personalities, she said, and sometimes they took exception to the people inhabiting them. *This* house had become tired of being a refuge for the Lord family and very likely knew that it had been left in the hands of two incompetent girls who often had to tell Mr. Soaper, the agent who came around on Thursdays for the rent, that he would have to wait a week.

Then one day when they were trying to move Sidney's rolltop desk downstairs, it tore loose from them and thundered down by itself, carrying away most of the banister. So there, the house was heard to mutter.

"Let's move," Sidney said.

She had met an Olive Flateau, who rented rooms up at the Cross. Anytime you're looking for a warm bed, dear, Olive had said. So what the hell were they doing in this mausoleum miles out of the city in dreary Turramurra *any*way? Kings Cross was where they belonged, that was where there was life and vitality and artists and writers and *musicians*. Mignon was musical, had a beautiful singing voice. They packed their suitcases, they left the dirty dishes in the sink, left the front door open to the wind and weather.

"Ta ta, house," Sidney said.

Kings Cross was the place, all right, the twinkly lights, the traffic, the bright-seeming people on the streets.

"You're just across the hall from the bathroom," Olive Flateau said, dropping cigarette ash onto her ample bosom, "and the only other one to share it is Miss Thirlwell and being a writer she doesn't use it much."

They would manage the rent between them somehow and the room was large enough for the two sizable beds with cotton coverlets and there was a glassed-in little balcony where they had a makeshift kitchen with a gas ring and a hanging meat safe, the big old-fashioned wardrobe was roomy and the orange silk lampshade cast a warm aurora on the dappled wallpaper and at night its shadows hid the milky traces of mildew on the green carpet. They were ecstatic, it was the first home they had ever had. Those old houses of their childhood did not seem home to them, merely places where they had had temporary lodging at someone else's behest and where there was constant wrangling over what belonged to whom. But this was their own room. They bought cups and saucers and a chipped china teapot. Outside their window Kings Cross rumbled with traffic and enticement. They saw a woman smoking in the street and were delightfully scandalized. They loitered along Macleay Street and Darlinghurst Road looking into the shopwindows of fruits and sweets, greengroceries and stalls of mandarins and bananas, coffee dens and restaurants with enticing names like The Oriental and La Scala, and once, hand in hand, wandering through a huddle of little back lanes where lights showed dimly through slatted blinds and women sat fanning themselves languidly in doorways, they were stopped by a friendly cop who said, "Now you girls get on home, you shouldn't be hanging around with this mob," and when they told Olive Flateau she laughed and said, "You must have been in Kellet Street where all the prossies are, no wonder."

Usually Sidney rose at six and made herself tea and wrote a short story, the typewriter on a pile of towels to deaden the sound, then usually trimmed a hat, most often the same hat, a wide-brimmed panama which she then put on, and took the story down to town to submit to a magazine editor. Some of them she knew well enough by now to get inside their offices and address by first names. She perched on their desks in her newly trimmed hat and listened to their advice gravely. They called her "Sport" and "Chum" and chided her about her spelling and her misuse of the semicolon. To her they were Ed and Bluey and Flo, and they were more her family than any of her sisters had been except Mignon. Mignon was a great listener. She would prop her long oval face in her hands and drink in what Sidney was saying, or listen with deep concentration to a story being read to her. Possibly because they were the two youngest, the last two conceptions of a thunderous series of matings, they found themselves growing up in a cold climate of menopause and turned to each other for warmth. They had grown up dissimilar and yet so alike that people frequently mistook one for the other. They had both had their dark red hair Eton-cropped in the new postwar style being adopted and neither had much bosom to mention and being the same size they often wore each other's clothes and shoes. Seen together, it was clear that Sidney was the leader but also that little docile Mig had an eye on a mystic objective. She would be the opera star, Sidney the famous author, they both knew that and were content. They made their beds and fried their sausages and bided their time, confident of the glory that lay ahead of them. Mates more than sisters.

"What's for tea?"

"Sardines on toast."

"Scrumptious."

"I thought you'd prob'ly approve."

Eavesdropping outside their door, you wouldn't have known which one said what.

"Which story did they take?"

" 'The Girl and the Brumby Rider.' "

"That the one about the bushranger?"

"Yes."

"That's my favorite. What'd they pay?"

"Two guineas."

"Hooray, can we go to the pictures?"

Wanted on the phone, you girls. Lily (on the phone in the hall) said she was worried about them living up at the Cross, that they might run into who knows what kind of riffraff there and who *was* this Mrs. Flateau and were they warm enough at night, were there enough blankets and was the house clean?

Clean enough if they swept up the mice droppings now and then, and the only riffraff they encountered, worse luck, was Olive Flateau's other boarders, who came and went. Coming out of the communal bathroom, Sidney encountered Pearl Thirlwell, who had the big end room and who announced theatrically that six in the evening was *her* time to bathe because she wrote all day and the fact that she was a writer gave her the privilege of choosing her hour and—beg pardon, Sidney said, but she was a writer too so couldn't they come to some agreement. In the discussion that followed about working hours, it transpired that Pearl had been at work on her book for eleven years. Sidney was suitably impressed. Why, she said, you must be nearly finished then. Finished! Pearl gave a hollow groan. Why, she hadn't yet even reached the midpoint.

Riffraff. Lily needn't have worried. Pearl Thirlwell was over fifty and she was writing the life of the explorer Abel Tasman. Olive Flateau, née Butcher and the ex Mrs. Prince, Latona and

Pizzey, proved to be a surrogate mother at heart, always luring the girls into her well-stocked pantry with gifts of chocolate biscuits and buns, often "happening" to have a dish of custard left over and "happening" to be still up with her door ajar when they came home late. Sidney was listening to Olive's life story in long episodes and getting "material" from it in melodramatic hunks. Olive's first husband, Mr. Prince, must have been taken by a shark in front of her eyes, more or less, as the story went. ". . . early on in our marriage and we were spending a week with my cousin down in Seaview which is near Wilson's Promontory in Victoria and the beaches there are pretty deserted and Ernie suddenly strips off his togs and starts running down the sand calling out Whoosh Whoosh, and I said don't go in dear, it's sunset and it's the worst time for sharks and all he said to me was Whoosh and dived in and swam off and it was the last I seen of him. Oh, he must have been taken, all right."

"Did they ever find him?"

"Not a toenail."

"How awful; poor you."

"Poor me is right. I had to wait out the seven years to have him legally declared."

"He might have just drowned."

"There would have been the body washed up. No, the only thing bothers me is supposing he just wanted to get away from me. Of course I had the other husbands later, but none of the others could ever hold a candle to Ernie. Oh, find the right bloke, darling, it makes all the difference, take it from me."

"I intend to," Sidney said.

"And have a kid or two, darling. Oh, if only I had had children," Olive said.

"My mother had nothing but," Sidney said, "and it didn't seem to make her any happier."

"Perhaps she didn't care enough. It's always the same with that kind, they have swarms, while I can't produce a tadpole."

Sidney saw herself with the perfect mate, the ravishing child, a famous author. Meanwhile she got up at six and wrote stories and sold some of them to the kinds of pulp magazines favored by factory girls and frustrated spinsters while all the time she had her weather eye on *Ovid,* the cultured literary journal which cost 2/6 on the bookstalls bound in dark orange where printed on thick expensive paper was the output of such cynosures as Katherine Susannah Pritchard, Digby Hammond and "Banjo" Patterson. She ingested their stories and poems and admired the simplicity with which they were written. They were without contrivance and seemed more real than anything she had attempted. In them, people were not rescued improbably from fates worse than death at the eleventh hour, not always kissed in the golden glow of setting orbs. One of Digby Hammond's stories she much admired ended with the words "The bank shut forever the following Tuesday." She tried to emulate them and was encouraged when her first story written (she hoped) in the *Ovid* style was turned down by all the editors she knew. "What's got *in* to you?" they asked. So she resumed the train wrecks, bush fires and broken hearts which she knew would sell. But her heart was set on one day seeing her name in the beautiful black print on the orange cover of *Ovid* and she continued to dream about Royce Cable, who was listed as Senior Editor. Royce Cable! A name out of Ouida. She pictured him as tall and darkly handsome.

She set herself to work on a story devoid of melodrama and written in a terse succinct manner and with the laconic ending Digby Hammond used to so much advantage; she titled it "Beside the Point," which had a subtle double meaning.

When she was finished (she took more than a month working on it, retyping it twice, the longest time she had ever spent writing *any* thing), she trimmed her hat, put on her best blouse and skirt and went into town to do battle, she hoped, with the archangels.

Going up in the lift, her heart almost failed her. The *Ovid* offices were on the tenth floor and that was about as near heaven as she had ever been. Instead of the familiar cracked plaster and linoleum, desks piled with old newspapers and half-eaten lunches, and the noise and smell of printing presses, she emerged from the lift into a pristine brown-carpeted hallway at the end of which sat a middle-aged lady in mauve wool at a beautifully polished desk which bore only a tray for messages, a mulga wood desk set and a telephone. Beyond her through an open door could be seen legs and feet wearing tan and white kid shoes resting on a similar desk. This would be all that Sidney would see of Royce Cable.

"Do you have an appointment?"

"No, but I have a story."

"Mr. Cable doesn't see anyone without an appointment."

"If he'd just give me two minutes, I promise I can tell him all I have to say and be gone. I promise."

The wool lady was implacable.

"You may leave the story, it will be read by one of our editors."

"But if I could just give it to Mr. Cab—"

"Just leave your manuscript."

The wool lady indicated the message tray.

So there was nothing for it but to do so and go down again in the lift without having met Royce Cable, but from then on she lived in a nervous agitation that bordered on mild hysteria. "Was that the phone?" she would ask. "Has the postman been yet?" In order to distract herself she wrote six stories in six weeks and sold five of them to the other mags.

The printed postcard bearing the *Ovid* logo and leaving space for the date simply said, "Mr. Royce Cable will see you on ——— at ———." It was addressed to Mr. Sidney Lord. She clutched Mignon to her in an agony of joy, she ran downstairs to tell Olive Flateau "they've taken my story." As soon as she got the check she would take everyone out to dinner at the Oriental Hotel in the Palm Room, her shout.

Mister Sidney Lord presented herself at the polished desk on the tenth floor on the appointed morning, seven minutes early for the time of the meeting. Beyond the desk the legs and tan and white kid shoes of Mr. Cable showed themselves stretched out on his desk. After the wool lady tapped discreetly on his door and murmured the name, the entranced Sidney was shown in.

Unbending his long legs from the desk and getting up, it seemed to be, in sections like a giraffe, Royce Cable looked down on her.

"Oh, it's *Miss,* is it?"

"I'm afraid so."

How strange, he was an American. Tall, going bald, his black hair slicked down so that it looked painted on, he had rather mocking dark eyes.

"Sit down, won't you?"

Yes, an American voice and those shoes. He picked up her manuscript from a small pile on his desk.

"I don't ordin*ar*ily see the slush pile people, but I'm making an exception with you."

He must like it then, exceptionally. Sidney smiled brightly but he looked at her unsmilingly.

"Is this meant to be a parody?"

"I don't quite—"

"Your story seems to be a meticulous takeoff of some of our writers. You even copy their words and inflections. Is this deliberate?"

"Oh, I didn't mean to copy *exact*ly, only to—to—try to emulate—I do so admire—"

"Oh, then it isn't meant to be comic? One of our readers brought it to me and thought it was the most comical thing she had ever read—"

"Oh, *God* no—I beg your pardon—no." Heart beating.

"Because it has a lot of nerve in it, dreadful as it is."

The ceiling fell on her; he didn't like it.

"Or maybe *you* have a bit of nerve. But you'll never get anywhere trying to copy other authors, that's the first thing you've got to learn, and the second thing is not to strew exclamation points all through your work like pepper. Now everyone has to start as a raw beginner. Mr. Tarkington had to start as a raw beginner and I daresay even Mark Twain, but the reason these people are famous authors is they had something *original* to offer, they didn't copy anyone else, and the reason I had you come in to see me was to tell you that and also that down under all this artificial bunkum you show talent."

"Thank you," she said, getting up haughtily and taking her story. "I've been living on that talent for the last couple of years."

Thank you, she said to the wool lady outside. Thank you, she said to the lift driver taking her down. Thank you, she said to the doorman pushing the revolving door.

Funny how bad news could make you momentarily lightheaded. She swam up Castlereagh Street.

"Don't cry, love," Mignon said.

"I'm not," she said, weeping and then blowing her nose. "Oh, bugger that bloody Yank anyway."

But she thought about Royce Cable and his advice. It had been kindly meant and she wished she had not swept out of his office so precipitously. He might have had more to say to her if she hadn't been so intent on galloping off on her high horse.

"My dear, he's only an *editor,*" Pearl Thirlwell said after she had recounted her experience. "There probably was an editor who turned down *Uncle Tom's Cabin* if the truth were known!"

"Yes, but they're the bosses, worse luck."

Head down, chin up, she wrote and wrote; stories flowed out of her but were of no consolation or satisfaction. She no longer took any pride in seeing her name in the index pages.

Then Pearl Thirlwell asked her, had she ever been to Poto-vink?

"No. Where is it? Russia?"

"Pot of Ink."

"Oh. No, what's that?"

"The writers' club. Chum of mine is reading his poems there next Sunday evening. Like to come?"

The Pot of Ink was located over a Greek café near the quay in a shabby loft. It was crowded with seedy people, some of whom looked more in need of a hot bath than of intellectual refreshment. But the fact that they were authors and poets was of prime interest to Sidney. Who's what? Who's that over there? she kept asking Pearl but most of the names were unfamiliar to her. Pearl introduced her chum the poet, who gave Sidney a limp-handed wet palm and Pearl a wet kiss, and they sat down on hard wooden chairs under the dusty orange light that somehow made the faces around them seem more sensitive and intense.

By and by the speakers were introduced and the readings began. In all honesty Sidney thought the material was pretentious and downright dull but it was greeted by a hushed reverence and sustained applause which only encouraged the readers to excessive lengths. During the interminable performance she began to be irritated by the smoke from somebody's pipe behind her which caught her throat stingingly, and turning around she said, "Could you blow that somewhere else?"

It was Royce Cable.

Of course. It would have to be. Red-faced, she shrank back in her seat hoping he had not recognized her. But why would he? And furthermore what did it matter? She had existed on her own talent without him, as she had pointed out in his office, and she would continue to do so. She turned around again and gave him a dazzling smile and as soon as the readings were finally over she stood up and said, "I'm Sidney Lord."

He looked bewildered for a moment and then said in his contradictory way, "Of course you are."

"Oh, you remember me."

"The little girl with the nerve."

"Who showed talent," she reminded him.

"And who deeply resents being told."

"Oh, not really."

He was looking at her in a quizzical offhand manner which seemed to intimate that she was being a nuisance, but as she turned away he said, "Rushing off again?"

"No." She was looking around for Pearl, who had disappeared.

"Come here often?"

"This is my first time. Are you a member?"

"No," he said, "just passing by." He looked around at the raffish crowd. "Oh, they're mostly harmless hacks but it's a good idea not to take them too seriously."

"I suppose not."

He sucked on his empty pipe a moment and said, "They feed on each other, it's how they get their sustenance, I suppose, but don't you."

"Don't I what?"

"Don't try to get your sustenance from them, they're drones."

"Drongoes?" she asked, smiling.

"What's that mean?"

"Australian for no-hopers."

"I distrust their sanctimoniousness," he said.

You couldn't help but notice his clothes; they were different in a way, most certainly Yankee. His jacket was of some soft velvety material, perhaps made only in New York. She had the impetuous inclination to touch it. His tallness must necessitate having his clothes tailored for him. Again she wondered what he was doing here in Sydney tinkering around with a small monthly magazine (by American standards, surely) when he could have been a big editor with one of those glossy-looking Yank publications you saw on the stands in posh hotels, like the *Saturday Evening Post.* What was he doing so far away from home? Perhaps, she almost hoped, there was some secret, some broken romance that had sent him halfway around the world; there was a sadness in his eyes behind the shell rims, a mistiness. Or perhaps it was astigmatism.

He seemed bored to extinction with the affair and with her, he was about to turn away, she thought, when he said, "Going anywhere?"

"No. Well, home eventually."

"Want to walk a bit?"

"Oh yes," she said too eagerly, "I'd love some fresh air, it's so hot in here. But I'll just have to find Pearl and tell her, she's the one I came with."

It seemed realer later on. Waking up Mignon and telling her seemed more real than the actual happening but then that was often the case with Sidney: relating or writing it made it real.

Not that anything earth-shaking had happened.

Yet.

They had walked around the rim of the harbor on the edge of the Botanic Gardens and sat down near the rock known as Lady Macquarie's Chair and watched the lighted ferries go by and listened to the slurp-slurp of the water below them on the rocks. He said almost nothing the whole time except things like Is my pipe bothering you? And somehow, Sidney said, she knew it was one of the times to be quiet and let nature take its course, if it was going to. Oh, she wasn't afraid of *that,* she laughed, heavens no. She wasn't ever going to be afraid of *that* because when it happened it would be with the right bloke. The only thing was she was chilly, only had on a light coat and it was windy down there by the water, and what with that and her excitement at being alone with this important man in the dark she was afraid her teeth would begin to chatter and all of a sudden he said, looking at the great dome of stars over the backwater, I've come a long way to find this. She knew he meant that he'd made a long spiritual journey rather than sea miles by the way he said it and so after a while she asked him, What's *here?* and he said, Peace. I don't *think,* Sidney said, lighting a cigarette which meant she was agitated, he'd say that to just *any*one.

Then in little jerks, like the little strips of paper that go to make up a telegram, he had told her snippets of his life. He was from Bismarck, North Dakota, wherever that was but it sounded far off in the prairies, and his father had a small ironmongering business and the wind blew all the year round he said. They were poor and the winters were blizzardy, people froze to death standing up and he hated it obviously and when he was fifteen he got on a freight train and got to civilization and ended up in Chicago where he worked in the stockyards and then he got a job as copy boy on a newspaper and eventually got to be junior editor on a Sunday supplement and so on and so on (as he kept saying, brushing the years away like crumbs) until he got to New York where it all happens and eventually (it must have taken some time to have extracted this information from him in painful slivers, it now being one o'clock in the morning) to be editor in chief of what he called a "classy" monthly featuring the works of writers he expected Sidney to know by the way he spoke of them, obviously famous names in America.

Then why?

Exactly. What was he doing here on the other side of the world? Mind you, Sidney said, don't forget our father threw over England and came out to Queensland. But it's not the same thing, Mignon said. Like turning your back on a posh job in New York to come out and work on a little minor magazine in Sydney, Australia. There must have been some reason. Oh, I'm sure, Sidney said, but he had shut up like a clam and sucked on his pipe and said only that he had been caught here by the war and unable to get a boat back and he'd gradually assimilated it and now he doesn't want to go back to the U.S. Peace here, he said, or as much of it as you're ever going to find in this pinch-arse world.

Pinch-*arse?*

I think that's what he said. The awful thing was I suddenly wanted to pee like mad, Sidney said. He might have told her more, they might have sat there until morning, if he hadn't suddenly said, Is all this boring you? and she had said, Oh no, I'm fascinated, but to be absolutely truthful I've got to pee right this minute and he said, Behind that tree, I'll keep guard and he did and I did and we walked home.

"It turns out he has a flat in that gloomy Bayswater Hall in Elizabeth Bay, where the lobby looks like a funeral home, all black and white tiles and ferns in tubs. Fancy coming home to that every evening alone."

"No wife?"

"I don't think so. Not *here* anyway."

"So he's a neighbor, that's nice."

"He's coming to have dinner with us on Thursday."

"Here?"

"I told him it'd be very simple."

"Simple's not the word with our gas ring."

"If it's a warm night we can have something cold, ham."

They had stewed rabbit cooked by Mignon and served with boiled parsnips on dishes borrowed from Olive Flateau and after some heated discussion a bottle of gut-rot red wine. Plonk, said Sidney, raising her glass, but here's to your health anyway.

"And to you, and you," Royce Cable said to them. He ate every scrap of food as if he had not had a square meal for weeks, but without comment. After dinner he stretched out in their one and only armchair and lit his pipe while Sidney provided conversation which only Mignon would have known was with a certain effort.

"Silent, isn't he?" Mignon said after Royce Cable had left.

"Still waters."

"Dresses funnily."

"American. Don't be insular."

"Beautiful shoes, I *will* admit."

Mister Mystery, Sidney called him. Ran into Mister Mystery in the laundry, at the greengrocers. Always alone, always laconic, the dim American began to perpetuate himself in the backyard of their lives, not quite with them, not quite apart. But Sidney's method of adopting orphans was as spontaneous as combustion and useless to evade. She would be on the phone to Royce. Hello, this is a call from your Kings Cross girls who are cooking up a stew of sorts tonight, are you doing anything? Or: We're going for a walk in the Botanic Gardens, want to come? Sometimes Mignon stayed home. "I don't want to be gooseberry," she said. "Oh, don't be silly, he's like a brother." Whatever Royce Cable thought about it, they never knew. (I'll get to the bottom of him yet, Sidney vowed.)

Eventually they were invited to his flat one Sunday evening, which put Sidney into a ferment of excitement that it might involve meeting Miles Franklin and other celebrated writers who contributed to *Ovid.* She fluctuated between wearing this dress or that, a hat or not, invested in a shoulder spray of pansies and fairy fern which went limp immediately.

But they were ushered into an empty living room by Royce, who was wearing a tobacco-colored sweater. The flat, which was rented furnished, was as impersonal as a railway waiting room. Not so much as a snapshot betrayed an iota of Mr. Cable's private life. The priory-like atmosphere of the chilly room with its wrought-iron lighting fixtures and stiff oak chairs did nothing to relieve the lack of conviviality although the sherry was excellent and he handed them what he called soda crackers on a pewter tray. Then he sat back and smoked his pipe.

When they got home to their own cheerful room, Mignon

threw her hat on the bed and said, "When are you going to get something out of it?"

"Out of him, do you mean?"

"Yes."

"What would I be supposed to get?"

"Isn't he ever going to ask to see something you've written?"

"Should he?"

"I damn well think so, you've done enough for *him.*"

"Oh, a few dinners. I don't wash out his socks."

"You would if he wanted."

"Mig, it isn't a relationship like that. I mean, I don't ask for anything *back.*"

But underneath she cared. Mignon knew by the way she shrugged it off as unimportant. When Sidney de-emphasized something it was often of paramount importance.

It was during the walk home from a chamber music recital he had taken her to that Royce had finally said to Sidney, "Why don't you give me some of your stuff to read sometime?"

She had barely managed not to squeal and clutch at his hand. Not too much, he added, not more than two or three pieces.

She had pulled out two that had been published and one in manuscript and given them to him. For days she was palpitating.

He said, handing them back, "Yeah, well, they hang together nicely." He might just as well have complimented her on her typing but she hung on grimly. "If this is what you want to do. Lovers' quarrels, purloined letters, bush fires. But where's the real stuff? The best thing is the description of the young girl brushing her teeth in the mirror."

"Oh."

"Don't look so swallowed up. You're writing this purple

prose stuff to please a certain public and doing it okay but it isn't really you."

"Isn't it?"

"I don't think you trust yourself to be smaller."

"Smaller?" She could only reiterate everything.

"Everything is a thunderclap, you fall back on catastrophe."

"But catastrophes happen."

He looked imploded for a second, as if the air had been sucked out of him, and said quietly, "I know a man whose life was ruined by a knock on the door."

She was positive he meant himself. Moreover, that probably was the last she would ever hear of it.

About her work she couldn't help feeling that somehow she had been wrongly diagnosed. Or that somehow he had been reading somebody else's manuscripts.

"Are you a bit in love with him?" Mignon asked.

"I'll never be just a *bit* in love."

"But with Royce? Are you?"

"*No.*"

She was so emphatic that Mignon raised eyebrows.

But Sidney was steadfast in her faith that she would know instantly when the man came along; she would be propelled toward him and unable to resist and whoever he might turn out to be, he was not Royce Cable, not in the wildest sense. She loved Royce but in the same way that she loved her brother Fred (they had even exchanged parodies of love letters, she dimly remembered), and the thought of sharing the privacies of love with Royce was unthinkable (the pauses between sentences, the thunderous silences, would be so much more potent with both of them lying down). The exalted adventure still lay before her and she thought of it as too sacred to be rendered commonplace or lewd although she was in no way prim even in these, her still innocent years.

But not Royce; he was more significant to her as her mentor.

She was chopping onions and weeping when the knife slipped and cut her finger, not deeply but she was bleeding all over the kitchen table and while she was hunting for a clean rag, she heard her sister Lily say, "Oh, hold your hand up in the air, dear, while I get some cheesecloth," as clearly as though Lily stood with her in the tiny glassed-in balcony, and she sat down giddily, blood and all, with the vision of Lily tying up her finger while something boiled over on the stove and one of the other girls called out from upstairs wanting something and a cart was delivering bread at the back door.

She had her book; it was memory.

Lily looking after all of them in the big house in place of their absent mother. Only in her book the mother would be really dead. She'd been searching for this book for years, sometimes it had almost revealed itself disguised in foreign accents and taking place in England or Venice or someplace she had never been, but now she clearly saw the back veranda of their house in Turramurra with the morning glories and she heard the wire flyproof door slam as Mary came out of the kitchen and scraped plates into the rubbish bin and the clink of its tin lid, the smell of the kitchen sink which no amount of liquid phenol could annul; the marks on the drainboard and the green tin tea canister with a picture of Vesuvius and the thick white cups with nonmatching saucers they drank their breakfast tea out of; doors banged open when the cool Southerly Buster wind came in the hot evenings of summer and they lit the gas lamps in the early winter twilight (oh but not to leave on in an empty room, it'll run up the bill fearfully, oh the gas bills are fearful). Voices came back to her now and the shapes of her family singing round the old upright piano with the candle-wax droppings on the lid, Just a Song at Twilight and On the Road to Gund-a-*gai,* Lily of Lagoona and Fred's beautiful baritone with Mignon's crystal-pure boy soprano; the time Jess bought herself the pink celluloid manicure set with the money she'd been given to buy cough medicine, the time she came home from the Blue Mountains subtly changed into the grand lady and the morning they all came into church with poor Lily leading the way and bowing right and left to the neighbors only to discover she was still wearing her kitchen apron under her coat. Above all it was Lillian, sweet Lillian holding them all together through thick and thin, storms and sicknesses, worrying, dosing, losing sleep, bamboozling the bill collectors, praying for a lucky day while the possums took over the attic and the ceiling fell on the dining room table. How Lily held her fist up to the sky and said, "That's enough," and they carried on somehow.

By the time the onions were bubbling she had her title, *Mother Load.* She wrote under a spell. Her old Corona rocked and trembled under her eagerness to get it all on paper. After they'd washed up the dishes in the evening she read the day's work to Mignon and she could tell from the absorbed look on Mignon's face and the way she had of fretting with her nails that it was affecting her deeply. She had the ectoplasmic sensation of floating above the table looking on while the little book wrote itself.

Meanwhile she kept quiet about it to Royce. She was so exhilarated with this new phase of herself and so sure she was on the right track of something better than she had ever done before that she wanted it to be complete and between covers before she handed it to him, so absolutely sure she was that it would be published. So it was that the last thing she was to do was type "For Royce" on a clean sheet of paper for the dedication, after which she fell sound asleep for three days, waking only for meals. The book had been written at white heat in ninety-three days.

Believing that the two big publishing houses might not condescend to her family ups and downs, she carried the manuscript as though it were the Book of Psalms up two flights of uncarpeted stairs to the offices of Bookstands Ltd., a small firm that nevertheless had their outlets in all the big railway stations in the country, where their lurid paperback novels sold for a shilling, their publication costs being defrayed by pages of advertising for skin cream and Dr. Small's Wart Remover Lotion.

A Mr. McCracken, who looked like a heron, with a fuzz of marabou white hair and a large Adam's apple, received her in a cubicle, calling her "little girl," and peering through his wire spectacles, said, "Tell me what it's about in ten words, little girl," and when she did, looked crestfallen and asked was there a flood or a bush fire in it, "they like a good bush fire." By the way he slapped her precious manuscript onto a table burdened by old galleys and newspapers, she felt certain it would be there unread indefinitely. For weeks she went around in a slight daze, not always hearing what was said to her and giving erratic answers, sometimes yawning prodigiously, which was a symptom of her stress.

Once or twice Royce asked her was there something on her mind, she seemed so distracted.

If only they would *read* it and let her know something; the uncertainty was what was killing her. But most of the winter went by and she was resolved to put it out of her mind, convinced that *Mother Load* had been thrown out in the dustbin or eaten by the mice, when the note came from Bookstands Ltd.

"We are pleased to infirm you," the letter said in sloppy typing, signed "for A. McCracken, Joan Cole."

Sidney and Mignon hugged each other and had a blowout dinner at the Prince of Wales with cash put aside for the dentist. She was going to be a published author, she was clothed in white samite, mystic, wonderful.

On the morning she was to sign the contract, she got up at six and trimmed a hat with seashells strung on vermilion string from the chemist shop.

It was a disappointing little contract, only a page. She had been expecting to sign something more like the American

Declaration of Independence or the Magna Carta.

"It's the same we give all our authors," Mr. McCracken said. "It's the same we give Flora Fern and Gertrude Gully."

She agreed that it was her own work and contained no libelous portrait of any living person. Now about the money (Mr. McCracken looked very grave), it would be the same they offered all their first-book authors. It would be a hundred quid flat out or seventy-five quid and a penny per copy sold, take it or leave it. And when Mr. McCracken said, "per copy sold," he sighed heavily with the inference that if *Mother Load* sold ten copies he would be among the marvelers. She thought of the bills and took the hundred flat out. She signed.

When Royce, who usually noticed nothing, commented on her shiny new shoes she almost told him where the money had come from. She had been on a spending spree and of course half the hundred quid had gone to Mignon, they always shared everything. They had both bought an evening dress in the hopes that sometime they might be asked to the Bondi Palais de Danse. Except that most of the boys they met around the Cross would have been more prone to take each other dancing.

Mother Load when it appeared in October was something of a shock. Printed on cheap paper which already showed the tendency to turn brown, it boasted a cover showing the young "mother" in a Red Riding Hood cloak spread over her brood, clinging to her in a gigantic rainstorm. The title caught the eye in a shrieking orange but there was her name, "by Sidney Lord."

"When are you going to show him?" Mignon asked as they fondled Sidney's six copies.

"Wouldn't it be fun if we could bake it in a pie and serve it to him like four and twenty blackbirds."

In the end she wrapped his copy in plain brown paper and just handed it to him.

"What's this?"

He was unwrapping it when his telephone rang and a long conversation evolved with someone he addressed as Foxy about making cuts in somebody's story for *Ovid* while Sidney sat and looked down at her new shoes and waited impatiently. Then, with the brown paper half removed, there was a further interruption while his landlady brought in a parcel of laundry and he queried her about a missing lemon-colored shirt. He then delivered a homily on laundries, waving her book in the air. *Open* it, she wanted to scream, it's all due to you. When he did, he stared at it as though he didn't quite understand its significance.

"Well," he said.

"Devoid of catastrophes," she said proudly.

"Well, well," he said. He was fingering the pages between his thumb and forefinger as if critical of the poor quality of the paper.

"Look at the dedication," Sidney said desperately and when he did his face grew very solemn and his mouth took on a pinched look.

"Why to me?"

Had she done the wrong thing? He seemed coldly indignant instead of flattered.

"Because—because you were responsible, you said I was afraid of being smaller. You said I had it in me—well, this is it."

She was beginning to sound childlike and petulant; this wasn't the way it was supposed to go. She had expected at least some sign of his appreciation.

He was staring at the lurid cover disapprovingly. Finally he coughed and asked her did she get a satisfactory price for it. She told him.

"No royalties?"

"I took the larger advance in lieu."

"You took the bait, they diddled you."

"They only pay a penny a copy royalty."

"It can add up."

"Mr. McCracken didn't seem to think so."

"Naturally. He didn't want you to take the royalties. This outfit is famously tightfisted. Why didn't you ask *me* first?"

"I wanted it to be a surprise."

"You shouldn't be allowed out alone."

"I'm sorry, Royce."

She meant, suddenly, about the dedication, about menacing him with recognition that might be mistaken for endearment. She stood up.

"I think perhaps I'm a bit superfluous here," she said.

"Sidney. Now don't, don't *please*," he said and to her it sounded ambiguous as if he were trying to dissuade her from being pleasing. He sat down and began rubbing his hand across his forehead.

"Well," she said, "I mean I'm sorry, I seem to have done the wrong thing, which is not unusual."

The silence was stupendous. Eventually he tossed the little book onto his bed and looked up at her.

"I'm at a loss for words. Nobody's ever done anything like this for me before and I don't quite know how to handle it. I'm not graceful about things, I guess, I was born wary of compliments paid me and I find it hard to respond. Whereas you respond to everything. You make me feel very humble, Sidney."

"I wish I didn't," she said.

She was the one who felt humble. To her embarrassment she began to cry. He reached up and took her hand and pulled her down beside him and like a child she let him console her, and leaning against his shoulder she gave in to the tears. Then to her amazement he began to unbutton her blouse. Only when he lay down and began to thrust open her thighs did she resist a moment. "Be careful," she said, but it was just as surely an admonition to herself.

When it was over, they lay side by side as if they were both stunned by the unlikelihood of it, not even fingers touching to substantiate the fragments of dream with which they felt involved. For Sidney, who had for a long time imagined the solemnity of the occasion, the triumph of the flesh being awakened for the first time and her thrilling accession to it, the act was dumbfounding in its complacency. Even the slight hurt and discomfort had been minor compared to the predictions made by girls whispering about the first time and when Royce got up naked to light his pipe and sat down on the edge of the bed, turned slightly away from her, they might have already seemed a long-married couple until he said suddenly, "Don't be sorry, will you?"

"No."

"Sure?"

"Oh yes, I'm quite sure."

He was hoarse, saying, "You especially must never be sorry about the things you do. You are the true of heart."

But he sounded as though he almost wished she were not, as though it rendered her unreachable to some degree. He puffed on his pipe a minute.

"You're true too," she said. "You're about the most honest person I've almost ever met." She put out a hand toward his naked back but he flinched as if she had scorched him and said "No" so emphatically she drew her knees up to her chin protectively. Then one of the portentous silences followed, until he said more quietly, "No. Corruptible as hell. *Correcting* other people's mistakes, watchful over punctuation and spelling but the book is a tissue of lies from beginning to end. Ask Mona."

"Who's Mona?"

"Mona, my wife."

So this was being naked together; he was telling her things. He was married, was he? And where was the wife? In America? Sidney knew enough not to prod. It was almost more sacred than the act they'd just completed in bed, this revelation of himself. She waited.

After a pause of nearly two minutes he went on.

"No, not true, not honest. Born a hypocrite in one way, one essential way, and disguised as plainspoken. Taking revenge for what I was by unmasking other people, you see. I'm good at it. But I married my nemesis, a good woman. Probably on purpose because that's the masochistic side of me. Then what happened was that she found me out the only time I was being completely honest."

"What *did* happen?"

"A knock on a door."

She wouldn't have moved, budged for a hundred quid now. He had rested his arm on her naked knees.

"In a hotel named the Gladsome Arms or some ironic nomenclature in Garden City, New Jersey, where I was in a compromising situation, in bed with someone."

After waiting as long as she could, Sidney asked gently, "Was it there? The knock on the door?"

"Yes."

"Oh. Was it somebody's husband at the door?"

"No. Somebody's wife."

It took her a moment to put the people together. Then she saw it, saw the two people in bed and what he was. And the woman outside the door. Was this his ruin then?

"Was it Mona outside?"

"No, she wouldn't have called out 'Pigs, pigs' to awaken the dead, she had more dignity. No, it was *his* wife. The guy I was with. The guy I loved."

Quite easily now, quite simply, the painful arrow had been drawn out of the wound in the side, he was breathing more easily. "But the divorce was unquiet, I was named as corespondent. Such things are not condoned in the land of the free and the home of the brave. So my wife stopped speaking to me except to say that she was going at her mother's behest to

Reno, Nevada, and that she hoped that the man and I—"

His pipe had gone out, he whistled it for a minute.

"—would be happy."

"And the man? The other 'guy'?" she dared ask at last.

"No. There was nothing left of him. There was nothing left of either of us."

He got up and threw her his old weather-beaten dressing gown.

"You look cold."

By the time she was dressed he had resumed himself, looking down at her quizzically, critically. He had combed his hair and put on his glasses. He might have been intimating that she was overstaying her welcome.

"Well," she said, awkward at the last, "I'll push off."

Thank you for taking me, thank you for giving me yourself, your pride and your body and your secret. I love you for it.

"Yes," he said. "Okay. Oh," as if he had forgotten it was on the bedside table, "and I'll read your book."

Sidney walked up Elizabeth Bay Road and wondered, passing under the yellow streetlights, if it didn't show to passersby that she was now subtly and irretrievably changed. There were better ways of putting it but in the story of herself which she was constantly writing she would end the chapter, "She was now a woman."

The stout woman sitting opposite Mignon in the second-class railway carriage was reading Sidney's book. Which was not unusual considering the way *Mother Load* had caught on. The paperback was now in its eleventh printing and seemed destined to go on forever, and so Royce Cable had been right and Sidney had been a fool to sign away the royalties but how was she to know? She had tried to rectify the situation by quickly manufacturing a sequel and this time making damn sure it was all in the contract and by boldly asking for *three*-pence a copy. But perhaps because of the desperation seeping into it or a refusal on the part of the same characters to rise to the occasion twice, the sequel had not imitated the success of *Mother Load*, which continued to be prominent on all the railway bookstalls from Sydney to Coolangatta.

Mignon was on the night express, sitting up second class, to Melbourne on her way to a little dairy town with the unlikely name of Bacchus Marsh, nearby to Mary's farm. Mary was now Mrs. Jim Wilkins and had had two babies in quick succession but time enough in between to drop frequent postcards to her sisters. Mary was a family girl and kept in touch even when she hadn't much to say which was frequently. She never forgot a birthday and sent Christmas cards of snow and holly in the furnace of December "with love and XXX." "Come on, Mig darling," Mary wrote, "and stay a few weeks." Mig darling was hard put to visualize Mary (she saw a flurry of red hair and freckled arms) and for the life of her she could not recall having any conversation with Mary beyond the matter-of-fact topics of daily living but then as far as her sisters were concerned, with the dazzling exception of Sidney, Mignon might well have been an only child.

Perhaps because she was the last child, perhaps because of her innate secrecy, she grew up solitary. Except for Sidney no one knew her, certainly no one understood her. First it was "Oh the baby, isn't she sweet, oh little Mig, look at her trying to pick the zinnia." There was the family joke retold and tittered about for years about her being given a penny and told to go to the sweetshop and buy herself a strip of licorice and about how the little moon-faced thing handed the penny to the shopkeeper and asked, "Is there any change?" But then it became "Oh here's *Mig,*" the tone slightly altered, somewhat piqued at the mystery of her brown studies (what was she contemplating? found with one leg in one pant, one leg out, in a stasis of getting dressed, staring), and these preoccupations made people uneasy. Or perhaps it was her unique closeness to her father, a closeness none of the others were permitted, the fact of her name being in memory of some strange girl whom Father had known as a young man. Who on God's earth was Mignon de Beauvoir and what was she to them?

"Sometimes you bother me," Sidney said.

"How bother?"

"You don't seem to want to do anything, dearest."

"What is there to do?"

"There must be something you want to do or to be, surely."

Like the other girls was what Sidney implied. But the other girls had visions, routes to follow. Lily had her politics, Sidney her writing, Adnia (they had heard) had found religion. Jess had chosen to live on somebody else's velvet. Mary had fled away into marriage. Mig didn't want to do any of these things. The simple truth was that she didn't want to be anything special. It was amorphous perhaps. She just wanted to *be*.

"Perhaps," Sidney said in her kindest way but still not understanding, "you will suddenly become clear to yourself when you fall in love. Whenever you finally meet the right bloke." Sidney obviously hoped it for her, was conjuring up the right man then and there.

She couldn't imagine such a man. Breaking in and stealing her heart? He would have to be *some*thing.

She sang to herself; it was refreshing. When Sidney was out, Mig sang as she washed dishes and made beds and that was how she had been approached by Mr. Rinaldi, who had the ground floor rear at Olive's and who stopped her on the way out and asked if she minded him asking but had she had lessons? No? Didn't she know she had a high C as good as Melba's? Did she intend letting a talent like that go to waste and so on. The result was that every Thursday she went to his dark little studio in the Conservatorium of Music in the Botanic Gardens and had a lesson in exchange for doing Mr. Rinaldi's "smalls"—socks, handkerchiefs and long woolen underwear.

She sang like a wound-up toy bird, someone touched the

spring and out came this effortless sound, soaring and pure. But it was like her life: she made nothing of it.

When Mary's untidy letter came, Sidney said unexpectedly, "Why not go, it'd do you good to have a change and I've got ten quid put by, I'll shout you the train fare." Perhaps Sidney was trying to give her a prod toward her own destiny, though what destiny there could possibly be in several hundred acres of wheat fields was not easily discernible.

She sat now as the train rushed on in the dark, content to stare at the fitful dots of light coming through the window rather than read the book she'd bought, "mooning" as they called it. Someone had said once, "Give Mig something to stare at and she'll be happy all day," and it was true; she often lost track of time sitting on the "dunny" until someone rattled the lock and said, Going to be in there all day?

On the smoky little box train that took her from Melbourne to Bacchus Marsh she stared out vacantly at the bare fields. Her only feeling was that she wished she hadn't come on this trip.

Quite a crowd got off at the Marsh with baskets and paraphernalia and as Mignon stood uncertain of which way to turn, a strange woman began waving and pushing through the crowd, hatless and with straggling fiery hair.

Mary embraced and kissed her fondly. Mig wouldn't have known her sister even in a small knot of strangers. Mary had on an apricot cotton dress and navy blue sand shoes; there was a bruise on her forehead. She grabbed Mig's suitcase and elbowed her forward into the street, where a horse and buggy was waiting; in the buggy a small reddish-haired girl sat on dirty blankets sucking barley sugar and in a wooden box on a pillow lay a baby. "Bett and Bill," Mary said, giving Mig a hand up into the shaky vehicle. "Bett can ride on your lap, darl. This is your Auntie *Mig,*" Mary said, and picking up the reins and her whip started the reluctant horse. "Giddap, Doll."

"Oh, I'm so glad you came, love," Mary said. "I said to Jim, 'If I get down there and there's nobody on that train, I'm going to cry *nails.*" Mary gave Mig a hug with her free arm. "We don't have many visitors. You dear old dear," Mary said as if they had been close pals for years.

"The Glen," as the wooden painted sign read, was a small tin-roofed house with a rickety paling fence in a wide treeless expanse of reddish dust. Two large water tanks stood on one side and a windmill turned ceaselessly, making a thin tinny shriek. An abortive attempt had been made to grow some sickly geraniums, and hens scratched and chuckled in their shade.

Outside the kitchen door, a muscular short bare-chested man was soaping and sponging himself under the arms at a tin tub. "My Jim," Mary introduced, dimpling like a bride, and the bare-chested man took Mig's hand in a soapy clasp and almost broke her fingers in an iron grip. "Good on ya," Jim said and then looked away with painful bashfulness.

"Saturday night. He's going to a big beer-up in town. Worse luck," Mary said, showing Mig into the little guest room with a huge double bed which seemed to require a ladder to climb into. "But he works like a mule all week and you can't grudge him a pot or two of a Saturday night. Just as long as he doesn't drive the truck into the creek."

While Mig was hanging up her few dresses in the little cretonne-covered wardrobe, she heard what seemed to be an altercation taking place in the kitchen. "Oh, shove off," the man's voice said and then Mary's voice protesting something. "You give me the fuggin' tomtits," the man said and there were sounds of a chair scraping on the bare floor and what seemed to be a scuffle, then a door banged and a minute later a truck drove by the window and out onto the road. A family squabble? Perhaps the reason for the bruise on Mary's forehead.

Almost immediately across the hall came the slam-bang

of chords on a piano and Mary's high-pitched voice singing.

"Oh you bun-bun-bundle of para-dise," Mary sang and when Mig peeked into the front parlor there was Mary at the piano, pounding away with her red hands, deeply ingrained with the dirt and cuts of heavy work.

"Oh you ham-ham-hamper of sugar and spice," Mary sang lustily.

Deep in the middle-of-the-night sleep, lost in the ocean of bed and down pillows, Mig was shaken awake to a candle and Mary standing over her in her nightdress with a woolen shawl over it.

"Better get up, darl. Quick, love, Dad's come home awfully blotto and he's on the warpath."

"Who? What?"

"Jim's been on the booze at the beer-up and it brings on the shell shock and he thinks he's back at the front again."

Mary was pushing aside the bedclothes. "Where's your slippers?"

"Where are we going?"

"Where it'll be safe. He's gone over to the harness shed to get his rifle."

Mary was pushing Mig's bare feet into her slippers. "Quick," she said again. The fact that this was no nocturnal joke was becoming apparent as Mary took Mig by the hand and they started down the hall.

"What about the children?" Mig asked.

"They're asleep so it's all right. He usually treats them as Red Cross."

So it wasn't the first time, it was a usual occurrence when Jim got on the beer, and it was deadly serious.

Outside, the warm darkness was romantic and they might have been children out on a prank. The outlines of the sheds and fences were dim contours in the milky blackness. Mary led the way through the outlines of scattered stables toward what

135

seemed to be nearby paddocks as they stumbled over the ruts of dried mud.

"Where are we going?"

"Over by the water hole. That's where I usually go; down in the hollow you're protected more."

They clambered over a rise and then Mary pulled Mig down on the soft dry earth. At the same moment a barn door opened and a beam of lamplight broke the dark, showing the silhouette of a short man holding a rifle that seemed to be aimed right at them. It was too unreal to be frightening, Mig just felt curiously detached lying there in the dry mud; a faint night wind ruffled water behind them and otherwise there was silence until Jim called, "Who goes there? Boche?"

He took a few steps in their direction and pointed the rifle once more. "If it's the Boche, they shall not pass. Hear me? They shall not pass. We are the Seventh Infantry Division Anzacs and we're going to blow you fugging huns to the other side of the river. They shall not pass."

"He thinks he's back at the Somme," Mary whispered as there was a sharp ping behind them and something hit a small gum sapling.

"Keep your head down," Mary said. "He nearly always misses but better to take care." They might have been playing some hobgoblin game on Guy Fawkes Night. Except that instead of harmless firecrackers these were bullets. Again there was a crack in the air and then silence, again a crack, a ping in some stones to the left. Jim shot, recharged, shot. Mary seemed to be counting.

"It'll be the end of that round in a minute," Mary said. "Once he's finished a round, I usually surrender."

Jim had fired the volley and was standing still in the beam of light. Then he turned and waved his arm to a seemingly real band of men in the trenches behind him. "Advance," Jim called and at the same moment Mary stood up and ran forward, waving her woolen shawl and calling out, "Surrender, surrender."

The rest of it was indistinct to Mig; the figures melted into the barn lamplight and apparently the war game was over. Cautiously Mig got to her knees and then stood up. Nothing happened. There was only the silence of night and the feathery feel of the tall grass around the water hole as she made her way very slowly toward where the dim light was coming from the open door of the shed. There, clasped in each other's arms and mouth to mouth, were the Australian and German armies. "Excuse me," Mig said, passing by them and going toward the house, where a glimmer behind blinds showed where the kitchen was, and coming inside, mud all over her slippers, she could almost have believed that she had been the victim of a wild hoax.

If it hadn't been for the sight of her dirty feet in the morning, she would have known she had dreamed it.

"Spuds with your eggs, darl?" Mary asked cheerfully as Mig came into the kitchen, where the Seventh Infantry Division was having breakfast and looking painfully woebegone, its face washed, hair combed over the stretched skin of misery. Mary came around the table and poured more hot dark tea into the tin mug in Jim's shaky hand, and leaning over him, caressed him lightly. In her eyes, in the way she looked at the young man, there was rapture so unmistakable that Mignon almost gasped with the conviction that the surrender last night had been total.

"You must remember," Mary said a little later, when Jim had driven off to church ("Oh, he wouldn't miss church for anything, hung over or not"), "that he didn't *have* to go. The farmboys were exempted. But he joined up and fought in the war and saw them blown to smithereens right and left. Sometimes he calls out in the night that they're going over the top and I have to hold him and hold him." There were tears in

Mary's eyes but a minute later she was "pounding the ivories" as she called it. Gay as a lark.

"Oh you bag-bag-bagful of sheer de-light."

Sometimes in the middle of the day it got so hot that it seemed the tin roof would melt and the distant paddocks quivered in a liquid sizzle at ground level. The only place they might feel cool was lying on the linoleum in the hall with all the doors shut and there they would stretch with little Bett and the baby crawling around them, cool damp cloths to dab at their necks and foreheads until the late afternoon brought the temperature down from over a hundred to a cooler ninety. But there was no surcease for Mary in the hell of her kitchen with the wood stove going day and night in the fever of Australian January. In the evening the big men tramped in for "tea," the harvesters helping Jim with the crop sat down to the kitchen table for a supper of boiled mutton and potatoes washed down with scalding tea, and after they were finished Mary and Mignon had theirs, by which time Jim was already snoring in the front bedroom. "Harvest's always hell," Mary said but never seemed to mind that she didn't have a day off excepting Sunday all summer long and nothing whatever to look forward to as far as Mignon could see except perhaps more children and more drudgery. First up in the dark to milk the cows, last to go to bed after she'd raked out the fire in the brick oven, it was no wonder that she looked on Jim's war games, even compounded with bullets, as an occasional respite from the monotony.

Also there were The Four Dominoes, the dance band Mary had scraped together from local talent, two boys from Parwan on drums and saxophone and two others from the Marsh on clarinet and double bass. They got together and played for the local dances, with Mary leading on piano. They were to be a feature of the coming Harvest Moon Ball at the School of Arts in Bacchus Marsh, for which Mary was learning "the new tunes" sent up from Melbourne.

Mig said at first that she wouldn't go, she would stay at home and look after the babies, but Mary wouldn't hear of it. "Miss the Harvest Moon *Ball?* Not on your life; it's the highlight of the whole year here and young Lou Ganz rides over to stay with the kids, they're used to her."

The Saturday night of the dance, the men knocked off early and there were frequent comings and goings with jugs of hot water to fill up the tin bathtub in the dairy, where Jim, being boss, cock of the walk, ex-AIF, took the first bath and the others followed until the water was the color of tomato soup. Reluctantly Mig got into her only good dress, a simple white linen with black buttons, unsuitable for a ball, she felt. In the kitchen she ran into this milk-white powdered stranger with dampened hair crimped into unwilling spit curls and dressed in glaring sateen, green rhinestone brooch clamped to the shoulder. "How do I look, darl?" Mary asked.

The School of Arts on the main street of the Marsh was brilliantly lit with electricity and a great bulbous moon of gold paper had been hung on the stage and paper streamers and tinsel from the ceiling. On the stage, which had a flaking canvas backdrop of a sylvan glade and waterfall, the three other Dominoes were tootling and tuning up in ferocious discords.

Mig was introduced by Mary to Joe and Jack and Ginger and Daph, to Eileen and Gwen and Ern. Mary was in her element. "Hello, love," she shrieked to all and sundry; she waved and blew kisses. But once she sat down at the piano and nodded one two three to the boys and they crashed into "I'm Forever Blowing Bubbles," it took no more than a minute for Mig to discover herself stranded on the dance floor and to recognize that there was a cast-iron system prevailing which forbade any mingling. The girls sat on one side of the hall in their finery, shocking-pink taffeta competing with turquoise net, while the boys, pomaded hair slicked down, in overtight navy blue suits, stood smoking and shuffling their feet in a gaggle on the other. Then one by one the boys crossed the floor and took hold of the girls in solemn procession. No word passed between the partners; the girls stood up and were whirled away as if they all had numbers, the best dancers and prettiest-looking being the first away, then the less attractive and older, plumper ones and finally the hopeless, the plain, the inherent spinsters were left in their disgrace, Mignon among them. They sat, disguising their shame with tinsel smiles and tilting their proud chins in the air, scorning the fortunate ones fox-trotting by and passing little comments between themselves which they greeted with loud joyless laughter. Then, all hope abandoned, the taller girls rose and took the shorter ones as partners. Deadly serious, these twosomes stayed on the outskirts of the dance floor as if, the caste system prevailing, they were the pariahs. To Mig's dismay a thin tall bony girl with hay-colored hair tortured into corkscrews confronted her and said, "My name's Eileen and I'll be the man." There seemed no escape and Mig was unwillingly led to the floor and held in an iron grip but also kept at arms' length as though she might have been incubating something contagious, while silently, sullenly Eileen marched her in time to the music, merely walking in time to the beat.

"You Mary Wilkins' town sister?" Eileen asked abruptly.
"Yes."

On they went, marching, turning the corners like automatons, on and on went the music. Would Mary and the band ever stop, would nothing have pity on her, Mig prayed, held in a viselike clasp. There was no avoiding Eileen's glassy stare.

"We heard you was coming," Eileen said after a while and as the music at last stopped, escorted Mig back to her seat against the wall like a gentleman.

During the respite Mig escaped into the ladies' room and needlessly combed her hair, staying away from the dance as long as she dared, and coming back to her seat, was made aware that she was being avidly discussed by the sudden silence that ensued and the fussings over straightening stockings and fluffing hair. When the next dance began, she rose and walked boldly up the steps onto the stage, where she took a seat near Mary, determined not to move again until the evening was over or at least until supper was served, and Mary seemed to understand, she nodded gaily and called out, "Having fun, darl?" Mary seemed sympathetic to the discomfort and disgrace; she probably had been through it herself when she arrived here newly married to Jim and had had to conform to the rigorous chauvinism of Bacchus Marsh. Between numbers, Mary would call out to the band "Sheik of Araby" or "Three O'clock in the Morning" and twitch the sheet music onto the piano. The band played without music, seeming to follow her lead as best they could, but the clarinetist's eyes stayed on Mig and every time she glanced at him the eyes were laughing at her and her high-and-mighty posture of pretending not to care a fig. Her foot tapped to the music. See if she cared.

Oh, I see through you, the eyes said.

Mind your own business, she telegraphed back.

One eye winked. She looked away haughtily, then back. Another wink. Toot toot tootsie, the clarinet went. Tum tum she loves me, I know she loves me because she said so . . . on moonlight bay . . . in my arms adorable . . . gee but you're glorious . . . in my dreams . . . I'll be loving you . . .

"Sing it, darl," Mary urged. " 'With a love that's true, *al*ways.' " Maybe the eyes had got into her throat; she had no breath, only a wisp of a voice came out quiveringly. "Come *on*," Mary said, "sing out, love. She's got the voice of an angel," Mary told the band. "Stand up and give us a song," Mary commanded but all the defeated Mig could manage was a faltering note or two and red with shame and despair she begged off, saying she had something caught in her throat.

When he put down the clarinet in the break for supper, he gave her an audacious bow. He was extravagantly good-looking and cheeky. She felt he was looking under her skirt and pulled it down, then wished she hadn't. While she was standing in the crowded basement trying to drink a cup of scalding milky coffee, he turned up next to her and said, "Not nervous of a bunch of hayseeds, are you?"

"Certainly not," she said and turned away because the eyes were boring into her and they were mesmerizing.

"Which?" Mary asked in the ladies' room, putting on more white powder in clouds. "Oh, the clarinet bloke, that's Lowden Ganz. They own the bakery. It's his sister Lou who's looking after the kids." If only Mary had taken Mig's temperature then and there and found it was a hundred and three point eight, if only a hurricane had blown the School of Arts away before the dance began, if only she had stayed home, never left Sydney or Sidney, if only Jim Wilkins had not got so pissed he couldn't drive.

All that occurred to her only later, in an aftermath of sorrow. But there was no sorrow at the time, only a tightening around the heart.

"Lowden's going to drive us home in his van because Dad's blotto," Mary said as they came out of the hall and they saw a tottering Jim being assisted into the back of a horse-drawn yellow van with the legend GANZ BAKER on the side. "Wait till he finds out who drove us home tomorrow," Mary chortled. "He hates the Ganzes, they're German. Oh, but they're a nice harmless lot, all except Lowden."

And up up into the high seat in front next to him while he went gee-up to the horse and they jogged off under the incredible carpet of stars along Geelong Road and she could feel an electricity coming from him so that she shivered slightly and Mary huddled beside her on the other side said, "You can't be *cold,* it's January."

And in the lamplit kitchen, awakening the sleeping Lou, he looked less threatening, the dimmer light exhausting the impertinence of his eyes, and then arousing his sleeping sister, askew on the horsehair couch, he seemed to transpose impudence into tenderness. "Wake up, love, wake up, beauty," he said to his sister and it was gentle as a kiss. The enormity of his sweetness was intensified by lamplight and giant shadows.

After Mary had got Jim's boots off and tucked him still in his shirt and pants under the quilt, she and Mig had a cup of tea.

"Oh, it's the usual story," Mary said. "He got a girl in trouble. Then vamoosed and she drowned herself in the Walleroo. Only she never named him. One of the Dobbs girls. Never said who, so it's only surmise. But everyone *knew* it was Lowden."

Tootling on the clarinet and winking at people as carefree as the wind even though everyone knew. And a wretched girl had thrown herself in the river. But somehow it didn't alter one's perspective about him or blot out the picture of him awakening his sister and the gentleness of him, how they went out into the moonlight with their arms around each other and how he helped her up onto the van beside him and they had driven off down the road with her head on his shoulder.

He was capable of such sweetness. It was a dangerous thought.

Mig determined she would put him out of her mind.

First thing in the morning she thought about him, before even opening her eyes, and he recurred to her on and off all day, setting the butter to cool on the dairy stone floor, gathering eggs from the henhouse. He materialized at the dinner table over the dishes of Mary's tripe and onions. One waved away the thought of him like a fly and like a fly he was back the next minute.

It was as if, fed some exotic food she had never tasted before, she longed for more. If he worked at the local bakery, then didn't they ever buy bread down in the Marsh? Didn't the baker ever deliver? The baker's cart hove in sight one morning and her heart did a rataplan until she saw that the squat driver was only a weak facsimile of Lowden, his brother Bert.

She could have announced that she was going home. Why didn't she? He had done nothing to encourage her in the least, barely spoken six words to her. Why was she behaving so strangely for *her?* Now it was like being slightly ill with flu and unable to throw it off. She would have wanted to be wearing black and pearls when she met him again, which might have given her a somber advantage, but she was in an old cotton print frock and a battered panama of Mary's because Mary had said "Pegs." Said flour, raisins, citronella, marking off a grocery list, and they drove into the Marsh without warning one Saturday afternoon while the boys were still in the paddocks. When they came out of the general store there was Lowden sitting at the wheel of the family tin lizzie and Mig nearly dropped the parcels she was carrying at the sight of him and the discomfort of being caught in such a tatterdemalion outfit.

"Hello, Mary; hello, Mig."

" 'Lo, Low," Mary said and began to guffaw at something he said. Mig was not listening. She stood beside the horse and buggy in this detached state until she realized that both Mary and Lowden were staring at her and that she had been asked something.

"What?"

"Do you want to stay in town and go to the pictures tonight?"

Pictures? She came out of her brown study.

"It's *The Gold Rush,*" Lowden said.

Usually Mary played the piano at the picture show but not during harvest. Don't you want to stay? she asked with what seemed to be a wink and a nudge.

"I'm not dressed," Mignon said.

It was like Sidney had said, she was never ready for anything, she never had anything planned. Here came the opportunity and she was in the wrong clothes.

"Oh nonsense, silly," Mary said. "Lowden doesn't mind what you have *on.*" Mary laughed at her own joke and added that what she really meant was that the girls didn't really dress up to go to the pictures Saturday night.

And Sidney would have said go, grab whatever might be coming your way and if you decide you want him, grab *him.*

But it wasn't true that none of the local girls bothered to dress up for the Saturday night flicks. When they got to the Kookaburra Café, girls looked up from tables everywhere in their Saturday best. One girl was wearing a little white bunny fur toque. Her name was Lettice, Lowden said, but he pronounced it Lettuce.

"How's tricks, Lettuce?"

"Oh, hello, Lowden," Lettuce said. She looked Mignon up and down, Mignon in her faded print dress, carrying the old panama hat to hide it.

She and Lowden sat down at the table next to where Lettuce was having her dinner alone, all dressed to the nines.

"Going to the pictures?" Lowden asked her.

"I don't know yet," Lettuce said.

"Got so many dates I suppose that it's hard to make up your mind."

"I may have," Lettuce said. "When it turns out to be any of your business, I'll let you know."

"Oh, you do that, love. Let me know. I'll be on tenterhooks."

Lettuce's glance was scornful but her eyes lingered on Lowden, and Mignon wondered if the white bunny hat had been worn with a view to running into him.

"Steak or dags?" asked the fat girl waiting tables.

"Steak with a couple of cows' eyes?" Lowden asked.

They were served steaks the size of small saddles covered with greasy fried eggs, and thick white cups of boiling black tea. It was a meal for bushrangers and she was not even mildly hungry.

The Mechanics Institute Hall was hot and crowded and they had to push their way to seats in the front row, under the screen. Ah, there Ruby, ah, there Gwen; Lowden said to old girlfriends, who returned his greetings with manufactured disdain.

Someone wound up a gramophone and a tinny record of "Dance of the Hours" accompanied the flickering newsreel showing the Prince of Wales and a woman in a cloche hat launching a battleship while crowds silently cheered and waved Union Jacks. "I thought we'd *had* a war," Lowden said. They sat through African warriors dancing and seals performing and when finally *The Gold Rush* came on he reached for her hand and she let him hold it, not knowing whether to withdraw it or just allow the presumption. You were damned if you did and if you didn't. But he held it lightly as a glove as though to reassure her that nothing concupiscent was intended. He laughed heartily at the film. Handed her afterwards into the tin lizzie without ceremony; she might have been a distant relative.

Only one headlamp worked, which cast a bleary lemon light on dusty trees and wire fences and into the startled eyes of occasional rabbits. After a few miles a tinny metal smell arose and Lowden said cheerfully, "She's overheating, poor old girl. Let's hope she gets you there."

Just in sight of the farmhouse, he leaned across the wheel, and putting one arm in a protective manner on her knee, with a quick graceful movement he kissed her on the lips.

When they drew up in the yard in a series of bangs and snorts, Mary opened the kitchen door in a beam of lamplight and he called out to ask if he could have a jug of water for the car. Mary came with the jug and they filled up the thirsty Ford.

"Good night then, Mig."

"Good night, Lowden, thanks."

He drove off.

Mary, setting the lamp back on the kitchen table, asked was it a nice evening, had she had fun? Oh yes.

"He didn't try anything, did he?"

"No."

"Good."

There was much to think of, going to bed. But oddly enough she put off thinking about him not so much out of fatigue as out of wanting to perpetuate the day. Wanting to have it to consider in the light of sensibility tomorrow. But there was no luxury of a gentle reminiscing granted her. He was too bold, he got into the bed with her with her sleep and she turned to embrace him gently when she awoke alone in the early morning light.

Life was a contradiction. Here was Mary, at times with a bruise or a sore arm which couldn't always be the nocturnal accident she claimed it to be, singing to herself over the stove or feeding the baby with that translucent look in her eyes which could only be from deep happiness, a happiness of total gratification, and Mig knew from the way she teased and chided him loudly over his coarse table manners and uncouth habits (he would walk from the dairy where he took his Saturday night bath to the house stark naked in his untied boots) that Jim ravished her. And here was Mig, ripe for such happiness and being safeguarded from it as though she should be inviolate. Somehow the hypocrisy of people toward sex was exemplified in Bubba and Ray Stone's shivaree, Mary explained.

"We all get tin plates and billy cans and wooden spoons and whistles and we creep up on the house at night and bang, we let them have it, bang wallop."

"Let whom?"

"The newlyweds."

"Why?"

"Oh, I don't know. It's the custom."

"Did they do it to you?"

147

"Oh, you bet. But it didn't stop *us*. We went right on doing it." Mary rolled over on the bed and guffawed.

"Why would they want you to *stop* it? You're married."

"Oh, it's only in fun, darl."

Naturally Lowden was the ringleader the night of the shivaree. They all met at the Anderson place nearby the newlyweds' but far enough away for them not to hear the sound of cars and buggies arriving, and as they all followed Lowden in the milky dark under an overclouded moon across a fallow paddock and through a wire fence down the road for half a mile, carrying their tin plates and spoons and stifling giggles, brushing against each other and everyone saying shush shush, hiccuping with the fun and excitement of it, Mig could not help the feeling that they were all sexually communing with each other in this wild display of discouraging nature.

When they got within a few yards of the darkened farmhouse they gathered in a knot outside the front veranda and when Lowden signaled one two three, they let loose with the cacophony in a relief that imitated the orgasm that was in everyone's mind, and rattling, whistling, spanking, they released themselves all over the quiet neat front yard until lights went on inside the house and the newlyweds, correctly dressed in nightclothes and wrappers, stood blinking in the lamplight, sheepish and obedient to the accustomed rite, pleased to get it over with and get really down to the business of being married, and asked everyone to come in for beer and cold frankfurters.

Stumbling into the light in the procession of grinning faces and into the heavy-handed jocularity of ribs being dug, Mig found herself being helped up the steps by Lowden, who then put an affectionate arm around her neck in the attitude of strangling her, and winking at her said, "Hello, Pup. How are you, Pup?"

They shared a seat in the crowded living room where everyone toasted Bubba and Ray over and over again and Mary led the mob in "Tea for Two." They all sang "You Are My Sunshine" and rocked to the music, and it was then that Lowden's arm was around Mig's waist and they rocked together, easy and sweet, and looking at the dreamy lustful faces around them it was easy to see that the shivaree was merely the sexual license given to everyone under the guise of good-natured fun: hands were being placed on hands, knees rubbed against knees, covert kisses were exchanged, even their giant shadows on the walls and ceiling took on libidinous shapes, the moonlight against the drawn blinds, the very notes Mary was playing on the piano, the words of the euphemistic song "Gimme a little kiss, will ya, huh?" From time to time Mig felt Lowden's clasp around her tighten.

"Don't get shickered now," he said when she accepted her third glass of pilsener.

"I'm all right," she told him, looking directly in his eyes.

"You all right?" he asked again later, murmuring into her neck.

"Perfect," she replied and leaned back against him.

Somehow in the melee of leaving, they lost Mary and Jim. Tripping over stones and cow dollops in the dusty road in the dark of moonset hand in hand with Lowden, she let herself be led to whatever was coming, to wherever he had hitched the horse and bakery van, and be helped up onto the seat beside him and driven off somewhere into the depths of night as if she were merely dreaming it. This time, outside the fence, under the big blue gum where Jim usually killed and cut up the sheep before cooking, where the earth was stained blue-black with blood, Lowden kissed her very lightly on the mouth and she kissed him back with fervor.

"I believe you're a tiny bit stonkered, my pet," Mary said as she came unsteadily into the kitchen, blinking in the light.

"It's not the beer," Mig said.

No? Be sure now, Mary's glance said, warning of the Lowdens of the world, of second natures.

But he was casual, inviting Mig to drive over to the Parwan football grounds next Saturday and see the woodchopping contest. He was offhand about taking her to *The Big Parade* at the flicks and afterwards to the Kookaburra Café for a ginger beer. Nevertheless to the local word of mouth "it was on," they were mistaken for lovers, not only by the outsiders but by themselves, partly for their tentative motions toward each other, the way he let his hand slip casually under the belt around her waist or the manner in which she held on to his hand a moment longer than necessary when he was helping her down from the bakery van. And they seemed to read more into conversational exchanges than was there.

It was her assumption that the reason he never laid hand on her sexually when their late meetings were often rife with opportunity was that he had classed her in a bracket above his usual fly-by-night relationships with girls and surely, she told herself, he didn't take every local "Sheila" he'd been roistering with behind the wheat stooks to meet his old grandparents, Lutheran stern in their grim parlor, to suffer through a tea of hard scones and gentle interrogation.

"Don't take it to heart," he said, laughing when she lamented that she had not been able to think of anything entertaining to say to old Mr. and Mrs. Ganz. "In a way they never left Stuttgart," he said and crushed her to him roughly. Such roughneck caresses came easily to him, perhaps were a protection against having to say he loved her. Always the half tackle, the arm around her neck in a parody of the football maneuver, never the serious word and if it came, halfway soberly ("You look pretty in that shirt"), it was instantly obliterated by a guffaw.

But when the true gesture was made (she thought) it was rigid and conventional. It was his turn for Saturday delivery of the bread. "Care to join me?" So his ultimate acceptance of her, there seemed no doubt in the tone, was of her sitting alongside him on the van as they drove around from farm to farm and of her reading off the penciled list as he filled the baskets: "Three white, two brown, one raisin." "Four long whites, two whole wheats, four custard tarts." How Sidney would have hooted! When all the time under the green of her imagination Mignon had been halfway priming herself for Lohengrin, investing the armor and the swan with a reality, seeing the profile of the beautiful manly chin and the power of the body under the steel while all the time she had been projecting this onto the baker. But the baker kissed her good night. "Sweet dreams," the baker said.

She was writing to Sidney: ". . . hardly believe it but what you said to me was maybe right and I'm beginning to think I am on the way to finding out about myself in a new way. There is a bloke—" She was interrupted by Mary screaming and running outside, found that little Bett had somehow got out the side gate and was wobbling her way toward the water hole. She and Mary rushed across the paddock and were in time to clutch at the tiny pinafore just as it might have disappeared into the muddy depths. Such a lot of crying and comforting had to ensue that Mig put away her letter to Sidney for a more convenient moment, not aware that the moment was about to strike.

Not aware that the future, hers and Lowden's, had been settled in fire and stone at the birth of the planet.

"I'm a surprise," Sidney said.

She was standing by the gate in the evening light. She had on her brown linen, crushed from being sat up in all night, and the smuts from the train engine were still painted around her eyes. Mary was at the pump, getting the water for boiling the evening vegetables and laughing.

"Drove out from the station with the postman," Mary explained joyously. "Not a word of warning, trust our Sid, didn't want to bother, but chummed up with Bluey Whistler and drove out as if she lived here." Mary gave Sidney a bear hug with one free hand. "You'll have to share the bed, you girls."

"My sister Sidney, Lowden Ganz," Mig said and as one might perhaps have at one time introduced Paolo and Francesca.

"How do you do?"

"G'day, Sidney."

Of course, typical of Sidney. Why wouldn't she just get on a train and come? On a whim. Missed you, darling, she said and embraced Mig heartily. Dull as dishwater in the city. "I woke up one morning and longed to hear the sound of magpies and smell the gum trees." Besides, she'd finished her book and turned it in.

"It's American."

"But you've never been in America."

"Nor have my readers. But don't forget, I've got an American pal and Royce is going through it to make sure it's true-blue Yankee. You're so *brown,* you look like a real farm girl. Have you had a good time? You never sent a card or *any*thing. Typical of you."

I'm Sid, she told the farmhands at supper and sat down with them to cold mutton and pickles and later won at dominoes from Jim, who pleased her by calling her "cobber" like an old friend.

"Oh, it's sunshine having Sidney around," Mary said over the washing up.

Sunshine every day from then on. Sidney was a wave that lifted everyone along with it and bore them up beyond their limits and yet was never intrusive. "I'm not taking up too much of the bed, am I?" she asked. But that was prior to Mig's beginning to feel any encroachment. Lowden stayed away all the first week but they may just have been busy at the bakery, Mig hoped, and at the end of ten days grew tense at the sound of approaching motors on the road. The end of harvest was customarily celebrated by the Parwan horse races held in the

Jorgensens' big field, to which everyone came to lay a bet and eat a picnic lunch.

Coming back with Mary from the tent where hot water was provided for the billy cans of tea, Mig saw that Sidney and Lowden were standing together at the fence near the starting post with their heads together, choosing a horse from the card he was holding, and appeared to be so deep in concentration they never saw her and Mary setting out the tea things on the tree stump until Mary yelled, "Tea for *two,* you two," whereupon they turned around and Lowden, seeing Mig, straightened up rather formally and said, "Hello, how are you?" in an offhanded way and then spoke to Sidney in an undertone.

"I'd love a beer," Sidney said.

"I'll be back with a couple," Lowden said. "Wait here, will you?"

"Right ho."

"Stand right there so's I'll find you, will you?"

"Right here."

"Right there, *promise?*" He was so waggish it was pitiful and they were both giggling as he went off, adjusting his digger hat to a more cocky angle. "He's mad," Sidney said, laughing and peeling a hard-boiled egg. "This is fun, Mary. You country people know a thing or two about a good time."

"Oh, there goes Jim into the beer tent." Mary laughed. "Better look out for someone to drive us all home, girls."

All the signs were there, of course, as if it had been arranged by God or the devil that these two would mesh like wheels in a clock. Need he, Mig wondered, stand so close to point out the lineup at the starting gate, and need Sidney lean back on him in that provocative way or was it that they couldn't help touching every moment or two?

The indignity of the jealousy was such that it made Mig feel physically in pain. That of all beloved people in her world she should be jealous of Sidney, that it could be Sidney who had trampled on her idyll, treading on roses and birds' eggs as it were and not seeming to notice or care, Sidney with her usual intuition and insight. Yet what Mig saw with a cruel clarity in the days that followed was that Sidney had succeeded with Lowden where Mig had failed, in his heart.

Every little gesture he made, passing her the tomato sauce, helping her off with a coat, seemed intended to gratify and please her but not in his usual jocular manner; more often grave and introspective. It was clear to Mig now that his gestures toward her had been perfunctory, even his kisses had been avuncular.

She began waiting formally for the moment when it would be clarified, as if an announcement were to be made about Sidney and Lowden, even a mention of them in the "About Town" topics in the Bacchus Marsh *Gazette.*

One night, up later than usual, Mary said, yawning, "Leave the lamp for the lovebirds," as they left the kitchen to the ticking clock. For a moment, the cup in Mig's hand almost flew across the room and shattered, but she put it carefully down in the sink.

She lay in the dark in bed waiting for Sidney to come home and was half expectant that the lateness indicated something of importance, perhaps tidings of unutterable joy and of despair. She was almost asleep when at last she heard the distant bangs and chortles of the lizzie stopping outside and later Sidney's soft steps down the hall and then the muffled sounds of her undressing nearby and then felt her get into the bed and sigh. There was the awareness that each of them was awake and then Sidney spoke.

"Are you awake?"

"Yes."

"Something to tell you."

After a long pause: "I'm his."

"I see."

"Happened this evening."

"I see."

"You knew it was going to, didn't you?"

"I suppose so."

"Had to tell you right away."

"Yes."

"You all right? You sound a bit muffled."

"Yes, okay, I'm fine, just sleepy."

"Sorry, but I always have to tell you things first, before anyone else, you know that."

"Yes, course, course."

"You don't mind, do you?"

"Me? Mind? Why should I *mind?*"

"I just wondered. I had this funny flash you might have— just suddenly, just now—that you might have had a crush on him."

"Heavens *no.*"

"Promise?"

"Don't be *mad.*"

"I'm so utterly happy I can't tell you. I'm in a state of bliss, utter bliss. You see, I think we're meant for each other and we've been waiting for each other all this time and everything up to now has just been a rehearsal of living."

Sidney settled comfortably and then said, "I don't think I'll ever sleep all night what with bliss and reliving it, the lovely thing. I suppose this is being in seventh heaven."

"Yes."

"Well, sixth."

But in a few minutes the regular breathing announced Sidney was asleep. It was Mignon who saw the first faint light outside the curtains and heard the first rooster crow.

Sidney did not appear in the kitchen until half past eleven in the morning, by which time Lowden had already driven up with the excuse of sweet buns accidentally left off Mary's list and Mary was cautious enough to concede them. "Stay and have a bite of lunch," she said to Lowden. "If you're not in any hurry."

"I'm not in any hurry," Lowden said.

"Oh, what are *you* doing here?" Sidney asked and, laughing, fell against him and into a fumbling mock embrace.

It was the divine inevitability that was painful, the blessing of some wanton gods that seemed to hang over Lowden and Sidney, and Mary seemed to recognize it and for once said nothing but served Lowden's buns with some honey and just smiled lovingly at them, and suddenly Mignon said that she felt like singing. "Let's sing something," she said, pulling Mary up from the kitchen table and pushing her toward the front parlor. "Come on," she called to Lowden and Sidney.

Oh, anything, she said to Mary, leafing through the sheet music on top of the piano, and twitched out, of all things, "My Hero." Then Mary plunked out the introductory chords and Mig took her revenge on Sidney and Lowden. She sang to them with all her heart. She sang that she had a true and faithful lover, that her arms were aching now to embrace him, come, come, she told him, I love you truly. And the two real lovers sat transfixed, caught red-handed, Lowden biting his fingernails and Sidney staring at the worn-out linoleum with a look of troubled compassion because naturally she understood, even though both sisters knew that no word would pass between them. All Sidney said when the last note had died away was "Well, you've never sung so beautifully in your whole life, you've made me cry."

Now it was better; now that she had exalted it, she felt she could breathe without pain, and Mig bent and kissed Sidney's wet face. That night over their mutton and potatoes, Mig announced that she was going home next day. Time enough, she told Mary.

"For what?" Mary asked.

Funnily enough it was Mary's Jim, Jim the obtuse, the slow-witted, who seemed to see through the mimicry of cheerfulness Mig projected, packing, humming, tittering at clumsy jokes. Pausing by the pump to wash his red dusty hands before tea, Jim looked for a long time at Mig and then said, "You're better off going home. There's nothing in this place in the long run for a girl but loneliness."

But she couldn't get away scot-free. Sidney and Lowden took her to the train and presented her with a bag of lemon drops.

Sidney kissed her fiercely, Lowden gave her the hammerlock.

"See you around, chum," Lowden said.

Mrs. Drum was making the sandwiches for the picnic even though Lily would rather have done so herself. No matter how much George excused the presence of Mrs. Drum on humanitarian grounds (she had nine children and the father was a brutal drunk), Lily still found her an intrusion; she left buttery knives on the sink and put tea leaves down the lavatory without pulling the chain and there was a demonic quickness about her which could be disconcerting: she was always where you didn't want her before you could get there.

The moment the phone rang Mrs. Drum flew down on it like a hawk on a field mouse, and relinquished the receiver with reluctance. One felt her presence all over the house, which was admittedly too large for just Lily and George; empty bedrooms testified to their childlessness, where Lily left the blinds pulled halfway down in a halfhearted apology; in one of them Mrs. Drum kept her ratty working clothes and occasionally took a "laydown" on the bed.

But after all, the big house in Kogarah was symbolic; after all George was the Labor Party member of Parliament for the Illawarra district and they had to keep up appearances. After all, George said they were helping out one of the electorate wives and freeing Lily for the intensive round of speechifying and public appearances that were necessary if George was to win in the forthcoming election. And people coming to the house (which they did day and night on any excuse: their pension, illegal abortions, the price of beef) would see that poor little Mrs. Drum had been given a job and a nice hot lunch to boot and with Mr. Barnes's generosity might even be able to one day get her upper and lowers.

Somehow Mrs. Drum represented (though Lily would never say it to George) the intrinsic failure of their mission. Everything about Mrs. Drum was halfhearted, including her sandwiches. Certainly her gratitude, which was perfunctory to say the least. "Ta," she would say, grasping the five shillings Lily put into her hand without glancing at it, and from time to time Lily caught a look of defiant exultation in Mrs. Drum's tea-colored eyes that together with her clamped toothless mouth set in its lockjaw grin seemed to say, "I'm as good as you any day." Of course the poor had a right to their own dignity the same as anyone else and Lily and George were fighting the battle for the poor, the underprivileged, their lives were dedicated to it, but just the same every now and then the poor made you wonder. Perhaps they hated you for it.

Lily had wakened this flawless summer day with a touch of headache: worry about the weather (would it *stay* good?), about Lowden Ganz (would he and Fred's wife get along? Grace could be dreadfully scratchy), about whether two dozen sausage rolls would be enough. Because interspersed with the myriad trivialities of life lay the fundamentals, love and dedication and blood being thicker than water, which fact had been made disconcerting by Lily's running into Adnia on the corner of King and George streets the week before. Adnia was handing out some sort of religious circular to passersby and when she thrust one at Lily as though Lily were a perfect stranger it exemplified how far Addie, poor lame Addie, had become estranged from them all. She had wanted to, of course. She had packed her tin trunk and she and it had been driven away in a taxi from the house in Turramurra without so much as a backward wave five years or so ago and although they all knew that she had a clerical job in the Pacific Light and Gas Company in Chatswood and roomed with some people named Hallbut in Cremorne, she might as well have been in Peru. On the odd occasions when Lily had telephoned her (asking the Hallbuts might she speak to Miss Lord, please, sorry to trouble you, it's her sister calling) she was met by Adnia's stratospheric indifference, indicated in a tone of bloodcurdling graciousness which Adnia used now, thrusting the orange circular into Lily's hand. It stated incontrovertibly that "GOD HAS SEEN YOU."

"Please stand to the side, Lily," Adnia said.

"How have you been?"

"I am *well,* of course, you needn't ask."

Sorry, forgot she'd been "translated" into another sphere of thought.

"We never see you."

Adnia nodded agreeably. She was wearing a green felt sliver of a hat with a long feather in it which gave her the look of a rakish Robin Hood.

"Sidney is getting married," Lily pursued. "He's a nice bloke, country boy, knows Mary. Name's Lowden. They're getting married a week from Saturday. St. Stephen's."

"Don't pass God by," Adnia called out, smiling. But most people glanced at the handbill and then crunched it up into a ball and threw it in the gutter.

"We're having a little picnic for them this Saturday," Lily went on, "at Figtree. You couldn't come, could you? Could you, Addie?"

Adnia's smile was that of a judge pleased with the disposal of a case.

"Go in Upward Thought, Lily," was all Adnia said.

That had been a week ago and Lily was still possessed by the thought of the family's disintegration and why things occurred the way they did.

She put Mrs. Drum's downtrodden-looking sandwiches in

the wicker basket together with the sausage rolls and fruit, the pink-iced cake from the Cakery in Arncliffe, and found George leaning on the front fence and talking to a small group of workmen who were repairing a drain. George was expounding on the wrongs of capitalism and royalty. One ruby from the coronation crown, George was saying, would wipe out the slums of Surrey Hills forever. As always when she saw her dear man talking to the common trusting working people, Lily's heart expanded with a quiet joy.

After years of marriage, these two awoke each morning in the same bed and with the same thought, it seemed. Lily could not remember a single moment (barring slight disagreements over the possibility of rain, the times of train departures) of disunity between them. They thought alike on all subjects, they leaned against the same ill wind, bore with courage the same vicissitudes, liked organ music, worshiped Lenin and abhorred the perfidious plutocrats, loved each other with undemanding reciprocity. They seldom touched in public but the cord that attached them to each other was so sensitive that if you touched one of them on a secret nerve, the other would instantly respond.

They treasured each other's responses, respected one another's silences.

They knew when the other one's silence contained foreboding. "What's up?" one would ask the other abruptly.

"What's up?" George now asked Lily on the train into the city, seeing her gazing too intently at the gritty brick and tiling of the Illawarra suburbs passing by. Uninspiring Mortdale.

"I was just thinking—I hope Sidney knows what she's doing —I *hope* she does. Otherwise why are we celebrating them?"

"I know what you mean," George said.

Sidney and Lowden had been living together in somebody's borrowed flat in Darlinghurst, which didn't shock Lily so much as worry her in regard to just how seriously Lowden regarded the act of marriage itself. Oh, he had buckets of charm, there was no doubt that he could charm a goanna, but where were the responsibilities? He seemed to lounge around all day while Sidney was out peddling stories and, it seemed, keeping the home fires burning, and when Lily had delicately broached the matter of the future, was Lowden seeing about a job of any kind, both Sidney and Lowden had burst out laughing and Sidney, putting her arms around her beloved, had said, "Oh Lily, don't worry, you are such a worrywart. He's got a million things on the stove bubbling away. We're inundated with possibilities." Some rigmarole about renting *sheep* to people to keep their lawns tidy because Low knew of some bloke who could get shorn sheep at a cut-rate price. Something about a small bakery in Cronulla. Surely Cronulla was too far out of town. In the meantime he was playing the clarinet in a jazz band Tuesday and Saturday at the Oxford Street Palais de Danse. Nevertheless he escorted Lily out to her taxi as if she were Queen Mary. Oh, he was nice as pie but —Sometimes it seemed to George and Lily that everyone except themselves was, well, peculiar. People were peculiar. Even one's own family.

At Circular Quay, waiting by the turnstiles at the Lane Cove ferry, were Fred and Grace, and they did nothing to fill one with confidence. To begin with, Grace was unsuitably dressed for a picnic, in severe ecru crepe with a muskrat fur piece and long gray suede gloves and wearing high-heeled gray suede shoes when they would be climbing over rocks to get to Bottlebrush lookout, where Lily had proposed the picnic site. Fred had lately become comical without intent. He had put on quite a bit of weight and was wearing a porkpie panama hat that was a size too small for him. Myopic now, he blinked behind gold-rimmed glasses. He was already pink and damp with perspiration, even in the shade of the pier.

"Hello, greetings, greetings," Lily said and kissed Fred while Grace rebuffed her embrace with a darting movement, offering a wan cheek.

"Well, isn't this nice, isn't it lovely, the *fam*ily," Lily burbled on.

"A boat just left," Grace said cuttingly. She had brought éclairs, she said, holding up a box with a contemptuous shrug. She had been dragged here against her will, her tenuous smile emphasized. Their clock had been fast, Fred was saying, so they had already been waiting three quarters of an hour. Never mind, Fred said, consolingly and in the flat tone of one accustomed to mistakes and minor inconveniences. He still stood pigeon-toed as he had as a little boy being introduced to parishioners in the old St. Kilda house; in small ways he had not changed an iota from the time he was seven years old. He looked at his wife hopefully and lit an Old Gold. "How's tricks, George?" Fred asked.

But even Lily's manufactured effervescence had gone as flat as probably had the ginger beer in the picnic basket by the time Sidney and Lowden arrived, nearly an hour and two missed ferries later. "We overslept," Sidney said and kissed everyone warmly. "Hello, troops," Lowden said in greeting. They were carrying a sack from which came the sound of clinking.

Lily knew it! The worst. Lowden *drank*. She had had suspicions about the tiny red lines on his eyeballs from the moment she had been introduced. And worst of all, he and Sidney had brought drink with them!

George was running for reelection on Prohibition. For a dry Australia. Although some of his most fervid Laborite friends looked askance (they took a drop of sherry now and then, a sparkling Hock on New Year's Eve), George and Lily had decided that they could no longer disguise their utter loathing of alcohol in any form whatsoever. Too many drunken husbands had beaten up their wives and assaulted and terrified their children, too many broken homes had been the result of a "harmless" evening beer. They knew of stories too horrifying to be repeated. Starvation and first-degree burns, incest, ringworm and associated fires accompanied every bottle of Resche's Pale Ale opened by the unscrupulous saloon-keepers. On the posters and in the newspaper advertisements George Barnes was shown gallantly shielding a terrified child from the menacing approach of a drunken father, with the legend VOTE FOR A DRY AUSTRALIA WITH GEORGE BARNES.

True, there were dissenters. Last week while George had been speaking at Rockdale Town Hall someone had called out, "What about America?"

George had smiled indulgently and said that the reports from America about gangsters and bootleggers and violence were all greatly exaggerated by the "wets" who wanted the Volstead Act repealed, and anyway fortunately Australia didn't nurture chappies like that Capone. Not on your life, not in dear old Aussie. The only danger to society lay in being "under the influence." (Cheers)

Now to Lily and George's mortification they were being confronted by demon liquor. Lowden had opened a bottle right there on the ferry and calmly poured beer into an enamel mug which he passed around amiably. Surely there must be people who had recognized the teetotaler candidate, Mr. Barnes, coming aboard and might wonder why he didn't strenuously object to the mug being passed around so vulgarly in public, and what if it got to the ears of Mr. Angus Fisher, the opposition candidate running against George on the Country Party ticket? Lily was sitting on tacks until the boat got to Figtree and they all disembarked.

They spread the tablecloth out on a large flat rock overlooking the river in a glade of wattle and wild heath and George and Fred got the twig fire going to boil the billy while Grace and Sidney unpacked the cups and paper plates. It was at least a tableau of family unity and in spite of Lowden's almost uninterrupted filling and refilling of the enamel mug, he didn't at first seem to be in any way affected. He passed the mug now and then to Sidney but the others refused.

"Oh, isn't this jolly? Isn't this *nice?*" Lily said and poured tea, passed sandwiches. No one agreed or disagreed. A constraint seemed to have fallen on them; they sat and ate their sandwiches and sausage rolls like road menders on a tea break; even Sidney seemed subdued. They flicked flies and ants from themselves. The brilliant day loomed over them, and it disconcerted them, they were made aware of their shortcomings and mortality even by the sights and sounds of life, the green and blue of leaves and sky, the everlastingness of rocks, the sanctity of air and water; their pulses were ticking away with the knowledge of their own evanescence, their little lives were rounded with a death. At moments like this there is nothing to say, a giant hand has come down, the reminder of time and the precariousness of mortal living, and it was no use George taking pictures. They huddled together grinning as he focused his Brownie, they put arms around each other and smiled into the burning sun to be captured lightheartedly for posterity. Laughing, smiling engagingly, Lily felt the awfulness of that smack of doom that comes infrequently with its omen of ill luck, the black butterfly, the goose walking over the grave, and thought, Which one of us? Somebody among us is fated to die. "Oh come, come, love," she said to George, "let Fred take one of *us* together," and put her arm around her beloved.

The interlude with camera having postponed their reveries, they all sank earthward like deflated balloons. Sidney and Lowden wandered off, George settled on a further knoll in deep thought, Grace Coin (as Lily always thought of her, never Mrs. Lord) lay flat on the rock and fled away into sleep, leaving Fred and Lily encompassed by the sky and accompanied by the ragtag and bobtail of white galahs. They talked for a little while of George's possibilities in the election and of Fred's position in the General Post Office (obtained for him by George). How *is* it going? Lily asked, looking out across Lane Cove with the deadest heart because of the hopelessness of such a future as Fred's in the Dead Letter office. Fred said,

Oh well, tracing a design in the dirt, and gave a little hopeless shrug as he might have shrugged off something as trivial as a slug or a gnat, all his education, all his formative years having come to this: he was merely a senior government worker in the post office with nothing to look forward to but the skimpy government pension when he retired, he and Grace didn't even own the weatherboard house at the wrong end of Edgecliffe, they had no children and he was going bald rapidly.

"But," Fred said and looked down cautiously at the sleeping Grace, "I have *her.*" Fred wiped a teary eye. "Lily, I have the prize."

"Yes, dear?" She could not help forming the question, the announcement was so formal and preposterous.

"Lily, I have the crème de la crème, the grade A; you know what I mean."

"Yes, dear."

"You can't imagine what it means to me, you can't really."

"Well—"

"It goes beyond anything I can say."

"Well, dear, I'm happy you're happy."

"Oh, *happy.*" Fred swept the word away crossly. "I'm not talking about *hap*piness. You see, Lily, I'm knocked about somewhat, I'm somewhat damaged in that things haven't worked out for me quite as I'd have wished. It hasn't been easy for me."

"I know, dear."

"But you don't, not really. You couldn't know how difficult it's been for me being the only boy and having so much expected of me."

"I'm sure we didn't—"

"Not meaning harm but never mind now, all water under the bridge, but—" Fred lowered his voice, glancing at the sleeping Grace. "Lily, she's made up for everything. Lily, can you imagine how lucky I am? I look around at other men and I have to say to myself, Well, Fred, you may not have quite pulled it off but by God you've got the honor to be married to a *pearl.*"

Only Lily and the birds, the white galahs, saw that Grace's lips tightened in her sleep and that an invisible caul, a membrane, was drawn over her calm face, on which had formed a look of contempt that was as grim as a death mask. It might have been only a play of shadows cast by moving leaves if it hadn't been for a tiny bead of moisture which formed at the corner of her mouth and a flickering of the eyelashes as though her body were silently convulsed by some emetic which at any moment would vomit up her sleeping rage.

"The prize," Fred said again and wiped his eyes. He was gazing at Grace with unreserved adoration, but whatever her mouth had indicated couldn't be seen by him because he was as usual looking at her upside down.

"Well," Lily said, *"she* hasn't made too bad a bargain; you mustn't run yourself down, dear."

"Oh," Fred said, disputing any defense. *"Me."* He edged a little nearer on the rock as though he had more private information to impart, and Lily wished he didn't.

"Lily," Fred said, "I've never told anyone this but, you know, our mother was unhappy."

"I'm sure—at times—"

"Remember the little sewing room at St. Kilda she used to sit in to get the afternoon sun? I suppose I was the only one in the house, you were all out somewhere and I'd been taking a nap and I had to go to the bathroom. I was in my stocking feet and she didn't hear me and as I came by the sewing room she was sitting by the window and she was holding a little sofa cushion to her and staring out at nothing really and then I heard her say in this terrible hard, unreal voice, 'Oh, won't you please come back to me, come back to me for God's sake.' "

Lily said, "Oh yes, well, she missed Father terribly after he died."

"This was before he died."

"Oh."

And there had been the voices Lily heard in the dead of night coming from under the parents' door, Mother crying, "Oh Will, Will," and what sounded like Father's stern reproval of her. But what business was it of theirs? Even one's parents should be allowed their privacy and a decent burial.

"What's the time?" Lily called to George, not so much because she wanted to know but because she felt a sudden need for him, wanted him nearer.

"Half past three."

Had their parents' love for each other dissipated? She wished it hadn't been brought up. She began packing the basket.

What had Mother meant, Come back to me? Whatever their temporary disagreements, they were passionately in love, weren't they? Only parted in death, surely, and right up to the dreadful moment when Mother ran out the gate and under the baker's cart. The disagreeable thing about these revelations people seemed intent on making was the doubt they sowed in your own sensibility. If indeed Mother and Father had had dark and perhaps irreconcilable differences, why had Lily transposed their life into beatitude? If it was a sham, then was hers and George's a sham too? Was their dream of a poverty-less world free of booze and crime just wishful thinking? Were all the worthwhile things, honor and decency, just subterfuges for dishonesty and greed? It was finding the wasps' nest under the eaves. It was the black snake under the picnic tablecloth when she and Grace shook it out, only that was real, it uncoiled and darted toward them, its little tongue projecting like a hairpin. "Get back," Lily gasped, but Fred had scuttled off the rock and George was looking around for a stick, while in the meantime, cool as cucumbers, Grace Coin had seized a thick branch of blue gum and whacked the thing amidships, whacked and whacked, and then looping the limp broken snake over the stick, calmly hung it on a low branch where it dangled harmlessly now out of their reach. "They don't die till sundown," Grace said and brushed off her hands as though killing a snake were the most everyday thing in the world. "Oh my God, dear," Fred said, "you were brave, oh darling, you were superb." He squeezed her arm in an excess of emotion and adulation, but Grace pushed him away and gave a little spasmodic shudder as if he had put the dead snake around her neck. "Oh what rot," she said, "what utter rot."

"There was a snake under the tablecloth," Lily told Sidney and Lowden when they appeared. "It may have been there the whole time we were having lunch."

But Sidney and Lowden were unimpressed; uninterested in anything that didn't directly impinge on their lives, even the snake in Eden.

And then on the ferry, as if this day had not been enough with one thing and another, Sidney beckoned Lily away from the others and catching hold of her with both hands and with eyes lit up like crystal said, "Lily, can I tell you the most secret thing, darling, the most beautiful sacred thing, love? I'm preggo."

"Oh, *Sid*ney."

"Oh, don't be prim about it please, darling, it's just a miracle of love, that's all, and you can't always time miracles. Anyway, what difference does a week make when you're going to have a little angel?"

Demure as maidenhair the following Saturday on George's arm coming up the aisle at St. Stephen's dressed in a pale blue taffeta and with a little lace hat and blue shoes, she carried the secret up to the altar, smiling radiantly at the sparsely filled pews (nearly all strangers to Lily and some of them pretty raffish-looking people, some of Sidney's bohemian hoi polloi, no doubt), and took her place beside Lowden while Mignon, also in pale blue, brought up the rear carrying sweet peas and forget-me-nots. But like a ray of sunlight coming through the stained-glass windows of saints and martyrs, the age-old words (the very same that had joined their mother and father in holy wedlock) sanctified and strengthened. Dearly beloved, we are gathered together. They were the simple promise to God that somehow commits human to human with divine authority; the bridge over the dark waters between the known and the unknown, between order and chaos, the very structure of life itself is marriage, Lily thought, and saw Fred was reaching for his handkerchief, standing there in this beam of light that now touched her heart, seeing George giving Sidney away, seeing Lowden hold out the ring. This is righteousness, she said silently, this is love and everything we were brought up to believe. This is blessedness (and thank God, now the baby is legitimate).

"—whom God hath joined together—"

This is the glory.

"—let no man put asunder."

"Amen," Lily said.

PART TWO

Miss Adnia Lord opened the gate and came into the garden of Eden. Eden being the name of the brick bungalow in Mill-grave Street, Mosman, where she rented a back room. There, damn, on her red tricycle beside the blazing hydrangeas was Smiley Hallbut, waiting. Smiley Hallbut, who had been christened June, was the landlady's child and she was the snake in Eden, often underfoot. Disguised as a pretty six-year-old, Smiley had the heart and disposition of a scorpion but unlike a scorpion there were days when she was harmless. There were also times when Adnia, with her lumbering walk, could make it from the front gate down the side path through the hydrangeas and damp hanging ferns to her own door without attracting Smiley's notice or get from her door to the front gate unscathed. But often just as you thought you could breathe free, the cherub face burst from bushes and confronted you on the narrow path with questions like "What ud yer sooner have on toast, rusty nails or butter?" and you said, like a fool, butter, at which she responded with a painful butt of the head in your groin and then danced around you chanting, "Miss Lord said to butt her." At other times she was a model of niceness, saying Good evening, Good morning and treadling away on her tricycle harmlessly. Once or twice though, when Adnia had misguidedly turned to look back, she had caught

Smiley watching her pegleg walk with a disgusting pity, her baby mouth curled into a smirk like the imitation of a grown person in pain. Now, as Adnia came in the front gate, Smiley turned the tricycle to block the path and stared up at her prey. There was no defense against children, the battle was lost before it started.

" 'Lo, s'Lord."

"Hullo, Smiley."

"There's a letter for you in the postbox."

"Oh, really?"

Perhaps there was. She lifted the flap and reached into the small wooden box by the gate. Something slimy moved in her hand and she withdrew it to find she had grasped and squashed a monstrous green caterpillar, the size of a man's finger, and that the disgusting ooze of it had run all over her hand and that the corpse with legs still writhing was stuck to her, and with a shudder she shook it off and turned to find the smiling Smiley. It was no use saying, You shouldn't or What a silly trick, because the caterpillar goo was all over you and there was nothing to actually prove the child had set the trap for you. Just the same, Adnia limped past the little girl, trying with her head in the air to disregard her, to reduce her to a nonentity, but heard the tricycle squeaking behind her all the way down the brick path between the hydrangeas and cinerarias until she reached her back wooden steps and fitted her key into her lock and came into the safety of her room, trembling.

It was ridiculous to have developed a fear of a six-year-old child, it was unnatural, but the perseverance of Smiley's little tortures was such that aggravation had become dread. Who had put the dead lizard on her steps? Was it always the wind that blew her washing off the clothesline into the bramble bushes? She had begun to suspect that the child sometimes came into her room when she was out (Mrs. Hallbut kept a key to the inside door for emergency); there was no outward evidence of anyone having intruded but there was a subtle but definite suggestion like a faint aroma of perfume. Was it merely coincidence that time and again when she had just settled herself into a nice hot bath (she had use of the bathroom understood in her rental) Mrs. Hallbut would knock loudly on the door and say, "Are you going to be long in there, Miss Lord? Smiley has to go on the throne urgently." Once when she had complained to Mrs. Hallbut about Smiley's leaving toys on the pathway where Adnia would trip over them coming home in the dark, Mrs. Hallbut snickered nastily (she had a kind of sinister jollity, she sang as she whipped egg whites fiercely in a bowl) and said, "That's all right then, because you're as free as air to find a room somewhere else for the little you pay, s'Lord." True, she only paid fifteen bob a week including gas and she had early morning sunlight in winter and her own little garden in the back where she pottered among pots of fuchsia and it was near a tram stop which precluded too much walking.

"If you prefer," Mrs. Hallbut said, whipping furiously. Adnia did not prefer, naturally enough. But why must the child be given a pet white rabbit and call it Limpetty? "Limpetty, *Limp*etty," called the dulcet child voice across the evening lawn when she saw Adnia come crookedly in the gate, and she seemed to have affected the other children, who gathered on the pavement playing hopscotch; they fell silent when Adnia approached, they stood there and it seemed as though a mute riffle went through them like a waft of air across a still pond. Absurd, but there were actually times when she stayed on at work at the Pacific Light and Gas Company on the frailest excuses so as not to get home until the child was safely inside and in bed. There was no doubt that Smiley was her earthly burden. "Unless thou bearest the earthly burden in thine heart, thou shalt not see the glory," Dr. Grimaldi had said and Adnia knew it to be true (even though try as she might she

could not find the quotation in the Book of Revelation or in any other book in the New Testament).

"Limpetty, Limpetty," sang Smiley to the rabbit and was suffused with silent laughter as Adnia limped by.

She had found Dr. Grimaldi and the Revelationists quite by accident (or divine intervention?) when one evening without her umbrella she had taken refuge ("from the stormy blast") from a sudden downpour in the dim hallway of a building near the gas company office and heard distant singing and seen the notice with the outstretched finger pointing upstairs that read "The Revelationists. One Fl. Up. Come Up and Be Ye Perfect." As if some golden trumpet drew her on, the voices above had begun to sing "Walk, walk in the garden of Faith," and as if obeying some silent call, she labored upstairs to where the door was open to a bare-floored room and possibly twenty or so people, mostly middle-aged women, sat in hard wooden chairs facing a small platform from which the eloquent Dr. Grimaldi was expostulating and "Sit, dear" a woman whispered hoarsely and indicated the vacant seat which had seemingly been waiting for Adnia.

"And round about the throne were four and twenty seats and I saw four and twenty elders sitting, clothed in white raiment . . ." Not exactly white, more brown and gray and dusty black with rather pitiful hats, but looking around at the rapt faces she saw a peace and contentment she had never seen in a church before, not even in her own father's congregation when he was at his very best. There was more a feeling of exaltation in this bare dirty white-walled room than perhaps in the whole of St. Paul's Cathedral in London and when they rose to sing "I know that my Redeemer lives" she found herself standing with them. She listened while one after another of the "Brethren" as they seemed to be called rose and attested to their faith and some told of miraculous cures from anemia, severe gastritis and even chronic asthma. But it wasn't so much the possible coincidence of cures, nor even the oratorical gymnastics of Dr. Grimaldi (a small man with silver hair and a heavy gold watch chain across his expansive belly), it was a presence she had not felt before in any church, a persuasiveness that was like the ring of truth behind the assertions that God was here. Sometime in her childhood, the fear of God had become oppressive and made her turn away from any confrontation with Deity, bad or good, the offering of supplication and psalms embarrassed her, even someone saying grace made her flush with sheepishness. But suddenly she felt freed from this crippling disdain and after the service was over she found herself in line waiting to speak with Dr. Grimaldi, who glanced at her pleasantly and said, "Yes, my dear?" and almost unable to believe what she was saying, heard herself say for the very first time in her life, "I am lame."

He paused before he spoke, then took hold of her hands (his own hands were dry and excessively warm) and said, "We'll see about that."

More than likely she would have laughed in his face but part of her metamorphosis was that she was transported then and there into hope, a hope that she had never had in her life. She waited on the cold rainy corner for her tram and for it to subside, to fade, as one might an alcoholic drink, but instead it persisted and she found herself in her little room boiling a kettle on her gas range with the same feeling of sublime sustenance, of *possibility.* She had less of it in the morning but nevertheless it was still there, like a faint beat inside her, and so the following Thursday evening she again clambered up the stairs to the little white-walled room and after the service she again stood in line to take his warm hands in hers. "Well, *well,* my dear," Dr. Grimaldi said and in such an ambivalent way that he could have meant she would be well or meant nothing except for the glow in his eyes which were magnetic and convincing in their assurance.

She became one of the Brethren; she helped with the floral

arrangements every third Thursday, she stood on corners and handed out the printed handbills. She waited for her deliverance, she knew it would come. She would hop, skip and jump.

Meanwhile the child laid traps for her and led her up the garden path.

The man sitting opposite her on the tram was dark and swarthy-skinned, foreign-looking with thick curly black hair, and he was in some difficulty with the inspector (they got on and off trams unexpectedly to catch nonpayers or people who had traveled further than the ticket specified). In this case it seemed that the foreigner had gone past his allotted stop and owed fourpence.

"Fourpence. Or else you shoulda got off at Spit Junction."

"Not understanding."

"Fourpence more."

The inspector held out a dirty hand. The little foreigner dug into his pocket and brought out a handful of change which he offered.

"Fourpence. Four pennies." The inspector was adamant. The foreigner gazed at the small change in his hand and moved coins. Adnia moved over and sat next to the confused stranger, and saying, "Excuse me," picked out a threepenny bit and one penny which she gave to the inspector, who tore off a ticket and gave it to the man and then, grunting "Dago," spat and pulled the strap for the tram to stop. Got off, whistling.

"I don't learn money," the man said, "yet."

"Poor fellow," she said.

"Yes?"

"Poor *fellow*," Adnia said and as the tram stopped at her corner, "Good luck," she said as she lumbered off. To her surprise the foreigner got off the tram behind her and then to her astonishment he seemed to be following her at a discreet distance. Could there have been some misunderstanding? She was not nervous of him, merely curious. It was, after all, broad daylight and he had an extremely polite manner. But how odd a coincidence. Did he know people in Millgrave Street? Once or twice she turned around but he merely smiled mildly at her and continued walking a pace behind her until she came to her gate, where he stopped behind her.

"Are you looking for someone?"

"Yes, I follow."

He smiled broadly at her; he had very fine white even teeth, she noticed. Was this some ridiculous mistake? He seemed to be expecting to be asked inside. For once, heavenly pity being on her side, Smiley was nowhere in sight.

"Well, I live here, you see. So goodbye now."

He was looking puzzled. He smiled again, winsomely it seemed.

"Yes? I follow?"

"No, no. This is where I live. We say goodbye now."

"You say follow."

"No, no, you're mistaken." Light dawned. "I said *fel*low. Poor *fel*low."

"Yes. Thank you."

What a ridiculous misunderstanding and now somehow she must get rid of him, he was standing waiting and smiling, he had taken off his small black peaked cap and his thick curly hair was disarranged.

She opened the gate and stepped inside. "If you're going to the ferry it's down that way," she said and pointed. He merely glanced toward the harbor and back at her. It was an absurdity, she didn't want to walk away and leave the poor thing standing there. She had no other recourse but to turn and start down the brick pathway but when she reached the hydrangea bushes she was compelled to turn around once more. He was still standing at the gate and now gazing after her with such a mournful expression that she was touched with compassion like a sudden warm rain on her skin and without drawing a breath of caution she said, "Would you like a cup of tea?"

He came up her steps on his big feet and creaked into her room, where he sat on the very edge of a chair as if it were deigning to receive him.

Kostos was his name.

Angelopoulos. Kostos Angelopoulos. It took her a minute to get it right.

Greek. Off the freighter *Ithaki* out of Piraeus. After a bit of circumnavigating in Greek-English accompanied by shrugging and gestures, with shots in the dark from her, she got the story. He had a Greek friend who had emigrated to Australia and ran a fruit shop in Mosman but when Kostos had finally found the address with much difficulty the shop was a dry cleaner and the friend gone, no one knew where.

Kostos gripped his teacup and slurped tea eagerly and devoured two stalish buns Adnia had been saving for the weekend. After the account of his adventure in Mosman there was little to say between them and vacant smiles prevailed until he asked suddenly, "You are marrit?"

"Married? No."

"No? Alone?"

"Yes. Oh, I have sisters galore."

"Where is that?"

"I mean—lots of sisters and a brother but I don't see them."

"Why?"

"We have drifted apart."

"I have two sisters and seven brothers."

"How nice. Do you all live near each other?"

"Yes, near. We are from Patmos."

How extraordinary. The Greek isle where the apostle John was said to have received the inspiration for and to have written the Book of Revelation, and it was the Book of Revelation on which Dr. Grimaldi had based his credo of Divine Authority. She saw Kostos's little house overlooking a glittering sea and hovering nearby St. John's woman clothed with the sun and with the moon under her feet. But trying to picture it without the Biblical poetry and the dream of St. John was more difficult. Perhaps it was in a glade of cedar trees and someone would bring them fish for supper. But the idea persisted that Kostos had come from Patmos especially to represent a sign of hope to her from God that her faith wasn't in vain. And miracles today didn't encompass smoke and fire and beasts rising from the sea with seven heads and seven crowns, miracles today happened on the tram going to Mosman wharf.

She said, "Kostos," saying his name for the first time, "if you will stay a little while, I could cook you some fish."

"Yes? Thank you."

It seemed that what he most liked was octopus, which was plentiful off Patmos; he especially liked *young* octopus. And something called moussaka. They moved into her little kitchenette and he ate every scrap of the piece of haddock she simmered in butter and milk and she herself ate warmed-up chicken soup. Outside, the daylight faded. Standing at her door twisting his Greek cap, he said that he would please like her name. How funny, they hadn't thought about it until now.

"Adnia."

"Andia."

It was near enough.

"I see you tomorrow?"

Ordinarily she would have refused point-blank on any excuse but this was the messenger from God and tomorrow was Saturday, another miracle. It seemed the *Ithaki* was in port loading for several days at Wooloomooloo and Kostos meanwhile was "putting up" (he said without a trace of irony) at the Sailors' Rest Home with the other stokers. Would he like to go to the zoo tomorrow? she asked. Oh yes, thank you, Andia. He had grabbed her hand and kissed it before she could stop him. After he had finally left with instructions as to how to get the ferry into the city and further instructions as to how to meet her tomorrow morning at the Taronga Park Zoo ferry, "at the gate," she sat down in order to try to accept the reality of what had happened. She had met a Greek sailor on a tram and asked him into her room and fed him supper. It was comparable with the scaling of Everest (only such a thing had never yet occurred and probably never would; those things remained forever in the vast unknown territory of hope). She could only believe that it was by the prompting of some inner power, but if she hadn't had his unwashed cup and dish in her hand she would not have believed it even ten minutes after he had gone.

She wasn't dressed in the morning, still in her old Japanese kimono and her hair in the iron curlers she rolled it in at night, making her morning tea, when there was a rap on the inside hall door and she heard Mrs. Hallbut saying (*What? No!* Couldn't be), "There's a man at the gate for you, Miss Lord."

Holding her kimono around her and limping in her carpet slippers up the path, she saw him in the distance through the blazing hydrangeas, standing meekly at the gate, twisting his Greek cap in his hand. He beamed as she panted up.

"No, no, Kostos. I said—I meant in town at the *ferry.*"

"You said we meet at the gate."

"Not at *my* gate, at the gate to the Taronga *ferry.*"

"Not here?"

"No, no. It's only *eight o'clock.*"

Two passing Mosmanites stared curiously at the frenzied woman in nightclothes arguing with this obvious foreigner.

"Yes, wait." She heard the squeak of the tricycle coming. What a windfall for Smiley. "I have to get dressed." She turned, ignoring the tricycle, and lumbered helplessly back down the path, with a feeling of ridiculous joy. She had pictured herself waiting at the Taronga ferry and no one coming. Even so the jaunt had elements of the bizarre, a lame spinster well into her thirties wearing a Robin Hood hat and dowdy coat with fake beaver collar and a twenty-something-year-old

Greek sailor in sky blue canvas pants and tanned dark with sun and sea, holding her arm attentively, smiling into her attenuated face.

But it was like entertaining a child; would be as easy as taking advantage of a tot if you took into consideration the large roll of Australian pounds Kostos kept peeling notes from; shore leave, she supposed. He was as simple and uncomplicated as sunlight. He was captivated by the lions and giraffes and especially by the brief appearance of the strange platypus. In the afternoon, back in town, they wandered through the great halls of the National Art Gallery but Kostos seemed less gratified by the Queen of Sheba visiting Solomon or by the plight of the Sons of Clovis.

"Why? Why they in bed on a river?"

"Some punishment."

Again he took her elbow.

"Nobody ever punish *you*, Andia. Too kind."

How extraordinary.

"Oh, I don't know about *that*, Kostos."

They stood outside on the steps looking at the darkening trees and the intimidating Domain where on Sundays the soapbox orators roared and threatened. How quickly the day had gone by; usually Saturdays passed like treacle.

"Where we go now for good dinner?"

"Well—" She remembered suddenly an office girl's engagement party and they'd gone to some sort of Greek place off Darlinghurst Road somewhere, Cristos or some name like it.

"Has octopus?"

"I doubt it but we can see."

"Has moussaka?"

"Very likely."

They proceeded along Darlinghurst Road, Kostos's hand under her arm under the garish lights of Kings Cross shops— PARLOR, CAFE, JAZZ RECORDS, GYPSY TEA ROOM, PIANOLA

ROLLS, NOW SHOWING: CLARA BOW—and as they were waiting to cross the street (she remembered Cristos was in Orwell Street), the transverse of two lives occurred as Sidney crossed against them, coming the other way.

Instantly, to her shame, Adnia bent to hide her face, pretending to straighten her stockings, bent, hot-faced but not wanting to be seen until Sidney had passed. Why do such a thing? Her sister. She was flushed right down to her neck and down her back with the shock of how widely she had become estranged from her family by choice. She took Kostos's arm in this moment of her weakness. Because Sidney would only have been pleased to see her. Sidney was warm. Sidney was also very pregnant.

What was the husband's name? Lobin? Longden? And Sidney still looked like a child.

The sensation of the past passing was so strong that Adnia shook, it was as if she had opened a door to a long-unused room and smelled the dead air. She felt momentarily sucked back into her past and held on tightly to Kostos to stay in the present. Long ago she had walked (or stumbled) out of that past, out of the family domicile ("What will you do, dear? Who will look after you, dear?") without regret or explanation other than that she had a job with Pacific Light and Gas way off in Chatswood, because she no longer wished to be subservient to their pity and concern for her. To be the object of a stranger's concern was not to be inhibited. The girls in the office never mentioned her leg, no one said kindly, "Wait for our Addie," and smiled that smile of sweet deprecation that sisters could and if anyone stood up in the tram to give her a seat it was with the assumed nonchalance of doing it for *any*body. Thus she had withdrawn from the cloistered sanctity of home to the safety of anonymity. It wasn't that she didn't still love her sisters, merely that her survival depended on maintaining a distance between her vision and their pedantry. It would have been easier explaining her faith to a stranger, to Kostos, than to any of her sisters. It would have seemed Greek to them.

On the other hand she was not intimidated by Kostos's familiarity; it was charitable. She only smiled when he asked, "You have lover?"

"Friend, you mean."

"Someone he loves you?"

"No."

"No? Why?"

Why? "Oh, perhaps I never found him. Or vice versa."

"Who is this visera?"

"Or the other way around."

Kostos's warm brown eyes were so concentrated on her that she felt enveloped in a sympathy that she ordinarily would have brusquely dismissed as impertinence, one of her gambits.

"You are good nice person, Andia, you have to be loved."

"Nobody *has* to be, Kostos."

"Oh yes, I think so."

"Is there somebody who loves you?" she asked. Never in her life had she asked such a personal question.

He brought out an extremely worn wallet and extracted from it a yellowing snapshot. It was of a young girl holding a cat in her arms and leaning against a tree. The girl was smiling for the camera but there was an air of dejection in the way she slumped against the tree.

"Your girl?" she asked.

"Yes. Despa. In Patmos."

And he was a sailor, consequently there were frequent goodbyes; no wonder she looked dejected.

They had been treated royally at Cristos, where Kostos had been instantly recognized as a fellow countryman (octopus was not available), and were treated to a glass of sour red wine each by the owner, whose name was Lambrinos. Adnia had taken off her hat at Kostos's urging.

"You hide your nice hair."

Guardedly she allowed a little of her astonishment to sink in. She was being liked. She was with a man who honestly liked her and wanted to be with her. The truth of it was, of course, that he was a lonely Greek stoker in a foreign country but the undeniable sweetness in the eyes testified to his liking her and it made her feel—really the most she had ever thought of herself, denying herself as she had all her life the luxury of any self-congratulation—pretty.

The wine had made her mouth dry, the lamb was fearfully greasy, but she felt as if she had suddenly grown straight and graceful, free of her infirmity. As though she had miraculously responded to a misconception or, as Dr. Grimaldi would have put it, a vision of herself as seen through someone else's eyes who wanted her to be her real self ("Take off your hat, Andia. Walk straight, Andia"), and ridiculous as it sounded, there was the sense of being quite normal that Kostos imbued in her. Kostos never questioned her walk, never glanced down at her twisted foot; asked personal questions—You are marrit? Does someone love you?—but never asked, as sometimes curious people did, masking it in sympathetic undertones, were you born with it, have they tried operating? What place is that? Kostos asked as they passed the lighted-up Glaciarium. Where they skate, she had said. Yes? You skate there? No, she replied, I haven't, but as though she might have considered it. That was the miracle, being treated as if she were possibly a skater.

Of course when they left the restaurant she lumbered along as badly as ever, but the constancy of Kostos's phantasm supported her. They held hands like lovers walking along Darlinghurst Road back to the tram and at Circular Quay they lingered, leaning against a railing watching the ferries come and go and listening to the slurp of water sucking against the mossy pilings, and she was thinking that some things are the same everywhere, the night tides came into Greek harbors the same as they did here, and Kostos, seeming to catch her

186

thought, pointed to the sky and said, "You see that star? And that one?" "Yes" and "Yes," she said, staring up at the firmament, and he said, "Like you and me, Andia. Very far away from each the other one but very near too."

"Yes, Kostos."

They walked in silence for a while and found a stone seat beside a horse drinking trough. Here they sat and listened to the subdued noises of the city from a distance and the feeling of safety, of being protected by him in this dark little square of isolated warehouses lit only from above by the illuminated Penfold's Wine bottle pouring red lights over them was permeating her warmly.

Kostos said, "Tomorrow what we do?"

Sunday in Sydney, blue day, bluenose, shops, cinemas closed, restaurants shut. They'd been to the zoo. Sunday ballooned up over them like a whale washed up on a beach.

"We could go to Vaucluse House and walk in the gardens and have tea," she said. "It's a very old house, very nice."

"Old, like in Greece?"

"Not that old."

"Yes, that I like. Being with you, Andia."

He walked her back to her ferry and saw her through the turnstile. They waved to each other and when she got on the boat she looked back and saw him still standing there as if to make sure the ferry was going to take her properly. This was where they would meet tomorrow at two o'clock. This time there was to be no mistake about it, Kostos *knew* which gate. And she would have all morning to think about it, like an unopened gift.

She went to bed in a mood very near happiness, so much so that, pulling the sheets over her, she realized that she had forgotten to brush her teeth.

Very early in the morning but, being December, already daylight, she was awakened by the noise. She couldn't at first identify it, it sounded like something dropped outside her door. But then dropped again deliberately and then again, and struggling out of sleep she sat up in bed and listened as it came again and there was no denying it this time, the sound of someone knocking on her outside door, someone on her steps surely was knocking *apologetically* for awakening her yet with the intention of wakening her. She looked at her clock; quarter to six. It couldn't be! But she knew it, without reason as she opened the door and saw he was kneeling on her step. He had a brown paper parcel under one arm.

"*Kos*tos."

"I am sorry I woke you but I go."

"What? What?"

"I see you for a minute? I go."

"Oh, come in," she said, "but be quiet, I don't want to wake up the Hallbuts."

He came in, taking off his Greek cap, his boots squeaking. She pulled on her wrapper. "What on earth—"

"I go."

"Oh, you mean your ship? Today? *Sun*day?"

"No, tomorrow morning, but I—" He made shoveling signs.

"Oh yes, I see, you have to stoke."

He shoveled again.

"I see," she said.

"Seven o'clock."

"I see."

"There has to be goodbye, Andia."

"Oh, and you came all this way to—won't you let me get you a cup of tea?"

"Has no time for it. Only to say goodbye."

"I see."

They sat a moment in the useless silence; birds had begun chittering outside. She saw suddenly that her ugly foot was in view and covered it with her nightgown.

"And to say I thank you for all this," he said, "and to say I like you, Andia."

"I like you too, Kostos. Very much."

"Yes. Very much I like you, Andia. I like you more than I love, do you see?"

"I think I see, yes. Thank you."

"Sometimes love is—" He made a gesture of extravagant embracing and then pulled a face. "And then over. But I like you more than love. If I don't see you again you are perfect for me always. Can I make it plain?"

"Yes."

"I like you forever, Andia, and you are perfect."

There was nothing more to say, it was like the end of her life. The moment was too gigantic for her to add anything to it like "Bon voyage" or "I hope you will have a happy life." They had met like stars crossing a galaxy, just as he had pointed out last night, and it was too momentous to add anything. Big or little, it would be anticlimactic.

She sat with her hands uselessly on her lap when he got up to go.

"Goodbye, Andia."

"Goodbye, Kostos."

Then he leaned down and kissed the top of her head, she felt it like a butterfly on her hair and closed her eyes and heard his boots go out and down her steps and away up the brick path and even the final closing of the front gate in the far distance.

After quite a long while she stirred and opened her eyes and then because she could think of nothing else to do, went back to bed. When she awoke again it was after ten and for a moment she fancied she might only have dreamed that he was there saying goodbye to her, but knew now that it had been actuality. As real as the sound of Mr. Hallbut mowing the lawn outside.

She made her breakfast tea and toast and lingered over it.

Then when she came back into her bed–sitting room to make the bed, she noticed that Kostos had left his brown paper parcel on the little sofa where he had been sitting.

Now what could she do? There was no way of getting it to him now.

It was fairly heavy and clinked. She undid the paper.

It was a pair of white kid skating boots.

Small, a woman's size.

She sat down heavily with the boots on her lap. Had he meant them for his girl? What was her name? Despa? But surely there were no glaciariums on Patmos and no ponds frozen in winter. Didn't Greece have a temperate climate, weren't there fig trees and olive groves, and so what would a girl living on a dry mountainside do with a pair of skates?

No and maybe they hadn't just been left by accident. An extraordinary thought was coming to her. You skate there? he had asked as they went past the gaudy lights of the Glaciarium.

You are perfect.

I like you forever, Andia, and you are perfect.

That was the way he had seen her. Unhandicapped. The boots were meant for her. This was her miracle. She stood up, holding the boots to her, the message he'd left for her. How he had bought them on a Saturday night, unless he had gone to the Glaciarium, she didn't know and didn't need to know. It was part of the miracle; you didn't ask where the loaves and fishes came from.

You are perfect and I like you forever.

Holding the boots to her breast she turned slowly in a circle, like a dancer, and then again the other way, turned, turned and gradually increased her motion, quickening her movement, moving her shoulders in time to some invisible silent music, entranced, exalted; she didn't see nor would she have cared that her outside door was open and the child Smiley was at the bottom of her steps watching this grotesque sight. She didn't hear a little table go crashing nor the child calling out, "Mum, Mum, Miss Lord's dancing. Come and see, Mum, old Limpetty's dancing."

Even when she fell with a sickening crunch to the side of her skull against the bureau, in the seconds before she recognized the fact of falling, she was still in the dream.

Nurse Storm popped her head around the door and asked, "Did you get your electric fan, dear?"

"Yes, thank you," Sidney said, "but where are my *children?*"

Nurse Storm laughed good-naturedly because little Mrs. Ganz's baby was nearly five days late now and this prompted a necessary brisk cheerfulness among the nurses at the hospital.

"Any day now," Nurse Storm said. "Sister will be in to see you later."

"And the doctor?"

"Oh, Dr. Trimble'll be in too. Don't you worry about a thing. Oh, what pretty snapdragons."

Nurse Storm showed her dentures in a smile that didn't conceal her disapproval of Lowden sitting on the bed in his street clothes next to Sidney and of their holding hands in all this heat.

"Perhaps it's like watched pots," Sidney said. "If we could get interested in something else, take our minds off it, the baby might come while our backs are turned."

"Only he's not likely to come *behind* your back, dearest."

"No, only I wish he'd get a move on. Next one I'm going to have in the middle of winter, please."

"Oh, you are?"

"Yes, please. It's not only the heat. The little bugger's interrupting my book too."

"If I brought you a pad and pencil—"

"I can't believe it if it isn't on the typewriter, sorry."

He was quiet, as he always was about her work. Her new

book was so important, her big book, she said; she was already two hundred pages into it and "only getting going" and the advance was paying for this private hospital out in the wild wilds but near to Lily and George if they were needed quickly and Lowden was off across the harbor or playing in the band. He shut up when it came to the bloody book; the bloody book was also going to see them through when the little monster showed up. Damn everything to hell and the bastard sheep he and Archie Ward had forked out nearly three hundred quid for penned up over at Rooty Hill, where they were pastured not earning a frigging razoo, the frigging sheep that had been his get-rich-quick scheme. Sheep-Clipped Lawns—No Mowing. But the jazz band, the Paid Pipers, was doing goodoh, they had two or three engagements a week now including the Palais de Danse out at Bondi; there was even talk they might get signed on at the Tivoli for the vaudeville.

"I'll shift the fan a bit, it's blowing right on you," he said and got up off the bed.

"Lunch in a minute," Nurse Storm announced, passing by the door with a tray for someone else.

"I'll piss off now, love," Lowden said. "I've got to meet a bloke in town. It's about the sheep. He thinks there's some Catholic college up the Lane Cove might want them. This chap could start things moving."

"Send him over to see me," she said.

"I might."

He leaned over to kiss her.

"Will you be in to see us this evening?"

"Will you be 'us' by then, monkey?"

"Might be if I think about something else. He's been moving around a lot."

"You forgot tonight's the night the band plays at Paramatta."

"Oh yes."

"Cash in hand."

"Oh yes. Well, you wouldn't have time if you have to get all the way out there, darling. Oh dear, so I won't see you until tomorrow then."

"Matron has the number out there if anything occurs. Be a good girl now."

"Come back a minute, darling. Just hold me a minute."

"That better?"

"Yes. Oh, I wish I could just hold you. Not do anything else the rest of my life but hold you forever."

"You do, as a matter of fact."

Fred said to Grace that this was the night he was to go over to Hurstville to the hospital to see Sidney, so he would grab a pie and eat it on the train. "I don't suppose," he added hopefully, "you'd want to come too?"

"Why?"

"Well, she'd be tickled to death to see you, Grace."

"Can't imagine why."

"She's fond of you."

"Of *me?* What rot."

What rot, what utter rot, was all she ever said if you offered her a compliment. Oh tosh. She was given to the mild expletives of her girlhood at the Presbyterian Ladies' College. Glory, how *awful* I look, was her declaration on looking at herself in the mirror, and in moments of dire distress in receiving unmerited praise, *God* no. She existed in a vortex of self-abnegation which tended to convince people eventually that she was right. She would frame an invitation with "if that's agreeable with *you*," said in such a grating manner that the invitee was often dissuaded from accepting, which further confirmed Grace's opinion of herself.

Grace Lord, the former Grace Coin of "The Towers," Darling Point, now a fashionable girls' school, granddaughter of Sir Humphrey Coin, once a governor of New South Wales, her mother a Pettigrew of the Cobbity Pettigrews when that name still meant something, Grace Lord now of 18 Druid Avenue, Edgecliffe, the wrong end of the road, and wife of the senior day clerk at the Department of Uncollected Post, the Dead Letter office of the General Post Office.

Grace Lord who now put the breakfast marmalade severely in its place.

Yet she was gentle with plants and animals. She wiped and put away good dishes as if they had feelings.

Tall and thin and usually dressed in coal black, she entered a room like a funnel of smoke, igniting, it seemed, a cigarette from her own sparks. Oh, don't move, she would say if anyone stirred, it's only *me*.

"All right if I send her your love?" Fred asked.

"Oh, if she *asks*, I suppose."

Grace lit the inevitable cigarette and dismissed him. Usually they forsook any demonstrations of affection when they parted or met. I'll be off then. Going, are you? You home? That you, is it? What sort of a day? *Dire*.

But occasionally he caught her looking herself, unaware, over the washing up or intent on a book and she was beautiful, in the most ethereal lovely sense, the aristocratic long face and dark coiled hair, the fragile bone construction around the deep-set eyes and thick eyelashes and the very thinness of the body, which somehow set off a spasm of tenderness in him that made him yearn to fold her in his arms protectively but which if acceded to would result in her squawking Watch out for my cigarette or even What's got *into* you? Sometimes when they'd been together in the dark that she preferred when love was made, he touched her cheeks and they were wet. He could never dare ask. Nor ask why sometimes when she stood looking out of the kitchen window, smoking, and then would turn and grind out the cigarette and he would see the flash of the tears.

He somehow believed that it was their lack of unification that had prevented their having children, the feeling that she only tolerated sex. Perhaps it had had something to do with her dreadful old mother, awful old Mrs. Coin, who fortunately had been hit by a Watson's Bay bus crossing New South Head Road on one of her errands of mercy to a blind friend, who had hated her with all her might.

"Never knew what hit her," Grace said, consoled, unrepentant of the long war between her and her mother.

Fred had been in his last year at Geelong University when they met. Home for the Easter break, was it? He couldn't remember anything about that day except meeting the dazzling Grace Coin. He had been at loose ends on Castlereagh Street and had run into his sister Jess and this tall elegant girl she worked with at the Red Cross canteen and they'd all gone to the Carlton. He'd fallen in love with Grace Coin that very day and remained so ever since. Bold as brass, he had asked for her phone number, which she had scribbled down with barely a look at him, but it hadn't been until after he had graduated with honors in Philosophy and Latin that he had begun seriously to woo her. Not until he was a junior master at a boys' boarding school in Moss Vale nearer to Sydney and could get into town overnight could he afford to take Grace "in the style to which she may have been accustomed" to restaurants or the front stalls at the theater. She had been offhand on the telephone (she kept asking rather querulously, *whose* brother was he? whose?) and frosty enough to further intrigue him when they met at Renaud's, where she ordered the *quenelles de brochet* without a second thought. There was something shrouded about her, she was a piece of sculpture not yet unveiled. Her references to her family were so scant that she could have been living in a nunnery. She would never permit him to see her home. "Thanks awfully," she would say at the end of the evening and dash for a tram like a gazelle.

Fred began sending her floral postcards with desultory messages: "Cold up here. Hope you are well and blooming."

Opening the rusty-hinged gate, he thought at first The Towers must be a hotel or hospital and checked again the address he'd written down hastily when she had invited him for tea "if you could *bear* it." Yes, 4 Longworth Gardens. The la-di-da-sounding address was a silent cul-de-sac almost hidden behind solemn yews, as arcane as Grace herself, and the house immense; it looked like the pictures of houses where murder had been committed. It was being devoured by ivy and a threatening crack ran down the archway above the front door like the finger of doom. An elderly maid took his hat sullenly and led him into the drawing room, where Grace and her mother were sitting in high-backed old tapestry chairs as if they were receiving Plantagenet kings. In fact, Mrs. Coin was so fussed out in black taffeta with a big bow on the behind that she might have been expecting to be asked to sing. She was a pink-cheeked little woman with faded blond hair curled over pads and very wide open innocent blue eyes. She had a burbling-brook voice and a tinkling laugh which had beguiled Fred at first into thinking her amiable until she said, on hearing that he taught up at Moss Vale, "Moss Vale, isn't that where the people who can't get *in* to Bowral society land?"

"Fred is Jess Lord's brother," Grace said.

"Oh yes, Jess," Mrs. Coin said, wide-eyed, "the one with the gloves."

The ancient maid trundled in a traymobile and then fetched an old-fashioned basketware cake stand which she set down, whereupon Mrs. Coin said amiably, "Eunice, the cake is *crooked;* take it out and lay it flat without that paper doily thing." Mrs. Coin laughed chirrupingly. "Heavens, Mr. Lord will think we're *aborigines* if we serve a crooked cake." Did he take milk and sugar in his tea, Mrs. Coin asked. *Two* lumps? Mrs. Coin managed to make everything sound slightly indictable. Oh really? she said pityingly on hearing that he had been rejected by the army because of a strained heart. Full of concern for his heart, Mrs. Coin offered him a salmon-paste sandwich, her blue eyes wide with concern. "It must be dreadful for you feeling so *safe*," she said. He thought it better not to mention that his sister Lily was an all-out pacifist and spokesman for the Women's Socialist Movement of Australia. Grace said nothing, but smoked one cigarette after another. Somehow the conversation wobbled on from heroics to poetry and he was asked what he liked best. Mrs. Coin graciously allowed him Keats. But Byron, well . . . Mrs. Coin laughed. Byron was another matter. She said, "Grace used to recite quite nicely. She used to do Shelley's 'To a Skylark,' and she was picked to recite it at her school breakup night but she forgot it in the middle, poor child. We all sat there and sat there." Mrs. Coin laughed indulgently at the recollection.

"Do you remember, Grace?"

"Yes, *thanks*."

"Perhaps you might *deign* to cut your guest a piece of cake," Mrs. Coin said, the crooked cake having been brought back flat. Grace sighed and reached for the cake knife.

"Grace cared more for hockey than poetry when it came right down to it, didn't you, dear? She was captain of the school team her last term. Of course, being taller than the other girls they naturally chose her. You could pick her out on the field a mile away by her height. They used to offer me field glasses and I used to say, 'Thank you but I don't need them to find *my* daughter.' But being so tall came in handy when she was chosen to play Oberon on the Play Night. She looked very fine in the black stockings and cloak. Grace, why don't you show Mr. Lord the photograph of you as Oberon?"

"Because I don't want to bore him any stiffer."

"Oh, am I boring him? I'm dreadfully sorry." Mrs. Coin looked stricken. "I didn't mean to bore you *pur*posely, Mr. Lord."

"Oh no, not in the least," Fred said.

"I must remember that I have to mind my p's and q's; you must forgive me. I'm a natural talker and I get carried away.

I was brought up to be gregarious, you see. I beg pardon, Grace."

Mrs. Coin sat back in her chair and submitted to her daughter, head prettily on one side, waiting, having graciously yielded the floor. But only silence followed. Grace merely stirred and stirred her tea.

So when Fred in desperation mentioned that the embossed teaspoons were quite striking, Mrs. Coin turned to him with a smile as charming as Persephone's reawakening the flowers after winter. How nice of him to have noticed.

"A falcon and a rose," Mrs. Coin said, "the Gillie coat of arms. My mother's Scottish cousin. There had been a Gillie who was a laird and they owned an island in the Hebrides. But the family is no more, alas. That is to say unless young Douglas—" Mrs. Coin looked to Grace with wide-eyed entreaty. "Am I permitted to tell?" she asked.

Grace said nothing.

"Young Douglas, the great-grandson of the laird, the last direct descendant, came out here a few years ago, just before the war, more or less to see if he liked it and might emigrate or so we were led to believe. The most charming boy, such style, such manners. Half the girls in Sydney were at his feet and Grace quite took to him or so it *seemed.* People told me he rather fancied her too."

"Mother, don't go on with this," Grace said.

"I *said* it was only hearsay. I'm telling Mr. Lord because he was nice enough to notice the spoons. I daresay I'm permitted to brag about my own family for a minute without being accused of talking out of school. Douglas was *my* cousin too. Well, she's too modest, Mr. Lord. Everyone said what a handsome couple they were at the Highland Reel when I believe he was in his kilts and full regalia which unfortunately I didn't see because when he came to pick Grace up I was in bed with flu. But I remember Grace had on a lovely dress, organdy, wasn't it, dear?"

"Sackcloth."

"Oh now, that's not funny, really it isn't. The phone rang all next day just with people telling me how nice they looked, otherwise I wouldn't have *known,* she's so quiet, and naturally people were hoping that perhaps he might decide to stay and something might come of it, naturally I was hoping *too.* But the Scots are a race unto themselves or it may even have been our wretched hot climate he was unused to, it was a roasting summer, but anyway my dream of reuniting us with our own family blood didn't eventuate because Douglas was seen no more, vanished. We dinna see him nae more and that was the end of the late Douglas Gillie."

"Oh I'm sorry," Fred said. "He's dead?"

"No," Grace said, "he came here to tea."

This time the women looked squarely at each other.

"Why, thank you, Grace," Mrs. Coin said, bitterly.

Grace set her cup down and said, "Perhaps you'd like some air, Fred."

The first time she had ever called him by his name. She thrust open a door to a dim veranda hung with darkening wisteria and stood waiting while Fred got up awkwardly and said to Mrs. Coin, "Will you excuse me?" Mrs. Coin looked like an assaulted acolyte, the blue eyes wide with hurt. "It seems *I'm* the one to be excused. For ruining lives."

Outside, Grace said, "If you'd like to cut along now, there's a side gate and thanks awf'ly for coming."

He said, "I'm sorry if it was my doing."

"*Your* doing? What rot. It was all deliberate. If you hadn't mentioned the damn spoons she would have found some way to embark on my failings. That's how we live."

She sat down on a bamboo couch and lit another cigarette and because he couldn't think of anything comfortable to say he just said, "Grace."

She said edgily, "You're lucky, you come from a big family,

the onus isn't all on *you*. I'm the only thing she's got, heaven help me."

He sat down beside her, wanting desperately to touch her but restraining himself. After a while she said in the barest voice he'd ever heard her speak, in the most despairing tones, "What can I do? Where can I go? I've never been taught anything useful. I can't go abroad because of the rotten war. There's only this hateful house and *it's* only a white elephant, mortgaged to the hilt, and we're on the verge of being stony broke. So what can I do? I have to grin and bear it. Sorry about all this."

She had taken out a wad of handkerchief and was holding it up to her face.

But she didn't cry, just dabbed furiously at her mouth as if to wipe away these revelations, with her back slightly turned to him, and without further hesitation he took hold of her elbows and said hoarsely, "Grace, I love you. I've loved you ever since I met you that day in the Carlton with Jess and that's the God's truth."

"Oh, don't be so mad," she said.

"I love you more than anything, Grace."

"Abs'lute rot."

"I'd do anything for you, anything I could to help you, be your friend, *any*thing."

"Jolly flatt'ring, really, but this is only the usual family rigmarole, dreadfully boring for you."

"And what I love even more is you confiding in me," he said.

"Me to go brimming over like that—*grim*mers, do apologize—"

"I just love you, Grace, that's all. That's just the beginning and end of everything."

"What *rot.*"

But she leaned her head on his shoulder and when he turned to kiss her, she didn't draw away. She leaned on him like a tired child. When she stood up and said, "I'll get your hat so you don't have to go back inside," he saw that her eyes were wet.

He took the train down from Moss Vale from then on every Saturday that he wasn't "duty master," and Grace did as he proposed, going with him to tennis matches and matinees and to dinners in less expensive restaurants. She was stiffly agreeable. Occasionally while he waited for her in her hall, Mrs. Coin, avoiding him with huge eyes, would pass by saying, "Good afternoon, Fred." There was no further communion between them from then until the day she was struck by the bus while getting off on the wrong side of the tram, about which she had been warned countless times. But by that time Fred had dared propose to Grace over a pallid Madeira in the Ladies' Salon of the Prince Edward Hotel and she had accepted him without any display of emotion; her final acquiescence was so subdued that it could have passed unnoticed by anyone else. They asked her at the registry office please to put out her cigarette and it was at the registry office that he learned she was six years older than he. No one from either of their immediate families was present, his by his choice, hers not unexpected.

Pronounced man and wife, they kissed parenthetically.

Looking back on it all, as he was wont to do at odd times, he wondered whether what was lacking in their communication was not only her abstaining from emotion but had also to do with his inability to express himself in simple terms. It had been his undoing as a teacher. Brilliant as a student, he nevertheless was unable to transmit his erudition to others. Moreover, there seemed to be no reason for this. He left his students in a state of dazed stupefaction which in turn he found hard to forgive. In his first dazzling opportunity, fresh from university, teaching his first year in Philosophy at Wadsworth College, he lasted only one term. In one of the final classes of the term it was unfortunate that Dean Wilson should have looked in at the moment when Fred was expounding on Plato and the one *eidos* to a classroom stagnant with unreceptivity and boredom. Fred, proceeding up and down before his lectern, was in the midst of saying that "Plato wrote that the *Demiurge* is the transcendental spirit that created the world as a living and animated organism. But," Fred said to them, hammering his palms together, "this is not the last and deepest reality." And one drooping student raised an academic arm and asked, "So what *is* reality?" "That I am losing patience with idiots," Fred snapped and it was at this moment that Dean Wilson had appeared.

"Not that we object to your reprimanding inattention," the dean said later to Fred, standing on the carpet in his study. "But if the results were to show that the class was making progress, which, alas, the end-of-term exams do *not* . . ." Fred had been hired "on spec" as it were; there was no disgrace in his dismissal and perhaps Elementary Latin at a boys' school in Moss Vale might lie more within the compass of his potential. In Moss Vale he lasted long enough to envision a permanence that enabled him to risk the proposal to Grace, but very shortly after their marriage he was let go in what was euphemistically described as an economy drive. It seemed that there was the same curious alienation between him and the boys, the "brats," he called them. Whatever it was, this manner of his, superior and exasperated, insulted them and they withdrew from him.

Grace and Fred scrounged out an existence in furnished rooms at first, moving frequently as Fred transferred from school to school, each move designed to be a step up but ending usually in a pronounced step down, and at the final school, Redbanks in Neutral Bay, having experienced the humiliation of being corrected in a Latin phrase by the headmaster in front of his own class, he resigned hotheadedly, declaring that he was done with education and would look out for a decent job "away from brats and the bloodiness of headmasters." Just to "tide him over," his member of Parliament brother-in-law, George Barnes, Lily's George, wangled a job for him in the General Post Office with the title of General Supervisor.

"Genial?" Grace asked. "You're certainly that."

"No, General," he corrected her.

Just for the summer, he said.

That had been eight years ago.

But he was still only in his early thirties, anything could happen, the world was his oyster.

"I *ima*gine," Grace had said.

What nobody had foreseen was that he had found his place in the sun. Where a lack of ability to communicate had formerly done him in, it now rehabilitated him—in the Dead Letter office.

On his way out to the hospital to see Sidney, Fred had bought her a small woolly bear with button eyes, dressed in a blue leather smock.

"Oh, I adore him," Sidney said, struggling to sit up in bed. "He's the very image of my child."

"Bit early to tell, isn't it?"

"Oho, not when you've been together night and day for nine bloody months."

"Suppose it's a girl?"

"Not a chance."

In spite of the fact that she was mountainous, she looked small, especially her hands; they looked like a child's hands and this reminded him of her as a child; in the face she hadn't changed much. It made Fred feel preposterously old somehow. There had been that sweet time when they had loved each other and written each other love letters. He and Grace had never written each other love letters nor exchanged so much as an ardent word on paper. Her few notes to him had ended "Affec. yrs."

"Darling," Sidney said, "would you reach me my comb? I feel I'm such a brier patch." She ran the comb through her short boyish cut and then lay back against the pillows. "Even *that* exhausts me in this heat. Oh, if only he would stop teetering around and ar*rive.*" She may have caught a look on Fred's face because she took hold of his hand and squeezed it and said, "Oh, I don't mean to complain, I'm so lucky to be having him. It's just that he knows he was a little prematurely conceived and he's determined to make us legitimate parents. The doctor said this morning, 'Look, do you think you could have it before I go off on my fishing trip so I don't have to be called back from the lakes?' I suggested we try TNT. He roared. They all seem to think I'm funny."

"You are."

Nurse Storm squished in on rubber soles. "Got your iced barley water? That's the girl. Hubby coming this evening?"

"No, his band's playing way out in Paramatta tonight."

"Oh well, dear, daddies have to work, don't they?"

"This is my brother, Mr. Lord."

"Djoodoo. Oh well, we're going to be sorry when she and the baby go home, she's got us all so entertained, the little dear." Nurse Storm squished out.

"They behave as if this were some seaside resort," Sidney said. "Oh, everyone's been sweet, even Matron's nice. But I wish Mig were here. Mig is the one I really miss. I sort of *need* her now." But Mignon could not leave the show. Such a chance for her. Singing in the chorus of *Rose Marie* at His Majesty's Theatre in Melbourne. But there were Lily and George in nearby Arncliffe, and Lowden came every single day, like the sun, she said.

"Grace sends her love," Fred said, intervening so that Grace should not be left out.

Sidney assumed a quizzical look; it was the look she used to give him when they were in love with each other and having one of their tête-à-têtes up in the attic.

"Fred, you are happy, aren't you?"

"Oh, God, yes," he said fervently, too emphatically. "Oh, you have no idea how much I love my cool lady," he said and laughed a little too boisterously.

"Cool, yes," Sidney said. "Remember the day she killed the snake while all the men stood around like mugwumps or so Lily said?"

"Yes, she didn't turn a hair, Grace didn't," Fred said.

Sidney looked away out of the window where a slight breeze seemed to be distressing the branches of a pale poplar in the evening light. "A Southerly Buster coming up, I think, talking of cool," she said and then, as she so often did, out of the blue to startle you, she said quietly, "Fred, you don't really like Lowden very much, do you?"

"Oh, yes," he said.

"No, you don't."

"Oh, we get on very well."

"Getting *on* with Low is easy," Sidney said, "but liking him isn't. For instance, Mig doesn't like him because she was in love with him. She doesn't know I know, but I do. He's a terrible person to love unless you can accept him at the same time, which I do. That's why it doesn't ever bother me what other people think about him, his never having a decent job, just playing in this band and trying to rent out his sheep to people for their lawns and nobody wanting them, and all his schemes which never come to anything. But that's because I love him absolutely and always will. What we have for each other and with each other is a kind of a miracle and it just goes on, it's perfection. I want it to go on until I'm about a hundred and three."

"It probably will, if I know you," Fred said. "You will get your way about it." He knew what she meant about the definition of failure.

And being capable of loving someone so totally that nothing was weighed in the balance nor made attributable to good or bad: that was the *real* success, the really great thing, a kind of glory. But most people wouldn't understand that, Fred was saying. He felt released by the power of Sidney's love and faith and lifted out of the self-doubts and the mystification as to why everything had seemed to go wrong in his life with the exception of Grace. But it was his love for Grace, like Sidney's love for Low, that— Sidney had been very quiet, lying still as though she had been taking in what Fred was saying, when she moved slightly against the pillows and said in a small voice, "Fred, would you look outside and see if you can see the nurse? I'm feeling rather peculiar."

He got up at once and went into the hall, where Nurse Storm and the matron were bent over a desk in conversation. "Mrs. Ganz—" Fred began, but the look on his face sent Nurse Storm flying. Matron bustled after her and when Fred came back into Sidney's room he was met by Matron's starched linen front as she barred the way and said, "If you'd like to wait, wait in the visitors' room at the end of the hall. It may just be another false alarm." Uncomfortable-looking sticky bamboo chairs stood round a table heaped with dog-eared magazines and Fred sat down and picked up a *National Geographic*. Through the door he saw Storm and the night nurse (Sidney called them Storm and Drang) wheel Sidney away and through some swing doors. Perhaps this wasn't a false alarm. Dr. Trimble, with an assistant tying on his hospital gown, hurried down the hall. Once when Nurse Storm came through the doors carrying a basin, Fred stood up to get her attention. "On the way," Nurse Storm said.

Except for the nurses coming and going in and out of patients' rooms, save for the evening trays being brought to people and an occasional telephone ringing in the distance, there was nothing but silence, the protracted silence of uncertainty. He tried to read an article about the Bosporus and the Blue Mosque of Constantinople but he could not keep his mind on it. Once he thought he heard the baby far away,

206

imagined the doctor holding up the red squalling little thing by the feet and whacking its bottom, but when he went to the door there was only the ticking of a clock in the hall. A quavery voice called out, "Nurse, I want the pan." He was almost asleep, exhausted by the strain of concentrating, the fatigue of keeping alert, and he had closed his eyes when the matron looked in and said, "Would you know where we could reach the father?"

Why? Was something wrong? Fred sat up.

"Mrs. Ganz gave us this number to ring but it seems to be a dance hall somewhere."

"That's right, he plays in the band."

"Oh, well, they never heard of Mr. Ganz, they said. They asked was he the drummer."

Typical of Lowden not to be reachable at this moment.

"Is anything wrong?"

Matron said briskly, "She's had a boy."

Oh, Fred said, realizing it, oh, with joy. Trust Sidney, she always got what she wanted. Hallelujah.

"Could I use the phone to ring my sister?"

"You mean Mrs. Barnes? We've already phoned her. She's coming."

Matron was gone before he could ask could he phone his own wife but never mind, Grace would know by now that something, possibly the baby, was keeping him. Grace never worried about him. He would just like to know Sidney was all right, resting, back in her room.

Occasionally a nurse or an assistant went through the swing doors where he kept waiting for them to wheel Sidney back, but nothing else occurred. He had begun to yawn and consider not staying any longer, had dozed off a second or two, when suddenly Lily and George were standing beside him in the visitors' room and Lily was peeling off her gloves and asking where was Lowden, hadn't anyone got hold of Lowden yet? Lily sounded worried as she always was. They had just been sitting down to dinner when the matron first phoned and said the little boy had come and they had just been putting on their things to go to a political meeting when Matron had phoned again to say come as soon as possible. Lily had brought alarm and a box of Old Gold chocolates which she now pushed at George. "Hang on to those for now," Lily said. "Did they tell you anything?" she asked Fred and when he said no, she added, to his consternation, "No, they never tell you anything, leave you in suspense." She had sat down on the bamboo couch but at that moment the matron came in and Lily jumped up and said, "I'm Mrs. Barnes, I'm the sister." The matron said, "Dr. Trimble will talk to you as soon as he's free. In the meantime, make yourselves comfortable."

"But is anything *wrong?*" Lily persisted.

"Doctor will see you in just a minute, Mrs. Barnes."

They sat stiffly, alerted to crisis.

Lily said, "The worst of these little private hospitals is they won't tell you anything."

Later she said, "You see, we wanted her close to us so that if she needed anything we could be there in five minutes."

"Yes," Fred said.

Ten minutes later she said, "We thought this would be best because of not being able to depend on Lowden."

George said gently, "Fred knows."

"These wretched little private hospitals; I said all along she'd have been better off in Kogarah Public," Lily said.

Twenty minutes more went by. They sat alerted and neglected. Then Nurse Storm appeared and said, "Mrs. Barnes? Dr. Trimble would like a word with you."

Lily went out into the hall and they could see her now with the doctor. The doctor was speaking very slowly and it seemed distinctly, as if she were a foreigner and could not understand much English. At least that is how it appeared in dumb show from a distance and Lily, apparently comprehending, was nodding her head and looking up at him. Then they saw her put

her hand up to her head and the doctor put out an arm to
steady her and then to guide her to a seat. Lily's head remained bent and every now and then she lifted her arms and
made a gesture as if she were shooing away flies and Fred and
George knew that whatever it was she was being told was so
terrible it had to be brushed away. Finally the doctor helped
her to her feet and groping in her handbag for a handkerchief
she came to the door of the visitors' room. She looked as
though struck in the face.

"Do you want to go in with me and see her?" Lily asked
as if they already knew.

"Is the baby—"

"The baby too. The baby only lived an hour."

"*Too?* Do you—how do you mean, *too?*"

Fred perversely just wouldn't take it in but bright micro-
scopic red dots had begun to float around and there was a light
sizzling sound in his ears.

"I think she just wasn't strong enough. He didn't say but
I think she wasn't able to—and the baby was so late," Lily said.
"And you see, they didn't know, he said they couldn't have
known, there was no way."

"No way what?"

"That she had this trouble, this thing. He wrote it down for
me. It has to go on the certificate. It's to do with the kidneys."
She squinted at a piece of paper in her hand. "Eclampsia."

Nurse Storm appeared, long-faced with discretion.

"Would you like to go in and see her now, Mrs. Barnes?"

"Yes, please," Lily said and turned to Fred.

"No," Fred said, "I'll wait here."

It hadn't happened yet and he would wait until he was alone
before he would let it happen, when he could be alone with
Sidney. At the moment the incredibility was too plausible.

He sat in the visitors' room while Lily and George went off
with the nurse, and he wondered if it could be the same
evening. Lily and George had a cab waiting, they had an-

ticipated catastrophe. ("I hate to think what the meter will be, but Mr. Josephson used to drive George and when the matron said hurry . . .") They dropped Fred at the railway station and Lily had a few ready tears.

"Oh," Lily said, "the dear, the little love."

"You'll let me know," Fred said in a firm voice, "about whatever arrangements."

"Oh, of course. You know what's ahead of *us,* don't you? We have to break it to Lowden sometime tonight, we can't leave him to find out from the hospital, poor Low. Oh, my God."

And there would be Mig and Mary, Adnia. Jess in England. So many of us are strangers, he thought. It takes death to keep us in touch. It takes the bright one to die.

He had to wait half an hour for a train; the Illawarra line trains were infrequent after eleven o'clock. Was that all it was? It seemed like five years since he had got off here at this station only this afternoon. A smiling red-lipped girl on a poster still offered him ARNOTT'S NICE BISCUITS.

When he arrived home there was a light on in the living room and to his surprise Grace put down a book and stood up; she was still in her day clothes as if she had been waiting for him.

He stood in the living room doorway a minute gazing at her and then he was able to say it for the first time.

"Sidney died this evening."

He dropped his hat on the carpet and blundered toward her and Grace held him, rather like a post holding him up but nevertheless held him, and he trembled and shook with the deep sobs that now came detonating out of him in great gulps; it was as though the heartbreak had been imprisoned in him from birth and now, opened to the light of pitiless truth, it was freeing itself at last from a lifetime of secrecy where he had buried it.

"The baby too," he said and clung to the post as she let him.

Eventually Grace freed herself from the embrace and said, "Look, I think what you need is a good stiff drink and I think we've got some whisky put away somewhere. I might have one too." That night in bed he held her until she went to sleep as though she were the one who needed comforting and it gave him a semblance of serenity. Toward morning he awoke with the sound of a word in his mind and, careful not to disturb Grace, he got out of bed and went into the living room where he switched on a light and got out the dictionary to look up the word the doctor had written down about how Sidney died.

Eclampsia, a shining forth. (*Ek*—out, *lampein*—to shine.) Attack of convulsions in latter stages of pregnancy caused by any of various toxic conditions of the body.

A shining forth. That was Sidney. And if she had had to die of anything, it would be bright.

When Mignon stepped off the night express and into Lily and George's embrace early in the morning, she appeared to be sullen about being summoned from Melbourne. This was only because she was cried out. She had cried ceaselessly all night, the sound of it mercifully hidden by the racket of the train. She was emptied out for the moment and able to function like an automaton, thanking them for holding up the funeral until she could get there.

They had been getting ready for bed at the San Remo Hotel in Little Bourke Street, where she lodged with some of the other girls from *Rose Marie,* when Helene, the manageress, called up the stairs, "Mig, Mig, phone. Shake a leg, pet, it's a trunk call. From Sydney." Naturally she had thought Helene meant that Sidney was calling her, perhaps to say she had had the baby, and she stumbled downstairs in mild surprise, only to receive over the whistling and crackle of the long-distance line the unthinkable information. Are you there, darling, are you still on? Can you hear me? Lily kept saying. We'll hold up the funeral until you can get here. Hello? Hello? I'll have to let you know, was all she could say, repeating it louder and louder over the bad connection. I'll have to see if they'll let me out of the show, Mig shouted. It was only after she had hung up that it occurred to her that she had asked no questions whatever, that indeed she might have been receiving the news of some stranger's death.

Two nights off would be docked from her pay, one night to go and one to come back. Shorty, the stage manager, was very firm about it even though he asked, "Close were you?" The girls were bricks, really, helping her to pack her suitcase and Peggy and Rita seeing her off on the train. She had been dry-eyed until she got into her sleeping compartment, where she was able to let go, and now she was dry-eyed again at the sparsely attended service which was at the same church where Sidney and Lowden had been married.

And all the way, the long hot drive through the airless afternoon out to the cemetery, she was like a somnambulist except that in her sleep she somehow resisted looking at Lowden, first at the church and later at the graveside. She knew that if she looked into those deprived eyes it would be her undoing. They had shaken hands outside the church while she looked at the ground. Lowden smelled of whisky even a foot away. When he dropped to his knees on the dug-up earth around the grave at the end of the short ceremony, she averted her eyes as if from an accident. Lowden had begun a low moaning sound and George and Fred were helping him back to his feet. The painful scene was made more graphic by the fact that the humid weather had condensed into threatening clouds from which thunder had begun to rumble, darkening the earth and whitening the gravestones around. Hardly the moment to make a small joke but she thought, listening to the thunder, it's Sidney, cross as buggery about dying and telling us so.

Rain and purple lightning swept down on the cars as they left the gravediggers to finish their work, small floods cascaded down the red earth, drenching "Beloved wife of" and "Dear Husband," pouring down on marble angels and alabaster doves, oblivious of the just and unjust and making it, thank God, difficult for conversation in the car in which Mig had been chosen to drive back to town with Fred and Grace and Lowden because all of them went in the direction of "the Cross" and although Lily had begged everyone please, please to come back to their house for tea, nobody honestly could bear to prolong the dreadful day.

Lily had kissed Mig and said, "Will you be all right, dear? What will you do until you get your train?" Oh, she said, she would go and see Olive, her old landlady where she and Sidney had lived. Nobody could stand the continuation of Lily's threnody for Sidney, even though she had bought an expensive cake, and everyone was conscious of the fact that Prohibition ruled in the Barneses' home and the thought of enduring the post-funeral rites without so much as a glass of sherry was unthinkable. Lily was hurt, her mouth was grieved in slight. She was heard asking the gravediggers whether they got overtime if they had to work in the rain.

So it was that Mignon and Lowden were left off by Grace and Fred at Kings Cross in the downpour under a tin awning outside a fish shop where rivulets of water cascaded inside the glass window against pressed ferns. Together with the rain outside, the whole world seemed to be weeping. "You haven't got an umbrella," Lowden said. "Let me walk you as far as you're going," and he opened his and so unable to refuse she walked beside him in the rain until they got to her old doorstep at Olive's house and for the first time she looked up at him, into the tormented eyes; the eyes were frightful to behold, the poor wretch, poor ghastly godforsaken wretch, and she knew instantly what he would say.

"Come home with me, Mig."

"I promised Olive I'd—"

"Please."

"But you know I can't."

"Please. Oh God—please, Mig. Don't let me have to go back to the bloody flat alone."

"Low—"

"Oh please, just for a little bit. Do I have to beg you for *her* sake to have a drop of pity for me? For Christ's sake."

He was standing there in the rain, utterly abandoned, crying, and the aloneness of him, the appallingness of the imitation glen plaid suit, the awfulness of the black silk armband, the unsuitable patent-leather shoes he had on, despair, ruin . . . If not for Christ, then for Sidney, she took his arm.

The little flat was dark and smoky, ashtrays overflowed everywhere; it seemed all he had done was to sit here in the dark and smoke in his agony and not even put away the reminders of Sidney—her sandals where she had kicked them off under the table, a little embroidered jacket on a chair. Lowden poured two stiff whiskies into already used glasses and passed one to her.

He said, "It's all so unreal."

"I know."

"Thanks for coming, Mig."

He drank deeply and lit another cigarette.

"She loved you, you know," he said.

"Yes, I know."

She sipped the burning drink and said, "Why don't you go home, Low?"

"What, to the Marsh, you mean? Oh, what for?"

"To your family there."

"They don't care."

"I'm sure they do."

"Not a chance, they don't understand. There's nobody understands, there's nowhere to go. It wouldn't matter where I went, I carry her with me; it's the same agony everywhere.

Look, nobody in the world understood me like she did and that's the truth, Mig. That's why I'm so bloody absolutely lost without her. Abso-bloody-lutely."

There was a brief spell of crying and Mignon just sat there knowing that no ordinary manifestation of compassion was adequate, no bland comfortings would suffice. But she knew what would.

Please don't move, don't go, he said every time she even stirred in her chair. You're dreadful slow with that drink, he said, getting up to fix his third whisky. Every time he got up he leaned over and pressed her hands warmly; coming back to his chair he passed his hands over her shoulder. Don't move, love, he said, don't be in a hurry, will you, please, he pleaded. His voice grew thicker and his eyes were bleary from drink and tears. Every now and then he gave her a fatuous smile. When she glanced at her little wristwatch she saw that it was already nearly six. Her train wasn't until eight but she felt that she must extricate herself somehow from this suffocating miasma of whisky and grief, it demeaned Sidney, but she could not explain that without being viscerally unkind to this hurting man. He would see her off on the train, don't worry, he said, don't move, Mig. He had embarked on a long anecdote about Sidney and something perceptive she had said while they had been rowing up a river on their honeymoon; it was interlaced with constant digression and by now the cigarette didn't always meet the lips, sometimes jabbed against his cheek, the eyes refused to focus and the story growing dimmer, trailing off, he said, "You know what is the greatest kindness you could do me, don't you?" and when she pulled away a little, smiling but firm, he continued doggedly, "You do, don't you? Don't you, Mig? You know the sweetest thing you ever did in your whole life would be to let me." "No, Lowden," she said and got up but he was already swaying, hanging on to her and saying in a hot breathy urgent way, "Oh, it's the only thing on God's earth that would let me be at peace. Oh, darling Mig, don't turn away from me, for God's sake. I'm burning in hell, darling. For *her* sake then, let me be with you, darling."

"Don't be rotten, Low, don't."

"Please."

Then just let him hold her, let them lie down and let him hold her. No, she kept saying, trying to push him away as they swayed together. Oh, Lowden, have some re*spect,* she said uselessly, please have some respect for your*self.* I have to get my train, she kept saying like a child as they fell down on the couch and he started to cover her neck with wet kisses and the reek of alcohol was so strong that she almost dry-retched and gradually, the room growing darker into twilight, the phantasmagoria took over as the substitute of whatever reality was left in what became mouths and touchings, and all of a sudden she felt herself responding with the ardor he had touched off. Even drunk, the skill of his lovemaking was bewildering; she was not even aware of how they were gradually dismantled of their clothes and of how the divinity of the fact got started, the pulsation of their bodies together as normal as heartbeat. Only occasionally he muttered something above her in the now dark and touched her face with a gentle caress that might have been parental, her father or mother passing her bed in the night and bending to kiss her lightly for a moment. It wasn't until later, streetlights from outside glinting on the ceiling, and he had rolled over and gone heavily to sleep, that she realized she must have long ago missed her train.

But so far gone was she into the country of his desperation that she couldn't begin to measure the fantasy with any realization of what had befallen her, that there was no train until tomorrow night, that she might well be dismissed from the company for not keeping her promise to the stage manager. Her betrayal of Sidney. None of it could be entertained. Not yet.

She slept.

When she awoke again her back ached from lying on this narrow ledge of couch pinned down by one of Lowden's legs. Very carefully she disengaged herself from him and got up; her watch said a quarter past five and already there was a faint crepuscular light from outside as she groped for her clothes on the floor. She was faint and woolly-headed from lack of food and her mouth felt stuffed with lint. Once Lowden whimpered in his sleep and turned with a seeking movement as if he were groping for her or anybody. She thought briefly of leaving a note but what was there to say? Not thank you, not love. There was nothing in this world for them to say to each other and it might even be easier for him in his hung-over condition to imagine that she had never been there. Just for a last moment she looked down at the naked sleeper, at the rumpled hair and the classic features, younger in sleep, but knowing that if the eyes were to open, the hands would go out to reach for her and pull her back and she would be helpless to resist the tenacious sorrow of him. Very quietly she let herself out.

Somehow she got through the endless day, unable to ring any of the family because of having to explain where she had been. She killed most of the afternoon in a picture theater, not taking in much of what was going on on the screen but vaguely recognizing Vilma Banky. It had no relation to the riot that was going on inside her. When she got to Central Station and picked up her suitcase from the checkroom she still had two hours to wait for the Melbourne train and sat down in the big waiting room, half afraid and half hoping that Lowden might appear. The ambiguity was tiring, moments when she felt that if he appeared she would run to him like a lost child, then other, saner moments when she ran from him. Safe at last on the train in her sleeping compartment, she finally was able to ask awkwardly for forgiveness as she fell asleep in her upper bunk and thought in her sleep that Sidney said "Don't be silly" over the sound of the wheels.

To her great relief her punishment at the theater for not being back on time was only a severe dressing-down by Shorty after he had listened to her lame excuses about not being able to leave her sorrowing family as quickly as she would have liked. Then as if nothing had happened, nobody had died, she had wet her eyelashes with blobs of mascara, painted on a scarlet mouth and put on her lemon chiffon dress and along with the other girls come on into the blazing amber light. "Pretty things," she sang, "unhappy girlie who has missed 'em."

Sometime in the winter, it must have been nearly four months later, when the company had moved to Adelaide, a letter arrived from her sister Mary from Bacchus Marsh reporting on farm affairs, their new rainwater tank, cattle with foot rot, children with mumps, and mentioning casually but with typical insensitivity that Lowden Ganz had married a local girl, Beryl Waterworth, a week ago last Saturday. They had known each other since they were kids, Mary added, and she had played piano for the dance that followed. Everybody had had a bonza time, Mary said.

PART THREE

The first impressions of Australia were of incompetence and jollity. Somehow in the muddle of disembarkation, Jess's beautiful cowhide shoe case (from Rawley & Shrove on Jermyn Street) was missing but everyone seemed singularly happy-go-lucky about it turning up.

"What was in it?" asked the customs officer.

"Shoes." *Na*turally, stupid man, her glare said. "Eight pairs."

"Eight." The customs man eyed her speculatively as though to say that nowadays there were people lucky to have one pair to their feet. "It'll probably walk back on its own," he said, chuckling.

Early in the morning, even before the *Orsova* had come through the Sydney Heads, they had been called into the first-class lounge, where the purser had explained that owing to a wharf strike, the cabin stewards would have to be delivering the luggage to the pier. The purser apologized for the possible inconvenience.

Standing on deck as the ship passed Watson's Bay Lighthouse into the harbor, Mrs. Dixon, the Australian woman, asked, "How long since you left?"

"Twelve years," Jess said.

"You'll notice a change," Mrs. Dixon said and laughed.

Change was not what Jess might have found disconcerting; she viewed the whole operation as change of the very worst.

"Going home?" English chums had asked.

No, leaving it, she wanted to say.

"Lovely, isn't it?" Mrs. Dixon said admiringly of the harbor. "I tell you I never fail to get a thrill coming home to it; there's no other place on earth as lovely, now *is* there?"

Oh, she could think of a few, Jess thought and screwed up her eyes against the glare of the hot brilliant sun on green water and white sailboats. After twelve years of the subdued grayness of England, the glare was a shock, strident, disturbing. It was the beginning confirmation of a paralyzing supposition that had begun in London that this trip back might prove to be the anathema she had been deserving for years. Jess lived with a conviction of her own hubris. There had been an element of the fatalistic in the needling way Cousin Jacquetta had said, "We have to go home, darling."

She felt that when the last moment came and she must walk down the gangplank and set foot on Australian soil, she would have broken the last beloved ties with England, and indeed when she reached the bottom of the swaying steps, she hesitated a moment before she stepped onto the wharf, until a voice behind said curtly, "Move on, please."

She had gone through melodramatic fantasies in which she had locked herself in her cabin and bargained with the ship's officers to be taken back to Southampton: feigned illness, madness, anything to preclude that dreadful moment when she must finally admit that she was back. And for how long? Nobody knew.

But now, hopeless, she could only automatically deal with the customs (in both senses) of her natal country. Nobody seemed in any hurry to do anything. Long after Jess's shoe case had been recovered, half hidden under a tarpaulin and suspiciously opened to reveal, just as she had declared, eight pairs of immaculate shoes tucked in two rows of ecru velveteen, and their cabin trunks and eleven suitcases and hatboxes had been collected in a pile, they had to wait in the sweltering tin-roofed pier for the chauffeur (engaged ahead of time from London six weeks before) to appear. When he finally did (name of Galbraith, Ernie if you like, he said, smiling), he wore no cap.

"Well, darling, here we are," Cousin Jackie said, smiling.

Nothing perturbed her, not even twelve thousand miles; for all her years of living abroad, she was as Australian as mulga wood.

"Yes," Jess said. Here they were. Now it was coming true, the recurring nightmare she so often had, sweetly to awaken safe in her bedroom in Wilton Crescent: the dream that she was back. Back and with no escape.

For without the allowance Jacquetta made her, she hadn't a penny of her own and never had had. She was the daughter of a poor Church of England clergyman with seven children, who had died young, leaving them with a noncommittal mother and just the clothes they had on their backs. And a second look at the family portrait taken just before Father died might have revealed that the clothes were probably frequently darned and heavily ironed.

But out of the seven she had been gloriously chosen by their mother's rich cousin, Mrs. Moss, for the vacant seat on the lap of luxury.

Probably had Jess been asked what it all boiled down to, she would never have mentioned the house in Wilton Crescent, luncheons at the Savoy Grill, Augusts spent in Scotland. Asked point-blank what luxury meant to her, Jess more likely would have said that it was the perfect cake of Houbigant's Quelques Fleurs soap which the maid always automatically replaced as soon as the embossed rose on it washed off. It was never sleeping on the same sheets two nights running. Things like that. Things taken for granted. After twenty years of luxury, the pinnacle of her achievement had been to become so completely unastonished by it that she almost never gave it a second thought. Occasionally a doubt passed across the sunlight of it like a cloud, causing her to wonder for a few moments what might happen to her when Jacquetta died (for after all, Jacquetta was now seventy-six), but she didn't dawdle in introspection because there was always something to do, somewhere she had to be within the next few minutes, and she had never been one to dwell on ifs and buts. She had been known all her life to have exceptional calm. She congratulated her youthful face in the mirror; careful living and expensive creams had kept her from looking her thirty-six years.

Presumably everyone thought of her as a very lucky woman, having a life of ease not complicated by attainments; she was unambitious, she had never really cared about marrying, marriage would have been a disrupting factor in her serenity, any forceful emotion or passion, even the thought of it, disarranged her composure. In this wall of composure there was only one crack.

That was the deep secret, the guilt.

The sapling broke, the girl's gloved hand holding on to it —Fall. Ghastly, the sound of a body crashing through trees, air. Bettina screaming help me. Bettina's hat had been knocked over her eyes as if to shield her from the awfulness of the drop under her. Help me Jess. The cliff face had opened under their feet with a roar of stones.

Try to reach her hand, not let her slip. Bettina's jacket was within Jess's reach but she had not—

So easily, almost restfully, the girl had plunged into the abyss.

Sometimes in the night Bettina awoke her with the forgotten scream which was echoed in the mountains around like the cry of a bird; sometimes when she was fully awake the recurrence took place while she was lunching with friends. Are you all right? they asked. My dear, you went ashen. No, I'm all right, she always said; she took hold of her little watch embedded in crystal that she wore on a gold chain and it always brought her back to reality and comfort after the recurrence of Bettina's death on the mountain path in the landslide when Jess had been only sixteen. She was never rid of Bettina, it could come back when least expected, and Jess knew for certain that someday she would be called upon to face indictment. She had committed murder.

In the meantime she congratulated her impassive face but she was secretly aware of the possibility of her own liability. So she corrected others. "Please put your cap on," she told the chauffeur when he opened the car door for them at the Wentworth.

"And send up tea right away for Mrs. Moss," she told them at the desk.

"We're here at the Wentworth until we can get into the house," she told her sister on the telephone. "The people who rent it have another month before their lease is up." She spoke pleasantly but in the manner of an estate agent. She knew Lily would tell people Jess is as standoffish as ever. But this was the way she was, this was the way they must learn to take her.

"Would you be going out to the grave anytime soon?" Lily asked.

"What grave?"

There was a little cough of incredulity from Lily.

"Well, Sidney's."

"I don't think so, why?"

"I thought if you were going up to Woronora Cemetery, we're on the way in Arncliffe, you could drop in to see us if you're going."

"I hadn't thought yet."

"No, well it's nice, the grave, now. We had a lovely marble book open with a marble bookmarker put up for her."

But this was exactly what Jess didn't want to know, this was exactly the kind of thing she had tried so hard to escape from. Marble gravestones and things expected of her by the family. Lily provided her with all kinds of information she didn't want about Fred and Grace, about Mig, poor old Addie. Jess almost broke in once to say that she hadn't seen or heard from any of these people for twelve years and so why was she supposed to thirst after news of them?

"Yes, or you'll come in and have tea or something with us," she said to Lily, remembering that drinks were out with Lily and George even now, even though their fierce dedication to prohibition had cost George his seat in Parliament. Imagine running for office on a "dry" ticket in as alcoholic a place as Australia, swimming in beer and wine, even though, as she discovered, it was snatched off your table at nine o'clock in the middle of dinner. "Wait, that's my wine," she objected to the waiter but he had given her that Australian look and said, "Nine o'clock, it's the rule, miss." If one wasn't careful one ran onto the shoals of dislike of anything foreign. She became used to hearing the ugly word "Pommy" used in her hearing, that denigration of the British. "You must have been abroad a long time," the lady in the Commonwealth Bank told her; "you've developed quite a Pommy accent."

And the unfair assumption that her accent signified snobbery. She clung desperately to her Belgravia accent as to a lifeboat, a link with England which, like her exquisite shoes, kept her English. Every day instead of feeling more at home she felt more foreign. Sydney itself wasn't greatly changed from what she remembered but there was a seedy air to it, too many buildings needed painting and reroofing and too many pasty-faced men played the violin or tooted on the cornet on street corners with a hat upside down beside them for any stray sixpence or penny. A little flower shop in King Street she had once frequented had become a dreadful affair with brown paper stickers on the window advertising jobs and about a dozen shabby men lounged around outside, smoking and rolling homemade cigarettes, hoping to be the lucky one that might get a drover's job up in the outback or even bottle washing. It was only after they had moved into the Point Piper house and she had begun interviewing women for cook and housemaid that it was made clear to her how desperate people were for work and how deeply the depression had struck. She could have engaged a full-time cook and housemaid for half what she offered them along with room and board. Pegeen and Annie, Irish sisters, both with ill-fitting dentures, but willing as fresh horses. The gardener she obtained over the front fence while she was trying to deal with wayward climbing roses that had begun encircling the gate with its iron escutcheon too high for her to reach; she was hooked by her dress on the thorny branches when this man passing asked, "Give you a hand?" and opening the gate, he managed to free her without any serious scratches from the encircling thorns. After Jess thanked him he looked around the neglected garden (really the Listers had taken no pride in the place; everywhere canna and salvia had replenished themselves riotously) and asked, "Mow your lawn for a couple of bob?" She showed him where the lawn mower was kept and he then mowed and raked the vast front lawn expertly. His name was Appleton, miss, he said. He looked hungry and she sent him around to the kitchen door with instructions for Annie to give him some of whatever they were having for lunch. The small act of kindness gave her dignity and a little relief from her misery. Appleton ("Tom, if you prefer, miss") said he would be glad to come once a week for five shillings or however often she wanted. He had difficulty disguising his rapture when she engaged him on the spot. "Just fancy if I'd walked down a different street," he said. His eyes shone.

Lily came to tea. She looked at the spacious rooms disapprovingly. She had aged, Jess thought, older than she need be with worry. But she had been a consummate worrier from the time she had come away from the womb. She was aggressively democratic with the maid from the moment Pegeen wheeled in the tea. "How are *you?*" Lily asked her, determined still on the myth of social equality but less assured than in the days when her oratory rang through the women's club meetings from here to Hobart. She seemed spent of the old fighting spirit which had propelled her and George in their struggle to assist the miners, the factory workers, the tinsmiths and sausage makers who had then voted them out of office for the sake of a beer. Lily's forgiveness of them was cosmetic at best, her smile wan. As for politicians, they were treacherous; some of the best Labor Party pals had proven fair-weather frauds and let George down after he was out of office, and it wasn't just the perquisites that had been taken away from them (the Hansard with the official record of parliamentary proceedings had ceased delivery), but the vacuum presented when a distinguished politician like George was suddenly left without a profession and a salary and was unqualified to find an ordinary job. Lily ate her cake like humble pie. But at last someone at the Trades Hall had got George a job there in the Office of Uniform Employment, whatever that was. She hadn't asked too many questions for obvious reasons, he just went off in the morning and came back in the evening. "But one day I took in his cardigan because it had turned cold and they directed me upstairs to where his office was and I saw it was just a cloakroom and he was sitting at a desk reading a novel. Imagine, Jess, this important man, this *champion* in his day, with a make-believe job. I couldn't let him see I'd found out. I tiptoed away with the cardigan."

There was nothing Jess could say or do about it but offer an éclair.

Cousin Jacquetta interposed. She had been listening to the forlorn narrative of lost hopes with nods and smiles, perhaps not taking it in; she had lately become more vague, smiling at woes. Now she leaned forward to Lily and asked out of the blue how was the poor lame one, poor lambkin, what was her name? Jess fled. When she returned with a silver jug of fresh hot water, Lily was recapitulating poor Adnia's end. Addie. There was no way that Jess could fit a face onto her, Adnia floated there like a great gray jellyfish, the other elder sister, more somber than Mary, less pragmatic than Lily. She was fetched back to reality with reluctance, only a little of her seeped into today. Addie would not, Lily was saying, condone having a doctor, there was nothing they could do to persuade her when the pleurisy turned into double pneumonia, so by the time she was forcibly taken in the ambulance . . . "But afterwards, when we went to clear out her room and go through her few little things, do you know what we found most carefully laid away in tissue paper?" A pair of skates, white skating boots. The mystery darkened the drawing room, even Cousin Jackie drew in her breath about the perplexity of human nature. Lily, bidding goodbye at the gate, frowning at the time, worrying that she would not get a seat on the train home, said suddenly, accusingly, "Oh Jess, you never married."

"No, thank God."

Lily looked affronted; there was no need to snap her head off this way as though one shouldn't be concerned about one's own flesh and blood.

But what she didn't understand, what nobody here "at home" seemed to comprehend, was that she, Jess, was nobody's flesh and blood but her own and only wanted to be left alone to pursue her own way and not become embroiled in relationships that were generally watered with glycerin tears.

Somehow or other she would have to get through the motions of family reconciliation by steeling herself not to adapt to its subtle entanglements. Fred and Grace were not too implicating, their attitude to each other imparted a sense of Sprat-like individuality. Fred had grown fat, Grace thin, Fred was solicitous, Grace scathing. They gave Jess dinner crowded around a small gateleg table one side of which constantly threatened to drop all the food onto their laps and perhaps symbolized the extreme fragility of their marriage. They addressed each other like polite strangers. "Would you

229

mind . . ." and "Could you possibly . . ." The dinner conversation might have been made up from a book of easy English phrases for the foreigner. Grace smoked between every course and Fred overate. Fred said that the lamb was very good. Grace, he said to Jess, is good at lamb. "Glad I'm good at *something,*" Grace said with one of her shudders at the thought of herself, but as she said so she glanced at her tubby husband with a strange light in her eyes and then rose and took out his dish like an acolyte serving a cardinal, and Jess knew in a flash that they had entered into a sacred pact not to reveal their love for each other. Extraordinary as it seemed, Grace, epicurean Grace, had found satisfaction with this flawed government worker; bereft of fulfillment, she had discovered something of her baptismal name in their private union; it was too inwardly precious to be outwardly admitted, that was the grace of it.

Jess fed on any scrap of grace in this hullaballoo land. She and Jackie cringed from the exuberance of everything. They lived like exiles from a more civilized society. They shaded the rooms from the brazen sky by day and dressed for dinner every night except Sunday even though nobody was ever invited. They had a fire lit even in the warm weather to remind them of home and sipped their preprandial sherries in front of it and after dinner their coffee and brandy while they played backgammon. The Australian servants learned to call them Miss and Madam and not to say "goodoh"; the *London Illustrated News* and *Tatler* reached them six weeks late but kept them in touch with English life. So deeply rooted was their Anglomania that once in her extended dream, coming home on the tram, Jess handed the conductor her fare and said, "Fulham Road, please." Once a month Mr. Sabeston, the lawyer, came for lunch, after which he and Jackie were closeted in the drawing room surrounded by strongboxes and documents tied up with pink string. These represented Jackie's "holdings," as she referred to her income, some of which had depreciated with the world depression and had been one of the reasons for the enforced return. Every time Jess handed Mr. Sabeston his raincoat and umbrella on crystal-fine days as he was leaving, she thought bitterly that his overriding pessimism was the reason they were back. "Ah well," Mr. Sabeston said in his nasal accent, "things could be worse before they're better."

Jess began collecting crumbs of comfort. One of them was Tom Appleton, who was now full-time gardener and under whose fertile thumb things blossomed Biblically as figs on thistles. Even on wet days he prospered, with seedlings in the potting shed. Sometimes he brought along his sixteen-year-old daughter to help, more likely, Jess thought, to be given a free hot lunch, as the two of them half rose awkwardly from eating when she came in the kitchen. But the sight of them digging into a decent meal of Annie's excellent shepherd's pie somehow replenished Jess too; it was mysteriously satisfying to a basic conceit to see them lapping it up, to be of help. She had so little opportunity to give where it was needed and she dug around among her cast-off clothing to find a sweater and an old wool skirt to give to the stringy daughter. But I also am indigent, she said silently, apologizing for her greedy generosity; oh, if you only knew how needy *I* am. Lost and far from home in a land where everyone else was glad to be living, even on the dole, and eager to tell you so at the drop of the hat. If you only knew how lonely I am.

Sometimes just walking up Martin Place or Pitt Street she was overwhelmed with the sense of alienation; even the sky looked foreign with its cerulean blue. If it wouldn't have amounted to a public spectacle, she would have sat right down on the post office steps and wept in her isolation. There was no one to turn to who could really understand.

Perhaps because they had never exchanged more than a hundred words in their whole lives, Mignon had invited someone else to help break the ice with Jess when she came to dinner at Mig's little flat in Roslyn Gardens.

"Imogene Blue," Mig said, indicating the woman on the sofa.

"How'd you do?"

The voice was unmistakably English.

And that luscious English complexion, cream of roses. "Yorkshire, originally," Mrs. Blue said offhandedly. And the tweed suit was old but exquisitely tailored somewhere on Bond Street; the hat was dowdy. But pinned to the jacket was a loop of diamonds and sapphires. She was the very reverse of Jess, she was an English expatriate, had been out here "for yers and yers," Mrs. Blue informed Jess in her euphonious voice, married to a grazier and recently widowed. Her son and grandchildren, however, lived "at home" in Sussex. She smoked English Craven A's, offered the red tin to Jess. She was trying to adjust to city life after being on a cattle station "all these yers." Mignon had found her not a bad flat in Hampton Court, that big new Tudor block of blue brick; that was how they'd met. Mig, it turned out, had gone into real estate after leaving the musical comedy stage, sick, she said, of waiting to go on for faltering sopranos and being told she was another Nellie Melba but living on cat's piss. There was something unused about Mig, a sense of rejection as though, if she had been a copper saucepan, shining on a wall, it had only needed someone to say, "This'll do for the beans, pity not to use it." Under the quiet of her there was something volcanic as if she were boiling with an inner rage and was exhausted by it, this formerly subdued child, an ethereal stranger known only to Sidney. Now she banged the oven door, assaulted pans, drank her drink as if there were only a few minutes left in life. She interested Jess. Perhaps everything trustworthy had failed her; something in her manner indicated there might be a young shrew in her waiting to punish people for forcing this demureness on her, and suiting her action to the tiger, she served dinner with a vengeance. "Here's the plonk," she said, banging down the bottle of Tintara red.

But Mrs. Blue was a cool water lily, it was restful just to accept her presence. Her small hands moved with unhurried grace, she blew smoke, she agreed with you courteously. Imogene Blue was the real thing, the thing Jackie Moss had persuaded herself years ago that she had become (and hadn't): the English lady.

No, she didn't particularly miss England after all these yers, friends told her that London was "crackingly awful" these days with the unemployment lines.

"Not as awful as—" Jess began and then substituted "as you may have heard," reddening.

"Do you hate being back?" Mig asked.

"I have to abide by it," Jess said.

"At least you *had* it."

"Yes."

"If I had a few quid put by," Mig said, "I'd get out of here. This bloody place, there wouldn't be a ship to take me fast enough."

Mig flung down dishes of shuddering jelly. Well, she implied, at least Jess had had the riches, she could be content with that, whereas Mig had had nothing. Jess had escaped, but romance and adventure had eluded Mig. But it wasn't the same need that Jess had had to escape, and it wasn't the same bone-cracking sameness she felt from day to day, this need of Mignon's. Hers was a superficial restlessness and giant impatience, whereas, as far as living was concerned, Jess had patience; it was her streak of aristocracy that always got her through in the long run, even when she manufactured it.

When she rose to go, apologizing for its being so early but explaining that Jackie always expected her home by half past ten or so, Mignon said, "Well, Jess, give us a tingle on the phone anytime if you're feeling blue and in need of a drop of the drop that cheers," and the sisters made a gesture of kissing as though blood might really be thicker than the Tintara wine.

Outside, shaking hands at parting, Mrs. Blue unexpectedly said, "Perhaps one evening you'd like to come to the Dickens Society with me."

Even more unexpectedly, Mrs. Blue followed it up, telephoning the following week and repeating the invitation. "I got hold of your number from Mignon as you don't seem to be in the book. Could you come with me on Thursday evening? It might be absorbing. We're going to try to unravel Edwin Drood."

Jess would, she said, thanks awfully.

"Nice woman I met with Mignon. English."

"Oh, English," was all Jackie said, spreading out the cards for Patience. But her buttoned mouth spoke out of school. She was vulnerable when exposed to the genuine article.

Frankly the Dickens Society was dull as dead moths, but when Imogene (it had quickly become Imogene and Jess) had volunteered the English Speaking Union, Jess had quickly accepted.

It was like being momentarily home, this enclave of modulated English voices. In the quietude of understressed statements and restrained opinion, never obtruding, never familiar, paraphrasing the same nostalgia which she constantly felt, Jess bloomed. Here in this pleasant oak-paneled room with its deep red carpeting and a fire unnecessarily but brightly going on this warm night, the raucous sounds of Sydney muted, they could have been within sight and sound of Park Lane. She was introduced to names like Farquharson and Twombley. A high-pitched voice belonging to the name of Esme was asking Imogene how she was coping with the ghastliness of Sydney. But this was a slice of England, this was Gilead right here in Bridge Street.

"But perhaps you'd care to join the Union, dear Jess"—it had become "dear" Jess—"perhaps you'd allow me to put your name up for membership."

Imogene never intruded, her invitations were always most casual, but there was the unspoken assumption that she and Jess were in the same boat. They were cautious strangers, careful of each other's propriety but in need, Jess of England, Imogene of companionship. Imogene provided opportunities. Would you like, could you bear to? Jess fitted in, she was ersatz high class but she knew enough to pass among Imogene's friends as the real thing. She was responsive to small requirements and so she often ran errands, can I pick up, let me phone for you, dear.

One night Imogene served them dinner in her little flat. She had crowded pansies into a flat blue bowl and between two crystal candlesticks she served iced consommé and an egg and ham pie as good as anyone would get in the Savoy Grill, apologizing for the unmatching china. It was as English and near perfect as the heart could wish; there was even a tinned plum pudding from Fortnum's.

"What about chestnuts?" Jackie asked. "Couldn't she rake up any?"

Like many stupid women, she had flashes of insight and this was one of them. There had been an unconscious comparison made between her and this Mrs. Blue.

"Why doesn't this woman," Jackie said, spilling dice onto the backgammon board, "get her *own* companion?"

"She doesn't need one."

"I suppose that means that *I* don't either."

What had brought this on? This spurt of jealousy. Had Jess unwittingly betrayed a preference for being with Imogene? Had she not listened attentively enough to some rambling story of Jackie's about a testy sales clerk in Beard Watson's napery department?

Jackie's little diamond earrings were quivering indignantly. Always out these days, Jess was, and when she was home she was no companion. She hadn't been a companion for Jackie couldn't *think* how long. And often not home until after eleven; she had heard Jess come in the other night long after everyone had gone to bed. Where was she? With that woman?

"Does she pay you as well as I do? I can't think why else you'd bother with her. You never did have any talent for anything except sniffing out where there's money like a bloodhound."

But the truth unfortunately was bleak and unconvincing. "She's just a friend."

And I'm lonely in this damned country.

The best thing was to sit and let it pour out like bile. Tears would follow.

Tears did and apologies, too much Napoleon brandy. Hugs around Jess's neck, being put to bed and childish whimpers. "I was a naughty girl to speak that way. Kiss, kiss."

But the following day she refused to get up, trays were brought to her in bed. The next day she got up only to bathe and went back to her new invalidism. Whether or not this tactic had been devised to keep Jess at home, it succeeded, as it had in various ways for twenty years. "Nothing seriously the matter," the doctor said, putting away his stethoscope. "Her pulse is a little weak, heart's more or less normal for her age." Jess went up and down stairs with distractions, books, crossword puzzles, *Punch*.

She had been napping on the morning room sofa when Pegeen opened the glass doors at four o'clock one afternoon and said, "Excuse me, Miss Lord, but . . ." Mrs. Moss looked peculiar.

The reason being that she looked as though she were silently laughing (having the last laugh), her top dentures having slipped down over her lip. She had apparently died while sucking on a stick of barley sugar; the sticky saffron-colored sweet was still in her hand.

Instantly the thought escaped from Jess like a bird into the quiet room, "I am free," and automatically she repressed it, ashamed of herself. She bent and kissed the cool forehead. She sponged and dried Jackie's hands, she pulled down the bedroom blinds, she telephoned to Dr. Ingram and to the lawyer, Mr. Sabeston, to tell them that Mrs. Moss had died late that afternoon.

Twenty years ago Jackie had chosen her out of the female litter of her cousin's pups to come and live with her, had opened all the doors to her, taken her to London, enriched her, not only with material trappings but with a sense of her own uniqueness; it wasn't only a matter of being known in the smoked meats and delicacies department of Fortnum's, it was a sense of a certain priority, a quality of being choice.

Yet twenty years are gone in an afternoon, during a nap, and with absolutely no qualms Jess sat down at eight o'clock and ate a three-course dinner; the only concession she made was not to put on an evening dress. The funeral was delayed a few days in order to give the Starks, Jackie's only close relatives, time to come from their ancestral home in Glenara Lakes, Victoria. Five elderly Starks, two brothers with wives and one elderly sister, knotted with arthritis, they smelled of mothballs and lavender sachets; they had not laid eyes on Jackie (nor probably anyone except themselves) for years. Cloistered in a huge drafty house that Jess had once visited painfully, the Starks lived with their money and complained about the price of fuel. They embraced Jess with their feeble arms and pressed their dried old lips on her cheek, calling her my dear, telling her what a consolation she had been to dear Jackie and to them, separated from her by a state. "Take good care of yourself, dear," the Starks enjoined her, being put into their limousine to take them back after the funeral to the Carlton Hotel where, they complained bleatingly, the breakfasts cost them five shillings apiece.

"Don't take them to heart," Mignon said, giving Jess an extra-large whisky and soda.

"That is the last place where I would put them," Jess said.

Jess sat down in a wide red leather chair in the lawyer's

office to hear her fate. She pulled off her white gloves and laid them on his polished desk. Mr. Sabeston, who had risen abruptly when she was ushered in, asked her was the afternoon sun in her eyes, would she like the blind down just a little? Mr. Sabeston seemed to be a touch overcourteous, which should have prepared her for what was coming but didn't. She crossed her legs and smoothed her simple black jersey dress while Mr. Sabeston fretted with papers and spread them on the desk around him, rubbed his palms together dryly while she waited. In the quiet room the ticking of the clock, the slight hum of the electric fire in the winter light; the tidal wave struck.

Everything was going to the Starks. Every last bean, almost, to the Starks. Jackie had left them her entire estate including the Point Piper house, her jewelry, her stocks and bonds, even the furniture. Riches to the rich, sweets to the sweet, farewell.

To her faithful and beloved companion, Jessie Lord, Mrs. Moss had bequeathed an annuity of two hundred pounds a year and a block of land at Mona Vale. It was to be understood (Mr. Sabeston's voice had the good grace to tremble) that all other gifts made to Miss Lord during Mrs. Moss's lifetime were to remain Miss Lord's possessions. Item: one crystal watch on gold chain, et cetera. Mr. Sabeston spread his clean dry hands over the papers in a deprecatory fashion and then took off his pince-nez and said, "The land will have to be assessed, Miss Lord, though quite frankly, I'm afraid that land nowadays, not being in much demand . . ."

The revenge must have been taken very recently and on account of Jess's lack of forethought over her trivial comings and goings with Imogene; there was no avenger like an old one. Mr. Sabeston must have been summoned to the house one afternoon when Jess was innocently lunching with Imogene on cold duck at the Queens' Club. Not knowing what to do now, where to turn, Jess picked up her gloves from the desk, and still not knowing what to do, put them down again.

When she could trust herself to speak, she asked, "When was this will made?"

"Nineteen twenty-eight, Miss Lord, with her London solicitors, Trevelyian and Couthby."

So.

She had been cheated and robbed four years ago while they were still in England. Treacherously, smiling at her over dinner, Jackie had robbed her while they were still living in Wilton Crescent, and Jess had not had an inkling, not a straw had flown past her in the wind that in the long run she was going to be paid off for all the years of service in seashells. Perhaps Jacquetta Moss had believed in flowers for the living and certainly Jess had had roses to burn. But Jacquetta Moss had also been a Stark and the Starks, childless, suckled their money to the family breast.

Extraordinarily, the shock made Jess icily clear-minded; she stood and took up her gloves positively this time and looked Mr. Sabeston right in the eye. "In the meantime?"

In the meantime, until the will was probated, she was to live on in the Point Piper house and expenses would be paid, the maids and gardener kept on pro tem.

Pro tem.

It gave one a sense of impermanence. As if one might encounter a bailiff sitting on the drawing room sofa or Starks in the bathroom. The grave tidings had to be announced to the staff and it had its immediate effect. Jess came down to dinner to find the dining room table laid only at one end, no candles lit, flowerless. "I thought prob'ly you wouldn't want to bother, miss."

Everything, Jess said, bristling, was to go on as usual, just as if Mrs. Moss were still here, is that understood? She was determined that the house would run on oiled wheels right up until the morning when she was obliged to move out. She discussed spring bulbs with Appleton as if spring were coming as usual and avoided looking into his sad eyes; his loyalty to the garden and to her were unshakable even by last wills and testaments.

An acne-skinned junior partner in the firm of Sabeston and Hayes was commissioned to drive Jess out to see the block of land that had been willed to her. A metaphor in itself, it would have been kinder to leave her in doubt as to its worth. The acre and a half lay at the end of a stony dirt road that had once been marked for development and indeed still had a faded sign at the end of the turnoff reading MYOLA VISTA, where some halfhearted attempt to develop this viewless area had been made and failed. Two desultory cottages, one of them untenanted, stood on desolate weedy plots. The wind riffled through paspalum and wild blackberry; a child's scooter without its wheels was rusting in the nettles.

"Who knows, there might be coal under it," the junior partner said, smirking. Trouble was, he explained, development of a new suburb had gone in the other direction.

Then, that evening, as though mercilessly timed by exultant gods, Pegeen and Annie gave in their two weeks' notice, having triumphantly landed a live-in job out at Hunters Hill with a "bonza" family, they said, chortling. So that Jess would soon be fetching for herself, without much to fetch except what would be in tins and jelly jars. The house grew bigger and so did the specter of the one-room dreary flat she imagined. She saw uncarpeted stairs and a basin full of her limp underwear soaking. Everything was gray.

Well, it's my punishment, she said to herself and gave it the hollow laugh it deserved. It was self-evident and had been a long time coming. But she had felt its presence as she left the ship on the day they had arrived back. Now there was no dismissing it. Now there was not a hand stretched out to save her because she had not stretched out hers to save . . .

She could never finish the sentence in her mind or name the name. It was too stony for words to frame the justification she felt imposed on her. Perhaps her father would have seen the

Biblical implication in her doom. She wondered if he might have quoted, "Vengeance is Mine, sayeth the Lord." And then, because even now and even to the likes of her miracles occur, Imogene Blue said, as modestly as she might have said Would you care for another slice of mince pie?, "Would you consider coming home to England with me, Jess dear?"

Jess didn't move an inch for fear that she hadn't heard right, for fear that she might startle the golden bird that had alighted on her. But then Imogene continued. She had to go "home," her son and daughter-in-law were insisting that she no longer stay so far-flung abroad. Imogene cried poor, her loop of diamonds shimmering in candlelight, deprecated her income: "I'm not very flush, we didn't get half what we should have for the property, but perhaps we could manage in a smallish flat in a nice part of Bloomsbury. We do really hit it off and after all these years I find I'm honestly not suited to living alone." What it meant was that Imogene couldn't afford to pay Jess perhaps quite as much as the emolument she had been getting.

Rescue is not always immediately recognizable and it took Jess minutes to grasp the full import of it, and only then, stunned, was she able to voice her mumbled assent, it sounded as though through grated teeth.

The offer made was so English, so diminuendo, made good-mannered with unconscious grace, that it could have passed unnoticed. Jess hardly heard the appendages Imogene added: "If you wouldn't mind awfully taking care of some of the untidy details for me," and "If you don't mind terribly just an inside cabin on the *Largs Bay* because I'm doing it on the cheap."

Jess nearly replied that she would gladly sleep on a shelf in the boiler room belowdecks to get back to England, that she could be packed by Friday, by tomorrow morning. The relief was so intense that it was almost unbearable, requiring solitude in order to digest and to weigh such an extraordinary turn of events in their true balance. Better not to look at such a benediction in the full light of its splendor and compassion; it might blind one.

So for a week or so she told no one, not even Mignon, of her windfall, partly so as not to arouse any particle of suspicion that some devious motivation of her own had set it in motion.

The nightmare about Bettina had returned in a deeper dimension and she had awakened to find that she had wandered in her sleep and was standing at the top of the dark staircase outside her bedroom, looking down into the well of night. This had never happened before and it alarmed her despairingly even in the sunlight of the next day. Although what possible connection there could be between it and her newly found deliverance, she could not fathom. Hardening her eyes at the shimmering morning harbor, she thought, "But I will only have to look at you for another six weeks."

The sparkling water seemed to wink back at her maliciously, the harbor breeze snapped, "We'll see."

Something was wrong. Something was not quite right.

She could not get this hump of depression off her back. No matter how often she reminded herself of the sailing date she could not visualize the ship, the colored streamers, the sailing up the harbor to the fulfillment of the wild dreams she had had about getting home to London. When she tried to picture Bond Street or Piccadilly she saw blank air.

It's just that I'm being cautious, she reassured herself, with so much happiness. She threw herself with enthusiasm and little faked cries of joy into the small jobs that Imogene had politely asked her to do, but in between, alone in Jacquetta's big silent house, she sometimes surrendered to a creeping unease.

Imprudently (because no longer was she able to have the bill charged to Mrs. Moss), she went to David Jones to buy a hat for the sailing and it was while she was faced with three quarters of herself in the three-way mirror that she saw, trying on the pretty straw with its bouquet of yellow primroses, that her face was ugly and morose, that her face was almost unrecognizable. It was the face of an aging greedy sycophant and in that revealing glimpse of herself she saw that the hat was identical with the one that had been pushed over Bettina's eyes at the moment that the sapling broke, and almost as if she had been stung by a wasp attracted to the silk flowers, she tore off the hat, crying that she didn't like it, couldn't stand herself in it, cried out so that women calmly trying on velvet and faille around her turned to see what had caused the rumpus, and thrusting the hat at the astonished shopgirl, she made her way out of the hat department, pushing into people in her urgency.

Of course there had been nothing remotely similar in the two hats or in the fashions, so vastly changed. But the fact that she had momentarily seen herself in the likeness of Bettina had transformed the nightmare into daytime reality.

But why now, after all these years? Was it because she had never in her life admitted her shame to anyone? Was it possible that even now the confessional might absolve her? If over all the years she had managed to change into this cultivated self, had she also striven so successfully to obliterate her guilt that it was no wonder she was fatigued to death and had nightmares? Late that night, sitting by Mig's little electric fire and hugging her knees to the warmth, she said at last, "I let a girl die," and told Mig about Bettina, about the hat tipped over Bettina's eyes and about Bettina crying out "Help me," the earth slipping away, and how the hand was outstretched within her reach, and how she did not reach for it, about the girl slipping terribly; the crack of the breaking branches, of how she still wakened in the night hearing it, sometimes crying out, and about the fantasy in the shop mirror which had so shocked her. And yet for the life of her she could not remember Bettina's other name. Mig was quiet for a long time but then she got up and poured herself a drink and said, "But you knew enough to save yourself. What if she had pulled you down with her? The world's full of dead heroes."

All the way home to Point Piper on the tram she thought about it and about Mig's practical, even casual, response. It had been another rescue, a rope thrown to her, but in her intense relief (she had almost thrown her arms around Mignon), she hadn't yet quite considered the real significance of what Mig meant, that she had saved herself.

The momentary, the stepping back from the abyss, had been self-preservation, the natural instinct. Nine people out of ten would have done the same thing at that moment. But now a different thought assailed her. Now that she had saved her life, what had it been?

If she had been the kind of girl to keep a diary, there would not have been one single day's entry that could have reported an instance of the slightest significance. It would have consisted entirely of notes about this or that luncheon, this or that dinner, some dull play, the Royal Academy show, fittings for sober evening dresses she never much liked, Empire Day fireworks, the dentist.

Only once in all that time had she ever had a night in London alone to do as she liked. In all those years, only one. One summer while they were in Cornwall, Jackie, in one of the willful passions which came on her like unexpected rages, sent Jess back to London to have a pair of buckles either put on or taken off (it was too piffling to remember) a pair of aging black satin evening shoes, and on account of the Wilton Crescent house being closed she was to put up at Brown's Hotel. And what had she done with her freedom? Had dinner alone in the hotel and then gone upstairs and washed her hair; her imagination had not stretched even as far as Albemarle Street. It had still been daylight outside the window when she got into bed and the only people she had spoken to were those at the reception desk and the waiter at the table. There had been nothing out of the usual in this; she had had no desire to contact any of Jackie's friends who might have been in town, and while having her after-dinner coffee in the hotel lounge she had studiously avoided meeting the eyes of anyone who might be on the verge of inviting conversation; she had drawn the cloak of anonymity close around her shoulders like the old green and gold jacket she wore on inconsequential evenings.

She had smoked one cigarette.

And for this she had let a girl die?

For a thousand evenings of backgammon with Jackie, or helping her solve the *Times* crossword? The Albert Hall once a month and to say at ten o'clock "Beddybyes"? Without being conscious of it, diminishing, diminishing until she could scarcely recognize the daring girl she might have been.

She'd kept herself alive for this, that she was almost dead. The shock of it so immobilized her that she sat on in the tram, frozen in time until she realized that she had gone two stops further than Wentworth Road.

A steady cold rain had begun and she was soaking wet by the time she reached the house. She let herself in and without even taking off her sopping blouse she went to the telephone and dialed Imogene Blue's number even though it was now nearly eleven-thirty.

"No, I was awake, dear, in bed but awake. What is it?"

"I can't go."

"Can't go where?"

"To London with you."

Why not? Imogene was monstrously concerned, was most probably sitting up in bed holding the phone and trying to pull on an angora bed jacket. Had something happened? Are you ill, dear? she asked. Surely something earth-shattering had occurred for Jess to make such a decision and at this time of night.

No, nothing terrible, not anything *suddenly* terrible, Jess said. She spoke calmly and with the strength of an inner certainty that already gave her a sense of dimension she had never guessed at.

Imogene was thunderstruck. Imogene persisted, "I thought you hated it here."

"I do. I have. But—"

She waited a moment to clarify it in her mind. The ruined days clattered past her like empty carriages on a dark train. What remained for her to find? She said, "It doesn't matter much where I am but I've got to find—" What she had to find lay about her like flintstones and rubble in the barren acre of land she had been left in the will. She could see it clearly in her mind: it was her state of life, the brine-smelling breeze riffling through the shreds of waste paper and old soup cans.

"—what's left of me," she said simply, without a trace of pity for herself.

She no longer had her innate weakness to rely on.

Then on the day before she moved out of the big house into the small flat that Mignon had found for her near Mig in Roslyn Gardens, she was emptying out the last drawers in a bedroom cabinet when something fell out of a sheaf of old letters and postcards onto the floor. Picking it up, she saw that it was the family photograph. There they were, all of them together, looking intently forward as though a door had opened suddenly onto their complacency in what seemed to be a Greek temple overlooking a sepia sea. *Le Mer Studios,* the legend read in curlicues. They had come into town then, on a cable tram in the heat of 1912.

There they all were, starched and frilled with their bouffant hairdos, all except the younger children, who had long curls and wore pinafores, ranged around Mother and Father in the perfect rendition of the loving clan. They looked up, serenely optimistic, burgeoning with youth and good health as if they stood on the prow of some splendid vessel cutting through a jeweled sea to an opulent destination known to each one of them by a different name and in a different latitude. Transparent as a dream, the faces of her brother and sisters, as yet innocent of the fact that they were bereft, waiting for a childhood that had been denied them. They radiated a heartbreaking innocence, a belief in the future, they looked out on it with their confident gaze. Jess, in her white muslin with the leg-of-mutton sleeves, seemed to have already grasped the intimation of her sumptuous good fortune; she leaned a little way away from the others as if to dispossess herself of any of their milder ambition. She was reaching out with her little white gloves to the possibilities she knew were already due her, her fortune, devoid of alternatives.

She sat down and put on her reading glasses and looked at the old photograph more intently. Here in the flick of a shutter was caught the glimpse of splendor they saw in themselves, the wished-for dream, the golden shore, there in front of them. But in the end they had been duped and deceived by elements beyond their imagination, whereas she, cocksure girl, her toe pointing toward the path she knew already she would take, had been aware all the time of her own monstrous deceit, the deliberate misappropriation of herself that had begun on a mountain pathway when she was sixteen.

But she was also lucky: harmed as she was, she had not been blinded, she had the vision of hindsight which transcended the mutable and frail. She had been granted a true appropriation of herself which could not be repudiated, she had been granted the opportunity of picking up the broken pieces and doing what she could with them. God knows it wasn't much but it was better than perhaps she deserved, this apocalyptic emergence of her real self, deplorable, decent; she could possibly abide with it, not as a restraint to curb her willful deceits nor to sanctify her (there were no more saints on the road to Damascus), but as an illumination of her future.